Naupaka Blooming

J.L. Eck

Copyright © 2016, J.L. Eck

Naupaka Blooming is a work of fiction. Names, characters, places, and incidents are the products of the authors imagination or are used fictiously. Any resemblance to actual events, locales or persons, living or dead, is entirely coincidental.

All rights reserved. No part of this publication may be reproduced, stored or transmitted in any form or by any means without prior written permission of the author.

ISBN: 978-1530348084

I dedicate this book to my daughter Megan. I started it before you were even conceived but I finished it hoping to make you proud. You inspire me to be a shining example of what can happen when you stop being afraid and just go for your dreams.

I lost my grandmother while writing Naupaka Blooming. *My grandmother always wanted to be a writer but never got around to it. I was able to share the first part of my novel with her before she passed and that was priceless. Without my grandmother this novel never would have seen the light of day, so thank you Nana! I hope you are smiling down on me from heaven.*

And to my husband, Ryan—I finally finished it! It's a miracle!

Table of Contents

Chapter 1 8

Chapter 2 22

Chapter 3 38

Chapter 4 57

Chapter 5 68

Chapter 6 76

Chapter 7 79

Chapter 8 89

Chapter 9 101

Chapter 10 108

Chapter 11 123

Chapter 12 130

Chapter 13 138

Chapter 14 155

Chapter 15 168

Chapter 16 181

Chapter 17	183
Chapter 18	188
Chapter 19	196
Chapter 20	205
Chapter 21	214
Chapter 22	226
Chapter 23	235
Chapter 24	260
About the Author	280

PART 1

Oahu, Hawaii

Sometime in the late 1600s

Chapter 1

a ʻohe pu ʻu ki ʻeki ʻe ke ho ʻu ʻo ʻIa e pi i

No cliff is so tall that it cannot be scaled.

Princess Leilani Kekoa stood barefoot at the edge of the rocky cliff, staring out at the blue ocean stretching endlessly around her. Strong winds whipped her long dark hair around her face. Far below, white-capped waves crashed up against the straight edge of the cliff. She closed her eyes for a moment and took a deep breath, letting the sun warm her skin. She smiled, opened her eyes and jumped.

Her heart pounded as she soared through the air, weightless for a moment. Then gravity pulled her down. She straightened her body and arched her back. With her arms at her sides, her toes pointed down, she held her breath. Her fall only lasted a few seconds and then she plunged into the cool ocean water.

Leilani let herself sink down to the ocean floor as she examined every detail of the incredible underwater world. Bright yellow butterfly fish darted off as she approached, and crabs scurried away on the colorful coral. And what a nice surprise! A giant *honu*, a sea turtle, swam lazily nearby. As soon as Leilani noticed it, the turtle turned and made its way toward her. The turtle looked to be as big as Leilani herself. Its shell was a light greenish color with radiating darker green markings. She froze as it approached. Was it her imagination or was the turtle smiling at her? She reached out and her heart skipped a beat as her fingers brushed against the turtle's shell as it swam by her.

Leilani surfaced for air and wondered about her encounter with the *honu*. The sea turtle was her family *aumakua*—guardian spirit and protector. This had to be an omen. Excitement and anticipation built up within her. Something big was sure to happen soon.

The *honu* popped its head up out of the water several feet away. Princess and turtle studied each other. Then the *honu* dived back under and swam away.

Leilani laughed. She floated on her back, closed her eyes and pondered the possibilities.

A snapping sound from the nearby shore caused her to turn, looking for the source. But everything was just as it should be. Tall palm trees swayed gently in the breeze and a few nēnē birds pecked in the bushes for food. She was alone here.

She sighed. This place made her happy. Unfortunately, she couldn't stay any longer. She had to make an appearance with her family at the big *luau* tonight. Of all her many obligations, she hated making public appearances the most. She hated being the center of attention, hated people scrutinizing her. She always had, ever since she had been a child. Now that she had become a woman, it was even worse. Her body had changed a lot over the last few years. She had become curvier and she had breasts now, which only increased the attention she received. But her mother would be angry with her if she didn't do what was expected, so she swam back toward the shore.

Back on land again, Leilani squished her toes in the warm sand as she admired the lush and wild landscape surrounding her. Sighing, she headed toward the path in the trees. Stepping over branches that had been carefully crossed over one another as a warning that this beach was *kapu*, off limits, she made her way to a nearby waterfall to wash the ocean smell away.

Leilani was momentarily breathless as she stepped under the cold water. Then she relaxed and enjoyed the water cascading down over her. She took her blue-and-green sarong off and rinsed it under the fresh water. Stepping back out into the sun, she wrung the fabric out and laid it out on a nearby rock to dry. She worked on wringing out her long hair with her fingers next. She tied her sarong back around her waist and took off running through the forest. With luck, her hair would be dry by the time she got home and no one would be the wiser.

Her mother saw her first as she approached her family's dwellings. "Leilani!" she scolded. "Where have you been?" She looked her daughter over and shook her head. "No, never mind, don't tell me. It's better if I do not know. It's time for the *luau*, and you are not even dressed yet!" She signaled for Leilani to follow her as she turned and strutted off toward the family huts. "Come!"

"I'm sorry, Mama, I lost track of time," Leilani muttered as she tried to catch up with her mother.

"Yes, yes. Typical!" Her mother ushered her inside the women's hut, where servants waited. "Here, let's hurry or your father will be angry."

Her mother instructed the servants, and they immediately began dressing Leilani. Her blue-and-green sarong was traded for a white one. The servants placed a *lei* made of ti leafs and naupaka flowers around her neck. A single red-and-white plumeria flower was pinned in her hair, which was dry now. Thank the Gods! Her mother wore similar *leis* and flowers in her hair. Leilani shared many of her mother's traits: big green eyes with thick, long eyelashes, high cheekbones and generous lips. The only differences between the two women were her mother's wrinkles and the gray in her hair.

Leilani hugged her mother, suddenly sentimental. "Thank you, Mama!"

"Oh!" Her mother blushed, forgiving her daughter of everything, and kissed her on the cheek. "My little heavenly *lei!*"

"Are you women ready yet?" Keoki, Leilani's brother, called impatiently from outside the hut. "Father wants us all to proceed to the *luau* together." He paused, and added sternly, "Now."

"We're coming, we're coming," Leilani's mother called back. She gave Leilani one more kiss on the cheek and a hug and headed out.

Leilani followed her mother outside, where her brother and father were waiting. Her father never showed much emotion, but Leilani thought she saw a small curve in his lips as she and her mother approached. Her father was the *ali'i*, the chief of the village, and as the *ali'i*, he wore the red-and-white crested helmet and feathered cloak of royalty. He stood nearly seven feet tall and tribal tattoos covered his arms, legs, chest and back. Each tattoo told a story about his life—his victories in battle, his rule over his kingdom and his family. His long, wavy, dark hair showed the first hints of gray. He usually had it pulled back, but it hung loose around his shoulders today. His dark eyes studied Leilani for a moment before he nodded his approval and then he turned and started off toward the village.

Keoki grinned at her and gave her a fake punch in the arm before following. He also wore the red-and-white feathered cloaks, and he was almost as formidable as her father. At seventeen, he had already been victorious in battle but Keoki only had a couple of tattoos. Each family member's first tattoo was always the turtle, the family *aumakua*, and Keoki had one on his right shoulder. He also had a tribal tattoo on his left leg, symbolizing his bravery in his first battle.

Keoki was promised to the daughter of another royal family on a nearby island, and their wedding was set for the end of the year. Leilani loved her brother and wished he didn't have to be married off so soon. She was a year younger than her brother and she knew she would get married off soon, too. The thought filled her with dread. But her mother told her it was a necessary tradition. They had to keep the *ali'i* blood pure, create bonds with other powerful royal families and continue to keep the peace for everyone. Her mother had been married off to Leilani's father at fourteen. If they could find happiness together, then perhaps Leilani would be able to find happiness as well.

Leilani had little interest in boys though. Boys could be pigs. She didn't like the way they looked at her and made comments behind her back. Hopefully, seeing the *honu* today had nothing to do with boys or getting married off soon. She wasn't ready for that yet. Would she ever be ready for that?

As she followed her family into the village, Leilani tried not to stare at the simple, small huts the commoners lived in. The homes of the *ali'i* were much larger and more extravagant, set on stone foundations and showcasing *kahili*, feather standards. She frowned. She didn't understand why the commoners had to live out their lives in such cramped quarters and without the luxuries that Leilani and her family had. Every time she questioned her mother about it, her mother always had the same response—the *ali'i* were descended from the Gods and thus were entitled to more. But that didn't sit well with Leilani. The way she saw it, everyone was descended from the Gods, not just the *ali'i*.

Leilani suddenly smelled the delicious aroma of fish cooking over fire and her stomach grumbled. She hadn't even realized that she was hungry. She put aside all of her jumbled thoughts. The Gods had been smiling down on them lately with an abundance of fish, fruit, mild weather and peace. But keeping the Gods happy required sacrifice and ceremony. The *luau* tonight was for the Gods.

The setting sun lit up the sky with brilliant shades of oranges and reds as *tiki* torches were ignited around the village center. It looked as if all of the villagers had come out tonight in celebration. Hundreds of people stood around talking and laughing while the children played. Everyone's spirits were high.

Someone blew a horn to announce the arrival of the *ali'i* and his family, and her father's warriors cleared a wide path for them. In silence, the villagers dropped to their knees and bowed their heads out of respect for the royal war chief and his family. Commoners were not supposed to touch the shadow of an *ali'i* or else his power would be diminished.

Once her father reached the pedestal at the center of the village, he faced the villagers. "My people!" he bellowed, his voice strong and deep. "We come together tonight to thank the Gods for taking good care of us this last year."

At this, everyone stood and cheered.

Leilani's father waited for the cheering to fade before he continued. "We thank Kane for our healthy, growing village."

The villagers thanked Kane, the God of Life, as one.

"We thank Ku for our strength in defeating the enemy."

The villagers thanked Ku, the God of War.

Leilani's father went through each of their Gods, thanking them one by one with the villagers repeating the thanks. Lono, the God of Peace, Kanaloa the God of the Sea, and many others, ending with Laka, the God of the *hula*.

Finally, her father opened his arms outward and announced, "We have more than enough good food and drink for everyone. So let us begin!"

The villagers cheered again and then the women and men separated for dinner. It was *kapu* for women to eat with men. As Leilani watched the men seat themselves at the feast prepared for them near the beach, she thought how silly it was that the men believed they were vulnerable to women stealing their *mana*, or divine spirit, while eating. But she didn't want to eat with the men anyway. She followed her mother to the women's feast set down the beach to the right of the men.

Leilani sat down in the sand in the middle of her mother, her grandmother and all her aunts and cousins. Giant bowls of poi, yams and breadfruit, platters full of cooked fish, chicken and pig and bowls filled with bananas, coconut and pineapple sat on mats of ti leaves. The women gossiped as they ate. The older women spoke in agitated tones about the troubles their children caused them. The younger girls whispered in excitement about the boys they liked or the men they were arranged to marry. But Leilani, bored easily with both subjects, tuned them all out. She thought of nothing more than her next opportunity to sneak away and play in the ocean again.

As the moon rose high in the sky and people finished eating, Leilani's father once again rose to address the villagers. "A most excellent feast!" he declared as he rubbed his belly. Everyone cheered in agreement. "Let us now thank the Gods with our finest dancers! Come!"

Drummers pounded out a rhythmic beat as Leilani's father led everyone down the beach to the dancers. The servants stayed behind to begin the monumental task of cleaning up.

Leilani lagged behind her mother, devising ways to sneak off for a moonlit swim. As she scanned the crowd to ensure that no one was paying her any attention, her eyes stopped on one man in particular. She couldn't take her eyes off him. He was obviously one of the *hula* dancers. He wore a white loincloth, and shark's tooth necklace, anklets and bracelets. A green leaf *lei* sat on his head and his long wavy hair flowed around his broad shoulders. Leilani was so mesmerized she almost ran into her mother who had stopped and was now talking with another woman. She'd never seen such a beautiful man! He was tall and muscular, but not quite as fierce as her father and brother. He had a strong nose and sharp cheekbones, but the most fascinating thing about him was his light brown eyes. They appeared to twinkle in the moonlight.

He caught her staring at him and for a moment, time seemed to stop. It was just the two of them there, staring into each other's eyes. Leilani's heart thudded uncontrollably and she forgot to breathe. He smiled at her as if he knew her, as if they were sharing a secret. Shocked, she ducked behind her mother to hide. Commoners were not allowed to look her in the eye, let alone smile at her. No one had ever dared to be so bold with her before!

After catching her breath, Leilani peered back out from behind her mother. The light-eyed man was walking toward the stage with the other male dancers. She watched him freely now. He seemed familiar to her in some strange way but she was sure that she had never seen him before.

He was no longer smiling as he took his place on the stage. His eyes were cast down. He was almost frowning but so were all the other dancers. It was all a part of the act of their *hula* dance. Despite the serious look on his face now, she couldn't get the image of him smiling at her out of her head. It made her feel funny inside. All jittery and excited.

The dancers started their *hula*, stomping their feet and slapping their chests, moving their arms and legs to tell stories. They mimicked the movements of rowing a canoe out to sea, casting a spear into the water, catching a fish and then gutting and eating the fish. They spoke of the sea, wind and rain with their hands. Their dance was graceful but also masculine and physical. The more the performance progressed, the more the men perspired. Leilani had never been so interested in a *hula* dance before. But she was really only interested in the man with the light eyes. He had the most beautiful body and more passion than the other dancers. Every move he made was perfect and filled with emotion.

He made eye contact with her several times as he performed. Leilani quickly looked away each time, of course. She didn't want him to get caught. He could be cast out of the village, or worse, over such brazen behavior. Leilani glanced at her mother. Surely her mother had noticed, usually nothing escaped her. But her mother was smiling and tapping her foot to the beat, captivated by the performance like everyone else.

The men ended their performance with a bang, slapping their chests, stomping their feet and letting out one final "Huah!" They then knelt and bowed their heads to their *ali'i*.

Leilani's father clapped his big hands together. "Laka is surely pleased with your performance tonight!" He then signaled for them to rise. All the men filed off the stage, taking their *leis* off and piling them one on top of another on a rock altar. Leilani tried to keep track of the man with the light eyes, but he disappeared into the crowd.

Women dancers, smiling sweetly and dressed in flowing yellow sarongs with white-and-orange flower *leis* around their necks, wrists, and ankles, assembled on the stage next. Once her father gave them the go ahead, they began a much gentler and feminine *hula* dance.

Nothing about these *hula* dancers interested Leilani. She thought of going swimming again. It was the perfect night for it with the full moon. She checked once more to make sure no one was paying attention to her. She secretly hoped to spot the light-eyed man, but he was nowhere to be seen. Everyone was entranced with the women dancers now, so she edged her way back from the crowd toward her escape.

Weaving through the trees in the moonlight, Leilani quickly made her way to her secret spot. The closer she got, the more the sweet feeling of freedom enveloped her. There wasn't time to climb the cliff so Leilani walked straight down the beach, into the small waves lapping at her feet and out farther still until she was submerged up to her neck. Then she allowed herself to sink completely under water.

Leilani surfaced and swam around, enjoying the feel of her muscles at work. She floated on her back, gazing up at the stars. The full moon seemed particularly big and bright in the sky tonight.

She heard a snap from the beach, the same sound she had heard while swimming earlier in the day. It was too difficult to see anything from where she was, so she swam in closer. In waist-deep water, she stood and searched the shadows for whatever had caused the noise, but still she saw nothing.

Annoyed, she called out, "Who's there?"

A shape emerged from the trees. A man. He meandered down to the beach and stopped near the water. Her heart sped up. The beautiful man with the light eyes stood there.

"You should not be here!" she scolded him angrily, but secretly she was pleased.

"Nor should you," he replied quietly with a smile.

He had her there.

"I saw you watching me tonight." His voice was softer and smoother than she would have imagined.

"I was watching all the dancers," she replied haughtily.

"Oh, yes, of course you were!" he laughed, somehow knowing she lied. "My name is Kanoa."

"Well, Kanoa, I am Leilani, daughter of–"

"I know who you are," he interrupted and bowed. "My princess."

"Then you know you should not be speaking to me."

He said nothing in response but tilted his head, studying her.

"Or looking me in the eyes," she added for good measure.

He shrugged. "I cannot help it; I am drawn to you. And your beautiful eyes."

"You will be in trouble if you are caught." Unsure how to accept his compliment, Leilani's voice rose.

"The whole village is back at the *hula*," he told her. "It is just us here now."

Leilani looked and listened for signs that they were not alone, but she saw and heard nothing. Then she had a troubling thought. She backed up and impulsively covered herself with her arms. "Did you follow me here?"

"I admit, I did," he confessed and then quickly added, "But do not be afraid; I mean you no harm. I thought you might need protection in the dark night." He sat down cross-legged in the sand in an attempt to make her more comfortable.

"I need no protection!" Leilani told him stubbornly, standing tall, her hands on her hips now, her head held high.

"I suppose you are right," he agreed. "You were magnificent this afternoon, climbing up that rocky cliff and then jumping off it."

Leilani gasped and he chuckled. "But still, I feel the need to protect you." He shrugged his shoulders again.

"You!" she accused. "You were on the beach earlier today!"

"Ahhh, I admit it!" he confessed again. "But I swear, it was purely chance that I was here earlier today."

Leilani grunted her disbelief.

"I happened to be praying over there," he pointed to a group of trees set back a bit from the beach, "to Laka for my performance tonight. You see, tonight was my first official performance as an *'olapa*. I have graduated with highest honors from the *halau*."

"Oh, well...." So he was a master *hula* dancer, just as she suspected. Leilani instantly forgave him for his intrusion. "You were very good tonight." The words were out before she realized it and she blushed.

"Thank you, my princess! I am honored by your praise." Kanoa rose from his cross-legged seat in the sand and bowed to her.

"So," he said, going back to his explanation, "as I was praying, I heard someone coming. When I investigated, I saw you climbing up the cliff. I was intrigued by a princess who could climb with such skill!"

"Yes, well...." Leilani took pride in her ability to do things other girls couldn't or wouldn't. "I've climbed that cliff my whole life." She added under her breath, "Despite my parents' wishes."

He nodded. "And when you jumped off that cliff into the ocean, I was in awe of your bravery!"

Leilani couldn't help but smile. She had no fear! She wished her family could see her strengths and abilities and let her do what she wanted. But that would never happen.

"You will tell no one about me. Or this place!" she commanded Kanoa in a stern voice. She needed this place and her cliff diving to remain a secret.

"No, of course not, my princess!" he assured her solemnly with his hand over his heart. "My lips are sealed."

Leilani couldn't help thinking about his lips then. She wondered what it would be like to be kissed by him. Surprised by the unexpected turn her thoughts had suddenly taken, she realized too late that Kanoa was walking toward her, splashing in the water with each step he took.

"What are you doing?" she asked in alarm, backing up to keep space between them.

"I enjoy swimming." He smiled that charming smile again. "May I not also enjoy this moonlit night in the ocean?"

"Well," Leilani thought about it, "if you promise to keep your distance, I suppose I can allow you to swim nearby."

"Thank you, my princess," Kanoa said graciously, diving under the water. Leilani waited to see him surface. She was wondering where he had gone to when he unexpectedly emerged right next to her, splashing her on purpose.

Outraged, Leilani coughed and attempted to wipe the water from her eyes. "How dare you!"

"What?" he teased with a big grin. "You were already wet!"

"How do you like it?" she asked and splashed him back.

He only laughed happily in response.

Leilani stood there fuming as he laughed and splashed her again.

Leilani growled. This was war, and she would win it! She splashed him with all her might, over and over again. But he just laughed and splashed her back.

After several minutes, she was laughing as well.

Kanoa stopped splashing her and took a step toward her. "You are so unbelievably beautiful when you smile," he said, turning serious.

Leilani could feel herself blushing again.

"I mean; you are beautiful even when you are not smiling." He stumbled on his words, trying to make himself clear. "But you look like a Goddess from the heavens above when you are smiling!"

"*Mahalo.*" She blushed deeply, the jittery feeling in her stomach returning. "You are not bad to look at yourself," she blurted out, not wanting to admit that she found him to be the most beautiful man she had ever seen, especially when he smiled at her.

He grinned, somehow knowing her true heart's feelings.

Just then, they heard faint voices in the distance. For a moment, time seemed to stop again as they looked anxiously at each other. They would both be in trouble if found in this *kapu* place. But Kanoa would be in terrible trouble if he was found swimming with Leilani. Without another word, they each dove under the water, heading in different directions. Leilani swam for the beach, and Kanoa swam in the opposite direction, farther out to sea. When she reached the shore, Leilani looked back, but saw no signs of Kanoa. She hoped he was a good swimmer.

Chapter 2

'A 'Ole E 'Olelo Mai Ana Ke Ahi Ua Ana la

Fire Will Never Say That It Has Had Enough

Leilani couldn't stop worrying about Kanoa. She participated in her daily obligations halfheartedly, as usual, but now instead of daydreaming about escaping and playing in the ocean, she daydreamed about Kanoa. While learning how to sew with her mother, she thought of Kanoa's strong, muscular body. He was most likely a good swimmer. She told herself she shouldn't worry about him swimming off into the ocean that fateful night last week. But she couldn't help it. While reciting history stories with her aunts and cousins, Kanoa's gorgeous light brown eyes haunted her. His eyes shined so brightly when he smiled and laughed. While visiting other royal families in nearby villages with her family, she thought of Kanoa's voice, the way he spoke to her. No one had ever spoken to her the way he had. That jittery feeling in her stomach each time she thought of him must be what the other girls called butterflies. Leilani felt as if her heart would explode from her desire to see him again.

She looked for him everywhere she went but she never saw him. This wasn't a surprise. After all, if he was as an *'olapa* now then he would spend his days and nights in the *halau*, away from the village. He would be busy teaching other young men the *hula*. He was an excellent performer, so he would probably be an excellent teacher.

One night, while lying in bed trying to recall every single moment of the night she met Kanoa, Leilani suddenly realized she hadn't been to her secret spot for nearly two weeks. She'd been so consumed with thoughts of Kanoa that she hadn't thought about sneaking off once! She decided it was time to get back there as soon as possible. Maybe it would help her forget about Kanoa. Or maybe she would run into him there again.

The next afternoon, after her mother had given Leilani a lesson in the art of making healing ointments, she found her opportunity. While her mother dealt with the servants, she ran down to her spot as fast as she could. She arrived breathless, fully expecting to find Kanoa there, waiting for her.

To her dismay, he was not there. Her heart heavy with disappointment, she climbed up her cliff anyway. Once she had reached the top, she took a moment to look back down at the beach. Could he be hiding in the trees? There was no sign of him. She jumped, but felt no joy from the flight as she usually did, or from plunging into the cool waters below. Ignoring the sea life swimming around her, she surfaced, hoping to see Kanoa swimming to her. He was not there. Leilani realized her secret spot was no longer the most important thing in her life. Kanoa had somehow become more important.

As she made her way back home, Leilani wondered why she always wanted the forbidden. She was forbidden from this beach and these cliffs and from swimming in the ocean. But nothing gave her more joy. And she was forbidden from Kanoa. But no one else made her heart race so.

Of course, rules had never stopped her before.

Deep in thought, Leilani was surprised as several men, including her brother, suddenly came crashing through the trees and raced past her, down toward the village lagoon. She heard them mention a body washing up on shore. Fearing the worst, that it might be Kanoa, Leilani followed after the men.

On the beach, a crowd had formed around the body. As Leilani lingered in the background trying to catch a glimpse, she heard whispers of a shark attack. She did her best to appear only mildly interested, but she was desperately hoping and praying it was not Kanoa. She couldn't stop picturing him swimming away that night. If he were lying there now, lifeless, killed by sharks.... It would be all her fault! Her stomach turned at the idea.

As the crowd parted and several men picked the body up to carry it away, Leilani could see that it was a young man's body, similar to Kanoa in height and build. She winced as she noticed that half the side of his body was missing, the flesh likely torn apart by sharks. It was a gruesome sight. Leilani shivered. But thank the Gods it was not Kanoa!

Two women, an older woman and a younger woman, wailed and grasped at the body as the men carried it away. Probably the dead man's mother and wife. Leilani didn't know these people, yet she felt their grief. What if it had been Kanoa?

Leilani decided she needed to see Kanoa right away. Her heart racing, she ran back inland, toward the *halau*. This new adventure would not be much different from her other adventures!

As she neared the *halau*, she forced herself to slow down. She crept silently through the forest, looking and listening for signs of others. When she heard voices, she ducked down and crawled behind a thick grove of tall bushes. Peering out from a narrow slit in the bushes, she saw a dozen young boys in the gardens in front of the *halau*. Kanoa was at the front of the group, leading them in their *hula* practice. Her breath caught. She bit her lip. He was even more stunning than she remembered.

Kanoa wore a blue-and-white patterned sarong around his waist. He looked stern, but she could see as he taught that he had a lot of patience. If a boy stumbled or turned the wrong way, Kanoa continued to work with him until he got it right. When the boys finally mastered one of the moves in unison, Kanoa lit up with a big grin, clapping and congratulating them all. Leilani smiled, too.

Kanoa looked over in Leilani's direction. He couldn't possibly see her, could he? Her face warmed instantly from his gaze. She crouched lower and didn't even dare to breathe for a moment as she waited for him to look away. He smiled, as if he knew that she was there, then went back to teaching his class.

Leilani stayed frozen for a few more minutes, afraid of making any sound and attracting Kanoa's attention again. Soon, Kanoa declared class to be over and all the boys gradually made their way into the *halau*, laughing, punching and pushing each other the way boys do. Kanoa remained alone outside, cleaning up the gardens. Leilani waited for him to look back in her direction again. But he never did. And then Kanoa went inside the *halau* as well.

Disappointed, Leilani waited a few more minutes to see if Kanoa would come back outside. But after a few minutes she gave up. She carefully and quietly started back toward the village, picking up her pace and weaving through the trees. Daydreaming of Kanoa and his beautiful eyes, she was not paying attention to her surroundings when suddenly Kanoa popped out from behind a tree. She ran right into him, knocking them both down to the ground. In shock, she found herself on top of him. He laughed, looking up at her with those big, beautiful light brown eyes.

She struggled to free herself from him, even though a part of her wanted to stay right where she was. His skin was soft. His muscles flexed beneath her. "What are you doing?" she demanded angrily as she rose. Kanoa tried to help her but she swatted him away.

"Saying hello!" he told her cheerfully, also standing.

"Ugh!" She grunted her disapproval. "You can't just sneak up on people all the time!"

"I thought you wanted to see me?" he asked innocently, but there was a teasing look in his eyes. "Isn't that why you came all the way to the *halau* today?"

"I was just ..." Leilani paused, trying to come up with a quick excuse. "... exploring."

Kanoa smiled at her knowingly. "Just exploring, huh?"

She nodded, glaring at him, daring him to contradict her.

"I thought I smelled you back there." he told her.

Leilani opened her mouth to prostest. She did not smell!

"The ocean." He smiled and winked. "You've been swimming, haven't you?"

Leilani bit her lip and nodded.

"And then I spotted you. Behind the bushes. Watching me." Seeing her eyes widen in alarm, he added, "Do not worry! No one else noticed."

"I just happened to stumble across the *halau* ..." she defended herself. "As I was exploring."

He couldn't help but chuckle.

"Why do you keep laughing at me?" Leilani demanded, her hands on her hips.

"I am not laughing at you!" Kanoa insisted. "I cannot help but smile and be happy in your presence. You make me feel so ... alive!"

Leilani tried to fight the grin forming.

"My world is so much more," he tried to find the right words, "exciting now that you are in it!"

"Oh...." She nodded, speechless.

He looked at her intently and took her hands in his. "I have been waiting for you to come find me. What took you so long?"

Leilani looked down at her small hands in his much bigger hands. The butterflies in her stomach were going crazy at his touch. She looked back up into his eyes again.

Kanoa studied her. "I hope you have been thinking of me as much as I have been thinking of you since the night of the *luau*."

"I might have thought of you once or twice," she said casually, knowing her blushing gave away her lie.

"Well, I'm glad you came to see me today." He kissed her hands.

Leilani panicked and hastily pulled her hands away. "I was just exploring." she insisted, sticking to her lie. She turned away from him, but couldn't resist peeking at him out of the corner of her eye.

Kanoa frowned. He looked hurt. But Leilani kept up her guard. She narrowed her eyes and held her head high.

"Very well then. I must have misunderstood." Kanoa shrugged, his whole demeanor changing. "I'll leave you to your ... exploring." He turned and headed back toward the *halau*.

Leilani watched him go, every fiber of her being insisting that she call out to him, stop him, make him come back to her. But for some reason she stood frozen in place, unable to do or say anything.

Eventually, long after Kanoa had disappeared into the trees, Leilani left as well, her heart heavy. She'd never felt so awful. The look on Kanoa's face when she had pulled away from him stuck in her head. If he could admit to his true feelings for her, then why couldn't she do the same for him? She had been terrified to admit she liked him though. Why? She had never been a fearful girl. Why was she suddenly turning into a quivering fool?

Leilani felt guilt, shame and regret for the first time in her life.

* * *

At dinner, Leilani's mother obviously sensed something was upsetting Leilani. She kept glancing worriedly at her throughout dinner. Leilani tried to avoid eye contact.

After they had eaten, Leilani found the courage to speak up. "Mama?"

"Yes, my sweet heavenly *lei?*"

"How did you feel about Papa? In the beginning?"

Her mother considered it. "I was a bit frightened by him at first; he is an intimidating man." She smiled at Leilani. "He had already won several battles by the time we were arranged to be married and had a fierce reputation. But I was drawn to him. He was a very handsome man. He looked at me in a way that made me feel funny. My mother told me it was love."

"Oh." Leilani took in her mother's words. So what she was feeling for Kanoa was love. "Did you think about him all the time?"

"Well, yes, I suppose I did." Her mother looked wistful.

"Were you afraid though?"

"Afraid of what?"

"I don't know, of letting him into your world?"

"Yes, I suppose I was a little afraid." Her mother looked thoughtfully at Leilani. "But I soon realized I had nothing to be afraid of." She smiled and gently stroked Leilani's cheek. "Love is a wonderful thing, and I promise you won't have anything to be afraid of either, my sweet heavenly *lei*."

Leilani bit her lip and studied her mother.

"Just allow yourself to be open and the rest will come naturally." Her mother kissed Leilani's cheek and then her forehead.

Leilani decided that her mother must know about Kanoa.

* * *

Leilani could not sleep that night. She lay restless in her bed, thinking about Kanoa and what her mother had said. She knew what she had to do now. She had to go back to Kanoa and confess her love to him.

In the early morning hours, as her family slept, she snuck off again to the *halau*. The sun was just beginning to rise as she approached the area. She hid behind the same bushes as the previous day, fidgeting and watching the *halau* for signs of life. After what seemed like hours, Kanoa exited. He yawned, stretched and then set off through the forest toward the temple. Probably to pray. She quietly made her way through the cover of the trees to follow him.

After several minutes, Leilani realized she had lost him. He must have been going somewhere else. She backtracked, frantically searching for signs of him. But she ended up circling around again to the spot where she first realized she had lost him. She sighed and cursed in frustration.

"I see I've caught you exploring again," Kanoa said from up above, somewhere in the trees.

Leilani jumped in surprise and cursed again.

She looked up, trying to find him, finally spotting him peering down at her from a tree several feet away, trying not to smile.

"You scared me!" Leilani scolded him.

"I did not mean to scare you. I was heading to the temple when I saw this mango tree and realized I was hungry." He bit into a mango and stared at her as he chewed.

She watched him for a moment, still afraid to admit her feelings to him.

"Well." Kanoa threw the half eaten mango over his shoulder and climbed down from the tree. "I will leave you to your exploring." He turned his back on her and started off in the direction of the temple again.

"Wait!" Leilani shouted after him, fear propelling her forward now. She would not lose this opportunity!

He stopped and turned, an expectant look on his face. "Yes?"

"I came here to find you," she admitted slowly.

"You did?" he asked with a slight grin.

"Yes!" she proclaimed haughtily, her royalty coming through again.

"Why?" he asked. As if he had no idea!

"I think you know why!"

"I am unsure." He tilted his head.

Leilani glared at him. Why must he make this so difficult?

Kanoa just stood waiting.

"Uhhh!" Leilani groaned in frustration. "Fine! I do think of you, Kanoa! All the time! There! Are you happy now?" She folded her arms and frowned at him.

Kanoa smiled from ear to ear and in two strides closed the distance between them. He gently cradled her face in his big hands. "Yes, I am happy now," he said simply, leaning in to kiss her.

Leilani's eyes widened, and she gasped as his lips touched hers. She had never been kissed by a man before. But she relaxed and forgot about everything except Kanoa as his lips explored hers. She closed her eyes then and melted into him. They clung to each other.

After what seemed like hours has passed, Kanoa pulled away. Leilani opened her eyes to find him smiling at her. She pulled him back to her and found his lips again.

She couldn't seem to stop kissing him. Her whole body was on fire.

Eventually, Kanoa pulled away again. "I am sorry," he said solemnly. "I wish it were not so, but I must be getting back soon." He kissed her softly on each cheek, then her nose and lastly her forehead.

Leilani had no idea how much time had passed, but the sun was shining brightly in the sky now.

"Me, too, I suppose." Leilani frowned. She would give anything to be able to stay here with Kanoa.

Kanoa kissed her gently on the lips one more time. "Let's meet again," he suggested with a grin.

Leilani smiled. She wanted nothing more! "When?"

"I can get away in two days' time, after everyone goes to sleep for the night."

Leilani nodded.

"At our secret spot?" he asked, his grin widening.

She knew exactly where he meant, as though he could read her mind, and she could read his. So her secret spot was now their secret spot? She liked that idea very much. Her two favorite things, together! It didn't get better than that!

She nodded. "Our secret spot!"

* * *

Everything felt different to Leilani as she made her way back home. The sun looked brighter and felt warmer, the sky seemed a brighter shade of blue. The green trees seemed more alive. For the first time, she really heard the sweet songs of the birds. The flowers even smelled sweeter. The whole world seemed better somehow, now that she had found Kanoa.

Leilani stopped to smell some naupaka flowers cascading onto the path. She broke one off and stuck it in her hair. Daydreaming, she turned back on the path home and almost collided with a girl running in the opposite direction.

The girl realized who she had just run into and immediately bowed down on her knees. "Princess! Please forgive me!" the girl begged, her head hung low.

"No, no! Please rise. There is no need to be so formal with me!" Leilani told her, feeling generous.

The girl rose. "I was on my way to see my brother. I am late as usual," the girl said.

"Who is your brother?" Leilani asked, thinking she already knew the answer. This girl had familiar light brown eyes.

"Kanoa," the girl confirmed. "Do you know of him? He is the best *hula* dancer in the village!" she proclaimed, her eyes sparkling with pride.

"Ah, yes." Leilani blushed. "You are right; he is the best *hula* dancer."

The girl cocked her head in interest at Leilani's reaction.

"Please, do not let me make you any later!" Leilani stepped aside.

"*Mahalo*, princess!" The girl bowed again and, with one last curious look, she took off running toward the *halau*.

* * *

Over the next two days, Leilani was even more distracted, as her thoughts of Kanoa became less and less innocent. She imagined being in his arms again. The butterflies in her stomach exploded at the thought of his lips on hers. She was sure that everyone could see what was going on in her head. But no one seemed to detect the change. Except her mother, of course. Her mother kept catching Leilani's eyes and giving her knowing smiles.

Leilani went to bed as normal the night of their planned secret meeting. She lay still, waiting for everyone else to fall asleep, waiting for her moment to sneak off. When she felt like enough time had passed, she tiptoed out of her hut and past her father's private hut. She could hear her father snoring inside.

As soon as she had cleared the village, she ran through the trees, down to the beach. Kanoa was already waiting for her at the base of the rocky cliff she always climbed. He smiled at her when she appeared. Returning the smile, she ran straight into his arms. He lifted her up off the ground and held her close, kissing her passionately. She wrapped her legs and arms around him and surrendered herself to him.

"I thought this night would never get here fast enough," he mumbled in between kisses.

Leilani mumbled her agreement back.

He smelled divine tonight, manly, musky and slightly of coconut. She nuzzled her nose in his neck, and he moaned. He put her down, then laid out a blanket for them.

They lay side by side on the blanket, holding hands and gazing up at the stars. The moon was only a sliver in the sky tonight, not full like it had been when they first met here weeks ago. Palm trees rustled softly in the breeze and waves crashed nearby on the beach.

Leilani turned and found Kanoa watching her. She realized she didn't really know much about him. Curious, she propped herself up on her elbow.

"Tell me about yourself, your family...."

"My father is a fisherman, and my mother is a cloth maker. I have a younger sister named Nani. She will also be a *hula* dancer. She is about to begin her training."

"Oh, yes. I know your sister. She is very pretty. She has the same eyes as you."

Kanoa nodded. "But your green eyes are much more beautiful and rare." He caressed her cheek.

Leilani blushed. "*Mahalo*." She was starting to get used to his compliments.

Kanoa leaned over and kissed her gently on the lips and soon they were wrapped up in each other's arms again.

They came up for air a while later.

"I heard about a body washing up on shore after our first meeting," she told him softly. "It had been eaten by sharks. I thought it might be you, and I had the most terrible feeling."

Kanoa smiled and shook his head. "My sweet, my family *aumakua* is the *mano*, the shark. So you see, I am safe from the *mano*."

"Oh," Leilani sighed. "That makes sense, with your father being a fisherman."

"And your family *aumakua* is the *honu*."

"Yes." Leilani thought about her encounter with the big sea turtle the day she met Kanoa. She had completely forgotten all about that! The *honu* must have been predicting her meeting with Kanoa!

"I saw a *honu* the day I met you!" Leilani sat up excitedly. "The biggest one I'd ever seen! And it swam right up to me and brushed against me. I swear it smiled at me."

Kanoa sat up as well. "Huh. I saw a *mano* that day. I had personal time in the morning, so I went out with my father fishing and a *mano* swam right up to our boat. My father said he'd never seen one swim up to the boat like that."

Leilani was speechless.

"Do you realize what this means?" Kanoa asked, grinning now.

Leilani smiled, too. Of course she did! Their meeting was destined by the Gods!

She wrapped her arms around him and kissed him again. They fell back on the blanket together, lips locked and arms and legs entwined.

Leilani was ready to surrender to him entirely when suddenly he pulled away. He looked flustered. He got up and just stood there, gazing up at the stars. Finally, he spoke in a hushed voice. "I took a vow, as a *hula* dancer, to never marry." He looked back down at her. "And now this happens."

"I know." She bit her lip.

"I was never interested in girls," he admitted. "Until you."

Leilani smiled. He was like her in so many ways; they were like two halves of a whole.

"And your parents are probably already arranging a marriage for you to some other man. A royal man, no doubt."

"Most likely." Leilani scrunched her face up in disgust. She groaned and stood up. "But I do not want that! I have never been interested in any man, least of all any royal men; they are pigs."

Kanoa laughed.

"And then you showed up." She echoed his sentiments.

He searched her eyes. "I am willing to give it all up for you."

Leilani nodded. "I don't even care about this place anymore!" She swept her arm toward the cliff and the ocean. "I want you more than I ever wanted this place."

"Oh!" He reached for her hand.

"I know." Leilani laughed, putting her arms around him.

Kanoa held her close. "What is it about you that makes me forget about everything else?"

"Well, look at me! I am a beautiful princess!" she joked, flipping her long hair back.

Kanoa slapped his chest and grunted, "And I'm a *hula* dancer!"

She laughed and pushed him away.

"I think I'm in love with you, Leilani," he confessed, pulling her back to him.

His confession surprised her, but she felt the same. "I ... I think I'm in love with you, too, Kanoa," she whispered in his ear.

"Run away with me," he whispered back.

She pulled away to look him in the eyes. "How would we do such a thing? Where would we go?"

"I can sail a canoe. We can go to a neighboring island. I have extended family there. Uncles."

She thought about his tempting suggestion. "No. My father would never let us get away. He would find us and kill you."

He grimaced.

"Let me talk to my mother. She may be able to help me persuade my father to let us marry."

"Really?" he asked doubtfully.

"Yes, I think she must know about you and I. My mother loves me and wants me to be happy. And she has influence with my father."

"I don't know...."

"We both saw our *aumakuas*! My father has to heed the signs! Otherwise...."

Kanoa looked up to the heavens, thinking.

"Just let me try," she pleaded. "If I can't get them to agree, then we can run away."

He studied her for a moment, undecided. Finally, he nodded.

Chapter 3

I ka ʻolelo no ke ola, i ka ʻolelo no ka make

In speech is life, in speech is death

During the next few days, Leilani anxiously waited for a good time to speak with her mother, but the two women were never alone. Late one afternoon, she got a chance as they worked on a sewing project. As Leilani watched her mother, she built up her courage.

Leilani finally broke the silence. "Mama?"

"Yes, my sweet heavenly *lei?*" Her mother continued to work at her sewing.

"I think that...." Leilani paused. "I mean; I know...." She scrunched her brow. "What I mean to say is that I believe...." Leilani groaned. She didn't know how to say what she needed to say.

"Well, spit it out!" Her mother glanced up from her work with a smile and then went back at it again.

"I'm in love!" Leilani blurted, her face warming at the confession.

Her mother put the sewing down and turned to Leilani, obviously surprised at her daughter's announcement. "With who?" she asked with unease.

"Kanoa," Leilani said, beaming.

Her mother's face paled at the news. "The *hula* dancer?" she asked in disbelief.

"Kanoa is an '*olapa*!" Leilani tried to argue, her heart suddenly pounding furiously in her chest. She had been so sure her mother already knew about and approved of Kanoa. But her reaction to Leilani's confession proved quite the opposite.

"Leilani!" her mother scolded. "You know you are forbidden from even speaking with Kanoa," She threw up her arms in exasperation. "Never mind falling in love with him!" She stood and began pacing back and forth, muttering to herself.

"But, Mama, the other night, when I asked you about Father, I thought you knew already."

Her mother stopped pacing, looking confused for a moment. Then she sighed and shook her head. "You have already been sworn to another. I thought you had found out about it."

Leilani gasped, narrowing her eyes. "Since when? Who is it? Why has no one told me of this yet? I am too young!"

"Last week," her mother interrupted. "Your father negotiated with Pika. You are to marry his son Kale. The arrangement is to be announced in a few days. The wedding will take place at the end of the year." Her mother put her hands on her hips and added, "And you are clearly not too young if you say you are in love with Kanoa!"

Leilani's stomach turned as she felt the bottom fall out from beneath her. She had to grasp at the nearby chair to keep from falling. She couldn't breathe or swallow. No way would she ever marry Pika's son Kale. That was the meanest, toughest family on the island. All the men in the family were known for shaving their heads with shark tooth knives. They prided themselves on their scars from battle wounds and they claimed they couldn't be killed. Not to mention, Pika lived on the other side of the island, where it was hotter and dryer, and mostly barren flat land. There were no cliffs to climb and jump from. Leilani could never live there. This was a total disaster! How could her mother and father do this to her?

"Mama, no!" Leilani pleaded, tears streaming down her face. "I cannot! Please do not make me marry into that vile family!"

"Leilani," her mother sighed.

"What about what I want?" Leilani screamed now. "What am I? Just a thing to be traded? I am your daughter! Do you not love me? Do you not want me to be happy?"

"I love you very much, my Leilani," her mother said. "But this is the way it has always worked."

"No!" Leilani shook her head. "I refuse to believe that! Father is the *ali'i*; he can do whatever he wants!"

"It is not that simple, my sweet heavenly *lei*."

"Ugggh!" Leilani stomped her foot. "It seems that simple to me, Mama! I can't be the first person who didn't want to get married off like this."

"You will grow to love your new husband the way I grew to love your father. The way every woman grows to love her husband."

"No, Mama," Leilani shook her head. "I will never love Kale." Then she took a deep breath. "I already love Kanoa."

The two women stared at each other. Then Leilani raised an eyebrow. "Think about how you feel about Father." she said. "Now imagine being told that you must marry someone else, someone you did not want to be with. Imagine that you were not allowed to be with Father."

Her mother crinkled her brow and continued to stare at Leilani for a moment, and then she frowned.

Leilani felt a spark of hope and kept going. She had to get through to her mother. "I have never had any feelings for boys, Mama, you know this. And now I have found Kanoa and I know that he and I are meant to be together!"

"Oh, Leilani!" Her mother rolled her eyes. "How could you possibly know that? You are so young. You have so much to learn."

Leilani realized that she had almost forgotten the most important argument in her defense. "Both Kanoa and I saw our *aumakuas* on the day we met." She paused, tilting her head. "You know what that means!"

Her mother gasped. "Truly?"

Leilani nodded and told the story of both her encounter with the turtle and Kanoa's encounter with the shark.

Her mother paced back and forth again, thinking, muttering to herself and talking to the Gods. Finally, she stopped and held her hand out to Leilani. "We must talk with your father."

Leilani let out a huge sigh of relief and threw her arms around her mother. It wasn't over yet.

* * *

The two women searched out the *ali'i* after dinner. He was in the courtyard of his personal hut, playing a game of *konane* with Keoki. The two men were sitting on opposite sides of a large flat boulder. The top of the boulder had sixty-four impressions where moveable white and black pebbles sat. Several uncles and male cousins sat on the side, watching in complete silence. Tiki torches surrounded the men, the shadows dancing in the firelight every time the breeze kicked up.

Leilani and her mother waited on the perimeter of the courtyard for the game to end. After nearly an hour, her father made the final move, winning the game. Everyone cheered except Keoki, who sat there studying the board in disbelief. Her father was a master at the game and always won, no matter who he played. He had long ago offered a prize to the first person who could beat him at the game. Keoki was determined to be the one to beat the *ali'i* and win the prize. But tonight was not his night.

Leilani's mother stepped forward, and the *ali'i* smiled at the sight of her. It was rare to see him in such a good mood. As soon as he noticed the serious look on her mother's face however, he immediately sent all the men away except her brother. Keoki looked questioning at Leilani, and she nervously smiled back.

As her mother filled the two men in with the news about Leilani and Kanoa, her father's smile quickly turned into a frown. Before her mother could get far, he slammed his big fist down on the boulder, scattering all the white and black pebbles and making Leilani jump.

He rose, towering over Leilani. "You are descended from Gods. You will not marry a commoner."

"Father!" Leilani cried out. "Kanoa and I are meant to be together!"

"Ha!" The *ali'i* scoffed at such an idea. "My daughter, the princess. And a *hula* dancer!"

"Kanoa is an *'olapa*!" Leilani needed her father to understand that Kanoa was a master at his craft. Her father respected men who were masters.

"I don't care." Her father waved his hand dismissively. "He is still a commoner."

"He is not common to me!" Leilani shouted, frustrated with this commoner nonsense. "I love him!"

"It does not matter!" her father growled, angry at being talked back to by his daughter. "You have already been offered to Kale, son of Pika."

Leilani groaned. "I know; Mama just told me." She stepped toward her father. "But please listen, Papa." She clasped her hands together, pleading as if her life depended on it. "The Gods themselves have brought Kanoa and I together, and they have given us their blessing; we were both visited by our *aumakuas* on the day we met."

Her father narrowed his eyes at this news and then glanced over at her mother, who nodded back at him. "We were visited by our *aumakua* on that same day, as you remember, husband. The day of the *luau*."

Leilani turned to her mother in shock. "Why didn't you tell me this earlier?"

"I am telling you now," her mother said softly and turned back to her father, nodding at him again.

The *ali'i* knit his brow and frowned deeply.

Leilani beamed. "The Gods must have a plan! Do you see now?" She looked back and forth from her mother to her father. "Otherwise, why would they have sent our *aumakuas* to each of us on that day? What else could it mean but that Kanoa and I are meant to be together?"

Her father continued to frown.

"Shouldn't we trust in the Gods?" Leilani continued to push. "They know what is best."

"Perhaps we should bring this matter to the *kahuna*," Keoki suggested.

"Yes!" Leilani said, smiling at her brother and silently thanking him. "His ruling on this matter would be considered final. Pika would have to abide by it."

Her father stared at Leilani for some time before he spoke. "I do not understand you, Leilani." he said, his tone softer now. "You have never done things the right way, ever since you were a baby."

Leilani couldn't help but smile. That was a compliment as far as she was concerned. She didn't know why she was different, why she couldn't just accept things the way they were. But she had to follow her heart.

"We will take this matter to Peleke in two days' time," her father finally decided.

"*Mahalo*!" Leilani threw her arms around her father, thanking him over and over.

He awkwardly hugged her back before pulling her away to look her in the eyes. "But first, I want to meet with Kanoa."

* * *

Leilani snuck away again in the early morning hours while everyone was still sleeping. She hadn't been able to sleep all night, and she wanted to update Kanoa before her father's servants got to him. She waited, hidden in the trees outside the *halau*, for what seemed like an eternity. Kanoa finally emerged near sunrise. He was alone, so she whistled to get his attention.

Kanoa double-checked to make sure they were alone and then ran to her. He picked her up and showered her with kisses. Leilani giggled and kissed him back.

"What has happened?" he asked with concern as he released her.

"I have told my family everything," Leilani explained with a smile. "And my father wants to meet you."

"Oh!" Kanoa's eyes widened.

Leilani laughed. "Do not worry! My mother and father were also visited by our *aumakua* on the day we met. They were unsure what it meant until I informed them of our meeting."

Kanoa nodded and relaxed a bit.

"You will meet with my father today after lunch."

"Today?" Kanoa's eyes widened again.

"Yes, my love!" Leilani kissed Kanoa on the cheek. "And we are all to go see the *kahuna* tomorrow to get his ruling."

"The *kahuna*!" Kanoa was alarmed now. "Why must the *kahuna* get involved?"

Leilani bit her lip. "My father has already arranged to marry me off to one of Pika's sons. Kale."

Kanoa rolled his eyes, slapped his forehead and groaned.

Leilani went on, "He cannot go back on his agreement now unless the *kahuna* declares it to be the wish of the Gods."

Kanoa squeezed his eyes shut and shook his head.

"Do not worry, my love!" She caressed his cheek. "We already have the blessing of the Gods!"

Kanoa opened his eyes and managed a small smile. "My love," he took her hands, "I will do everything I can to win your father over and persuade the *kahuna* of our destiny to be together."

Leilani smiled and jumped into his arms.

* * *

"I know of a better vantage point," Keoki whispered in Leilani's ear, startling her and nearly causing her to fall from atop the pile of rocks she had stacked up against the back fence of her father's private courtyard. An hour earlier, her father's servants had led Kanoa inside and then placed guards at the entrance.

She clumsily climbed down and punched Keoki as hard as she could in the arm. "You scared me!"

He chuckled and headed off around the corner of the fence. "Follow me."

She did as instructed, and Keoki led her to a forty-foot-tall banyan tree. He started climbing up, stopping briefly to look back at her, silently challenging her to keep up with him. It had been a while since Leilani had climbed a tree with Keoki, though they used to do it all the time as kids. Until Keoki had grown up and started training to be a warrior.

Leilani started up the tree, trying to catch up to her brother. She looked up just as he veered off to the left on a big branch above her. She scrambled up and over the same way. "Remember when we used to do this all the time?" she asked and then noticed someone else was already up there with her brother.

"Nani!" Leilani said, surprised.

"I brought Nani here to watch; she was worried when she found out what was going on with her brother," Keoki explained.

"How did she find out?" Leilani cast an accusing glance at Keoki.

"The rumors are spreading throughout the village, princess," Nani told her.

"What?" Leilani asked, shocked by this news.

"People in the *halau* started gossiping when two of your father's servants came to fetch Kanoa earlier," Keoki replied. "Word quickly spread to the village after that. Someone saw you near the *halua* recently. So everyone is guessing."

Leilani glanced at Nani, the only person she knew of who had seen her near the *halua*.

"It wasn't me, princess!" Nani swore.

"You aren't the only one sneaking around out there, sister," Keoki interjected. "Perhaps I should teach you how to hide better."

Leilani slapped her brother's leg with a frown.

"Ouch!" he teased her.

Leilani smiled at Nani. "Please, no more of this princess stuff! We may be sisters soon. You can call me Leilani."

Nani nodded, a grin spreading across her face.

Keoki nudged Leilani and pointed down to the courtyard.

Leilani had been so distracted that she hadn't realized what a great view of the courtyard she had from twenty feet up in the tree. She could clearly see the *ali'i* sitting at the *konane* boulder with Kanoa, and they were in the middle of a game. Interesting.

"Does Kanoa even play *konane*?" she asked Nani.

"He used to play," Nani said. "Our grandfather taught him."

"Is he any good?"

"Yes," Nani said with pride. "He is quite good."

The three conspirators watched in silence. It was difficult to tell who was winning. The *ali'i* looked more serious than he had the other night when he had played Keoki. Kanoa looked nervous. He seemed to be sweating profusely, even though they were under the shade of a Koa tree and the day was cool and breezy.

Kanoa made a move and sat back, looking at the *ali'i* expectantly. The *ali'i* looked surprised at first, but then he smiled and clapped Kanoa on the back. "Excellent! Excellent!" he said loudly, laughing. "I have finally found my match at *konane*."

Leilani looked over to see Keoki frowning. He had wanted to be the one to defeat their father at Konane.

"You three can come down now," the *ali'i* said, standing and looking up toward the banyan tree.

Leilani felt her face turn red from being caught. She climbed down and ran around the fence past the guards into the courtyard and straight into Kanoa's arms.

"I wasn't sure if I should play the game to the best of my abilities or if I should let your father win," Kanoa whispered in Leilani's ear.

"I'm so glad you chose to play fairly!" Leilani whispered back.

The *ali'i* cleared his throat, and the two lovebirds reluctantly separated.

"Kanoa has proven himself to be a formidable opponent. This is surely another sign from the Gods," her father declared. "We leave to see the *kahuna* first thing in the morning."

Leilani and Kanoa smiled at each other. One obstacle cleared, only one more to go.

* * *

Leilani and her family arrived at the foot of the trail leading to the *kahuna*'s temple before sun up. They brought along several servants and two of her father's warriors. Kanoa and his family showed up soon afterward. Right away, Leilani could see how much Kanoa resembled his father in his build, but he had his mother's eyes. Kanoa's mother seemed quite frail and nervous though. Leilani worried about her ability to handle the journey they were about to take. The *kahuna* lived in a remote part of the island in a *heiau* built just for him. The difficult journey would take several hours.

The *ali'i* started up the trail with one of his warriors, and the rest of the group followed. The other warrior took up position at the back of the group. At first, the path was well worn and easy to travel, and the group chatted amongst themselves quietly. The day soon turned warm and sunny. Leilani couldn't help but admire the scenery along the way. Rainbow eucalyptus trees towered over them and lush green tropical plants and colorful flowers bordered the path. Birds of different colors and sizes flew from tree to tree, each singing their own unique song. Butterflies and bees flew from flower to flower.

But soon the trees and plants grew thicker and the path narrower. The terrain became steeper. A stream flowed down the mountain next to the trail, and sometimes their path forced them to cross it. Kanoa's mother nearly slipped several times while trying to cross, but Kanoa and his father were always there to catch her. Leilani's heart soared as she watched Kanoa take gentle care of his mother.

She felt so free and happy that she almost forgot the serious nature of their journey. But every time she caught a glimpse of Kanoa's mother, the reality of the situation came crashing back. His mother's face became more drawn and pale the closer they got to the *kahuna* and his decision regarding her son.

At mid-day they finally reached a large, impressive stone structure sitting in the middle of a cleared open area. The *kahuna* stood just outside of the *heiau*, watching the group as they emerged from the jungle as if he had been waiting for them.

The *kahuna* looked much older than he had the last time Leilani had seen him. Deep-set wrinkles lined his face; his long hair and beard were now all white instead of black and gray, and he stood hunched over in his long white robes. He steadied himself with a crooked wooden staff made from Koa wood. He seemed much too frail for Leilani's liking.

"Peleke." The *ali'i* crossed to the *kahuna* as the rest of the group waited at the edge of the trees. "I come to you today for your help in a truly delicate matter. Only one who speaks with the Gods can solve our dilemma."

The *kahuna* nodded his understanding and then turned, slowly making his way into the *heiau*. The *ali'i* motioned for Leilani and Kanoa to follow the *kahuna*. The interior of the *heiau* was even more impressive than the exterior. The *heiau* had paved floors; even the *ali'i* didn't have paved floors in his private quarters. Statues of Ku, the God the *heiau* was dedicated to, stood in each corner of the main worship room. The *kahuna* attempted to sit down on a straw mat on a slightly raised platform in the center of the room. When it looked like he was about to topple over in his efforts, the *ali'i* rushed over to assist.

Once the *kahuna* was finally settled, the *ali'i* proceeded to explain the situation with Leilani and Kanoa. The *kahuna* nodded as the *ali'i* spoke, showing no signs of emotion or opinion. The *ali'i* described the predicament regarding the prearranged marriage agreement with Pika. After the *ali'i* finished speaking, the *kahuna* took a moment before he spoke.

"I will need to pray to the Gods for an answer." His deep, strong voice surprised Leilani. Maybe he wasn't so frail after all. He signaled for them to leave the *heiau*.

Leilani and Kanoa shuffled outside after the *ali'i*. Everyone turned toward them expectantly. "It will take time for the Gods to give us their answer," the *ali'i* told the group. "We set up camp for the night." He tasked his servants with setting up temporary shelters and then he, Keoki and his two warriors headed off into the forest. Leilani's mother made her way over to assist Kanoa's mother.

Leilani and Kanoa were alone at last.

"I'm so anxious to get this over with!" Leilani admitted as she took Kanoa's hand and smiled up at him.

"Me, too." Kanoa smiled back at her but the smile did not reach his eyes. He seemed more somber about the situation than she was. He looked down and took Leilani's other hand. Clasping and unclasping her hands with his, he studied the way their hands fit together.

"We are meant to be together, my love." Leilani squeezed his hands, trying to reassure him.

"I know we are." Kanoa smiled again.

"So," Leilani said, trying to distract him from his worries. "What exactly did my father discuss with you yesterday?"

"He tested me," Kanoa said.

"I know, and you passed his test when you beat him at *konane*!"

"No, before that. He told me if the Gods allowed us to marry, then he would accept their decision, but he would have to cut us off from the village. We would have to make it on our own somewhere else."

Leilani's eyebrows shot up. "He wouldn't!"

"I told him that I didn't care how or where I lived my life with you. As long as we were together, I would be happy and I would make sure you were happy, too."

Leilani threw her arms around him. "I just want to be with you, too! I don't care how or where!"

Kanoa laughed and pulled back to look her in the eyes. "We will not be cut off. Your father told me that I gave the right answer. He had worried that my intentions were not pure. But he could see that I truly love you."

Leilani huffed. "You're such a tease sometimes!" She playfully tried to push him away but he kept her locked in his arms. "What will we do though?" she wondered aloud. "Will you still dance the *hula*?"

"I'm not sure they will allow it," Kanoa said sadly.

Leilani pursed her lips. Now that they actually had a chance at a future together, they would have to figure out the details.

The *ali'i* returned soon with Keoki and his warriors, carrying several dead chickens and a squealing pig. The servants got right to work. Two pits were dug out in the middle of the open area and fires were built. The pig was sacrificed in the *heiau* to the Gods and then prepared for roasting. The chickens were prepared for the women to eat, since pig was *kapu* for women. Kanoa and Nani kept everyone entertained with *hula* dances as they waited for the pig and chickens to roast. As dusk settled and the food was finally ready, the men and women separated to eat. Bellies were filled and then the group settled in for the night. Laughter came from the men's group. Leilani watched as Kanoa easily interacted with Keoki and her father. They were truly meant to be together. She knew it in her heart. As she drifted off to sleep, she dreamed of her future life with Kanoa.

* * *

Pika crept silently through the trees by the light of the moon with two of his strongest men. His lips were twisted in a scowl. This little excursion had been unanticipated and inconvenient but absolutely necessary. Earlier in the day, when he had first heard about the *ali'i*'s visit to the *kahuna* and the rumors surrounding it, he had known he would need to move quickly to ensure that his voice was heard in the matter. His voice would definitely be heard! He had come too far to lose it all now. Especially to such a commoner. A *hula* dancer. He scowled even deeper and growled in disgust.

It was well past midnight as Pika and his men reached the opening around the *heiau*. He had already discussed his plan with his men. As one of his men crept into the *heiau*, he waited in the trees with the other. The man emerged a few minutes later with Peleke, who looked to be half asleep and confused about what was happening. Pika's man led him to Pika.

"What is the meaning of this—" the *kahuna* started to ask when he saw Pika, but Pika's man immediately put a knife to his throat, drawing blood. Pika put a finger to his lips and smiled ruthlessly. The *kahuna*'s eyes widened with fear. Pika turned and led the group deeper into the trees, away from the *heiau*, where they could speak without being heard.

When they were far enough away, Pika turned and faced the *kahuna*. "You were wondering why we pulled you from your sleep in the middle of the night."

The *kahuna* nodded hesitantly, eyeing Pika's man with the knife, who stood close by.

"It's a simple matter really," Pika began cheerfully. "I want you to confirm the marriage arrangement between my son and the daughter of the *ali'i*."

The *kahuna* looked nervously back and forth between Pika and his man with the knife. "I have been praying to the Gods this very night over the matter."

"Good!" Pika slapped him on the back.

The *kahuna* gulped. "But the Gods are in favor of the marriage of Leilani to Kanoa."

Pike narrowed his eyes and frowned at this news. "Are you quite certain?"

The *kahuna* nodded slowly, noticing that Pika's man with the knife was now polishing the blade in the moonlight. He was determined to follow the will of the Gods, even if it meant Pika might harm him. The Gods would do him more harm if he disobeyed their will than Pika ever could.

"I disagree," Pika said. "My own priests, who are very devout, have confirmed that my son is still favored by the Gods for the daughter of the *ali'i*."

The *kahuna* shook his head. He was the foremost authority on the will of the Gods. "I'm afraid that they are wrong. There have been many signs—"

Pika cut him off. "Yes, let's speak of signs!" He gave the *kahuna* another slap on the back. "Here's a sign for you to consider. The heads of your sister and her sons and daughters, and their sons and daughters, roasting over the fires on spits." Pika smiled. "That will be their future if you do not rule in my son's favor."

The *kahuna* paled at the threat. He thought of all his nieces and nephews; so young and full of life and promise. He couldn't bear the thought of any harm coming to them. He studied Pika. Would Pika really do this evil thing he threatened?

Pika smiled that terrible smile again. His eyes gleamed, as if he relished the idea of performing such terrible acts.

The *kahuna* knew what he had to do.

* * *

Leilani woke in the morning to the sound of the *kahuna* speaking in hushed tones with her father. She jumped up and hurried over to hear the news. The *ali'i* did not look happy.

"Father, what is it?" Leilani asked.

Everyone else began to gather around. Neither the *kahuna* nor the *ali'i* spoke for a moment. The *kahuna* stared down at the ground, refusing to lift his eyes. The *ali'i* paced, looking back and forth from the *kahuna* to Leilani. Finally, he approached Leilani and took her tiny hands in his.

"My precious daughter," he began sadly.

Leilani's heart dropped. She shook her head and put her hands over her ears, knowing what was coming but not wanting to hear the words spoken out loud.

"I'm afraid the Gods have declared the marriage contract with Pika's son to be final."

"No, no, no, no, no!" Leilani yelled out, wild eyed. She ran to the *kahuna,* who continued to stare at the ground. "This is not right!" She tried to get the *kahuna* to look at her but he refused.

Her mother rushed over and tried to soothe her, but Leilani would not have it. She pushed her mother aside and ran to Kanoa.

Kanoa looked sadly down at Leilani. *Let's run away*, she tried to tell him with her eyes. A tear fell down her cheek, and he wiped it away. "I will always love you, Leilani."

Her father's warriors separated them.

Leilani fought them off, kicking and scratching at them and ran back to the *kahuna*. This wasn't right! "Please!" she begged. "Ask one more time! I know the Gods brought us together for a reason!"

But the *kahuna* turned and walked away, retreating into his *heiau*.

Leilani fell to her knees, sobbing. "Father, please."

Her father pulled her up into his arms, embracing her as he never had before. "Leilani," he tried to soothe her, "we must honor the decision of the *kahuna*. I promise everything will be all right."

"No, everything will *not* be all right," she screamed and pounded her fists against her father. Reluctantly, he let her go. She took off running into the jungle.

She ran as fast as she could for as long as she could, tears clouding her vision. She ran deep into untraveled terrain, falling and cutting and bruising herself several times without even feeling it. When she finally collapsed from exhaustion, she was surprised to see her wounds. Not caring, she searched and found a small cave to hide in. It seemed no one had followed her. She sighed and hiccupped. This was a disaster, she thought as the tears flowed again. Her life was over.

Chapter 4

Pu'uwai hao kila

Heart of steel

Leilani woke to darkness. She sat up and listened for signs of life but heard nothing more than the wind. She didn't know what her next move would be, but she wasn't going back to her village. She was done with all of it. She was done with being a princess and following orders. She would die before she married Pika's son. She knew in her heart that her destiny was with Kanoa.

Where was Kanoa right now? She suddenly worried about him. Perhaps she could sneak to the *halau* to see him. No. She would surely be caught if she did that.

Her stomach rumbled. She hadn't eaten all day. By the position of the moon in the sky, it must be close to sunrise. She forced herself to get up to search for fruit. And water. She was so thirsty. Crying all those tears was to blame. She tiptoed quietly through the trees in case any of her father's men were camped nearby. They would be looking for her.

She found a stream and gulped greedily until she could handle no more. Then she washed away the dried blood from her cuts. Next, she found a mango tree and climbed it, picking the closest mango within reach. She sat on a limb, numbly eating her mango, and thought of the time she had found Kanoa in a tree eating a mango. Everything had changed that day. If only she could go back in time. They should have run away together. They might have had a chance together if they had.

Leilani considered her options as she sat in the tree waiting for the sun to come up.

* * *

Pika and one of his men watched Leilani from a safe distance.

"Let's take her now and tie her up," Pika's man said anxiously.

"No," Pika explained calmly once again. "We must wait for her father to get here. He must deal with her. Not us."

Pika's man grimaced. "What if we lose her?"

"We will not lose her," Pika growled. "She is just a girl."

* * *

Leilani heard someone coming. She pulled her feet up onto the branch where she was perched and held her breath, waiting to see who it was.

Kanoa crashed through the trees below and came to an abrupt stop. He looked around frantically.

Leilani's heart stopped at the sight of him but she waited a moment before revealing herself in case anyone else was with him. When it looked as if he was about to leave, she broke a twig from the tree and threw it toward him.

The twig hit him the head. Leilani gasped and bit her lip. She hadn't meant to hit him in the head. He massaged his head and looked up, and his irritation turned to relief as he spotted Leilani perched in the tree.

"I'm sorry! Is it safe?" Leilani whispered.

He nodded. "Yes! I am alone!" He extended his arms out for her. "You can come down."

Leilani dropped down to the ground and rushed into Kanoa's arms. He held her tightly to him and kissed her forehead, cheeks and nose. In his arms, she felt safe and happy again.

"Are you all right?" he looked her over and inspected her cuts and bruises.

"I'm all right," Leilani assured him. "Are you?"

"Yes. I told your father that I would help look for you," Kanoa explained. "We all spread out to find you."

"I'm not going back!" Leilani took a step back.

"No, I know." Kanoa stepped toward her, closing the gap. "I'm not here to take you back."

Leilani nodded. "I can't believe the *kahuna* ruled against us." She threw her hands up. "I thought the Gods brought us together for a reason."

"They did," Kanoa said, taking her hand. "I think Pika is behind this."

Leilani gasped.

"He is a ruthless man," Kanoa said. "He is the only one who has anything to lose if you and I are allowed to be together."

Leilani nodded.

"I think he threatened the *kahuna*."

Leilani raised her eyebrows. "Why do you think such a thing?"

"I saw the *kahuna* returning from the jungle late last night," Kanoa explained. "He kept looking behind him, as if someone else was back there. And he looked frightened."

Leilani bit her lip, considering this news. "I know he has a bad reputation," Leilani agreed. "But to defy the Gods?"

Kanoa shrugged.

"But the Gods favor us!" Leilani protested. "Won't the Gods help us?"

"I hope so." Kanoa looked up to the heavens.

"What should we do?"

"We must leave now. My father has a canoe. He taught me how to navigate on the open sea. I have relatives on a distant island. They will protect us. But we must hurry."

Leilani frowned. "We can talk to my father now, tell him what you saw, what you believe happened...."

Kanoa shook his head. "We could never prove it. Pika would deny it."

Leilani thought about it. There truly was no other way. "All right." she finally agreed.

Kanoa took her hand and led her back into the jungle.

* * *

They traveled back down the mountain in the opposite direction on a less-traveled path. Even though the terrain was more difficult and dangerous, they moved efficiently and silently. Every time they heard the slightest sound, they both stopped to listen, on high alert. But there were no signs of anyone following them and the farther they got, the braver and more confident they became.

The sun was just beginning its decent in the sky as they neared the lagoon where Kanoa's father had left the canoe for their escape. They stopped at the edge of the trees to survey the area. They waited, watched and listened. But the beach was deserted.

"Stay here while I go prepare the canoe," Kanoa told Leilani.

"No! I want to help!"

"It will only take me a moment. If anyone is watching and they see you with me...."

Leilani reluctantly nodded her understanding.

"Keep a lookout," he told her.

She nodded again.

Kanoa turned and walked toward the canoe, surveying the area as he went. When he got to the canoe, he quickly went to work preparing it for their voyage.

As soon as he signaled, Leilani ran to him.

Just as Kanoa was about to help Leilani into the canoe, four men emerged from the trees. Pika, his son and two of their men. Leilani's heart stopped.

"Halt!" Pika demanded, pulling out his infamous shark-tooth knife. Pika's son carried a shark-tooth club, and their two men each had long spears.

"Get in the canoe," Kanoa whispered to Leilani. He reached down to the bottom of the canoe and grabbed something hidden under the supplies. A spear! He turned toward Pika with it.

"No!" Leilani cried, trying to pull Kanoa away.

"I mean you no harm." Pika and his men stopped a few feet from Kanoa and Leilani. Pika put his hands up in a gesture of peace.

"You *do* mean us harm," Kanoa said. "I know you threatened the *kahuna*!"

"I did no such thing!" Pika turned to Leilani and spoke to her in a different tone, as if she were a silly child. "You know you must abide by the *kahuna*'s decision, little one. Your father is on his way. We are to keep you from doing anything rash until he gets here."

"You lie!" Leilani snarled. "How is it that you are even here?" Leilani didn't give Pika a chance to respond. She continued, "And don't tell me you just happened to be in the area. The *kahuna* was behaving very oddly yesterday when he told us his decision. He would look no one in the eye. You did something."

Pika merely shook his head and shrugged.

"The Gods are on our side," Leilani said. "And we are leaving."

One of Pika's men made a move to grab Leilani. Kanoa reacted by attempting to use his spear on him. The man ducked the shot and grabbed hold of Leilani's arm. Pika's son came at Kanoa with his club next. Kanoa ducked, the club narrowly missing him.

Leilani struggled to free herself from Pika's man, watching in horror as Kanoa and Kale started fighting. She was surprised at the skill with which Kanoa fought. Kanoa managed to strike Kale in the leg with his spear, leaving a long bloody gash down his left calf. Kale roared out in anger.

"Enough!" Pika roared, grabbing Leilani by a handful of her long hair and dragging her to him.

Leilani cried out.

Kanoa paled. "Don't hurt her."

"Drop your weapon," Pika ordered.

Kanoa hesitated.

Pika held his shark-tooth knife to Leilani's throat, and she whimpered as blood was drawn.

Kanoa dropped his spear.

Kale instantly moved in, hitting Kanoa over the head with his club. Kanoa fell to the ground.

Leilani screamed, and Pika lowered the knife. Feeling a powerful drive to survive take over, she thrashed and kicked at Pika, not caring anymore about getting injured. She would not be a victim. She would fight back. She managed to free one arm. She turned, intending to scratch his eye out, but Pika ducked and her nails clawed down the side of his nose instead. Pika roared in frustration and then punched her in the stomach, knocking the wind out of her. She wilted but Pika held her in a firm grip. She was powerless. She began to weep.

"Now why did you have to go and do that just as I had everything under control?" Pika shouted, directing his anger at both Kale and Leilani.

Kale shrugged carelessly. "He had it coming."

Pika wiped at the blood running down his nose and spat at Leilani.

Kanoa sprung up then with his spear in hand and stabbed Kale straight through the heart. The injured man stood there in shock for a moment, looking wide-eyed at his father and then finally he looked down in disbelief at the spear in his chest. He fell to his knees in slow motion and then collapsed on the ground, lifeless.

Pika was on Kanoa in an instant. "You should not have done that," Pika growled between clenched teeth as he slowly slit Kanoa's neck from one side to the other with the shark-tooth knife. Kanoa's eyes widened in shock as blood gushed from the fatal wound.

Leilani watched in horror as Kanoa's face went white, and his eyeballs rolled back in his head. She ran to him as his limp body fell to the ground. She tried to cover the wound with her hands, to stop all the blood from leaving his body. But it was impossible. There was so much blood. She tried to lift his head but his body was limp. He was already gone. She heard a strange sound, like an animal, coming from a faraway place then. In shock, she realized the sound was coming from her.

Several fat raindrops splattered on Leilani's cheeks and lightning crashed down nearby, lighting up the grisly scene for an instant. A loud crash of thunder came seconds later.

Pika jumped, glancing fearfully up at the darkening sky and then back down at Leilani, who was still wailing.

"What has happened here?" The *ali'i* had arrived, along with her mother, brother and his men carrying torches. Her father's men pulled out their spears and knives as they took in the dead bodies.

Pika said nothing but knelt in submission.

"You're too late," Leilani whimpered. She rose on unsteady legs, turned and then ran.

People called out to her, but she ignored them. She ran and ran, her only thought to get away, far, far away. A heavy rain fell. Soon she was at the base of her cliff. Looking back, she saw the torches coming, pursuing her. She didn't have much time.

"Leilani!" her mother cried out from below as she climbed up the cliff. "Please, for the love of the Gods, stop!"

Leilani slipped and almost fell at the sound of her mother's distraught voice but she continued on.

She heard other voices but they were getting distant now as she climbed higher and higher. More lightning lit up the night sky and deep rumbling thunder followed. The climb was slick from the rain, and Leilani slipped a few more times, but she was determined to reach the top. Nothing would stop her.

Once she reached the top of the cliff, she looked back down. Her mother was down there, yelling up at her, but Leilani couldn't hear anything she was saying. Several men were trying to climb the mountain but they weren't getting far. They kept slipping on the wet rocks. One man was steadily making progress despite the wet conditions. Leilani knew it was her brother and that he would make it all the way to the top.

She walked to the other edge of the cliff. She was soaked from the rain, and the wind whipped her wet hair around her face but she felt nothing. The waves below were more ferocious and violent than she had ever seen them before. She raised her arms to the Gods and looked up to the sky. "Why?" she demanded. There was no reply.

"Don't!" her brother called out, panic in his voice. He had reached the top.

"It's too late," Leilani said without turning.

"Leilani," he pleaded with her. "Let me help you!"

"No!" Leilani yelled.

"Kanoa would not want you to do this."

Leilani waivered. But she would never forget the look on Kanoa's face as he had died. "Kanoa is no longer here."

And then she jumped.

PART 2

Mohala ka pua, ua wehe kaiao

The blossoms are opening, for dawn is breaking

Modern Day

Chapter 5

"*Puanani Kekoa, your great-grandmother, has passed away and she left you, her only living heir, her home in Hawaii.*"

These words kept repeating in my mind as I sat on the plane headed to Hawaii for the first time. Two short weeks had passed since getting this news from Duke, my great-grandmother's estate lawyer. Apparently my great-grandmother had really wanted me to come to Hawaii. Her will stipulated that I couldn't sell the house until I had lived in it for two years. It wasn't a difficult decision for me. Within days of hearing the news, I quit my job and sold almost everything I owned for the move.

Hawaii! Who wouldn't want to move to Hawaii? Nothing was tying me to California where I had grown up. My grandparents and parents were gone, and I didn't have any siblings, aunts or uncles or close friends that I would miss. My job at a big CPA firm was both stressful and boring, if such a thing was possible, and I was ready to leave. I could easily find a new job in Hawaii. Hawaii would be a fresh start for me.

The pilot came over the loudspeaker, interrupting my thoughts. He announced that we were beginning our descent into Honolulu. I had booked a window seat specifically so that I could see the islands as we flew in. I peered out excitedly now, looking for my first glimpse of Hawaii.

The deep, dark blue ocean turned more turquoise and then suddenly white sandy beaches came into view. Lush green mountains rose up in the background. The spectacular view left me breathless. I couldn't wait to land and see Hawaii up close and personal!

The plane touched down with a bumpy landing and taxied to the terminal much too slowly for my liking. I tapped my foot anxiously. As soon as the plane stopped and the steward gave his okay to move about, I quickly gathered up my belongings and waited impatiently for my turn to exit the plane. As I followed the other passengers toward the baggage claim area, I was instantly struck by how warm and humid the Hawaiian air was. The airport was partially open to the outside, where palm trees swayed and lovely pink-and-yellow flowers grew. Hawaiian music played in the background, relaxing melodies with ukuleles and slack-key guitars. I started to relax and couldn't help but smile. Even though I had barely arrived, I already felt like I was home.

While waiting for my luggage to come out on the conveyer belt, I scanned the crowd for Duke, who was supposed to be picking me up and taking me to my new home. Duke had described himself as a tall thin man with graying hair in his fifties. He'd told me that he would be wearing a blue *aloha* shirt and tan pants. Just such a man suddenly appeared, smiling and waving at me.

"Liz?"

"Yes." I returned the smile. "Duke?"

"Yes! Yes! *Aloha*! Welcome!" He produced a white-and-purple *lei* and placed it around my neck. I stuck my nose in it and inhaled deeply. It smelled wonderfully Hawaiian to me.

"You have bags?" he asked, nodding toward the conveyer belt, which had started moving.

"Two big ones!" I admitted.

We didn't wait long before I spotted my bags. Duke grabbed them as they went by and then he helped me wheel them to his car, a shiny black Lexus, parked in the attached garage.

"I'll take you on a short tour of the island first, if you're up for it, on the way to your new home," Duke offered.

"I'd love a tour!" I grinned.

As Duke drove away from the airport, I gazed out the car window. The Hawaiian sky was a brighter shade of blue than the sky in California. The brilliant white puffy clouds seemed to move across the sky with greater speed here. Duke told me all about the sights as we drove. We inched our way down the crowded freeway until the Waikiki exit. Big hotels lined the street across from the ocean and hundreds of tourists walked around in sundresses, bikinis and board shorts. Some tourists carried surfboards; others carried bags from expensive shops. I had to laugh when I spotted an older guy with long gray hair pulled back in a ponytail, wearing nothing more than board shorts and flip flops, dancing carefree along the sidewalk.

"Lots of interesting people down here," Duke commented with a chuckle.

He headed back to the freeway and then drove us around to the lower southeastern edge of the island, where ferocious white-capped waves crashed violently against black rocky cliffs. Cars were haphazardly parked along the narrow edge of the road and people were hiking down the cliffs, trying to get as close to nature as they could. We drove past busy beaches where sunbathers were lying in the sand and surfers were out catching waves. And finally, we drove through Kailua, a small town on the eastside of the island, which Duke called the windward side, where my great-grandmother's home, now my home, was located.

Duke explained that the home was a couple of blocks from the Kailua beach, considered one of the best beaches in the world. The houses here were mostly older little one-level cottages set close together. Palm trees and surfboard occupied most yards. Duke parked in front of an older blue house with several tall palm trees in the front yard and a stone fence around the perimeter. It looked perfect!

After Duke helped me bring in my luggage, he took me on a tour of the house. The front room had big open windows on three sides and a wood floor. A faded floral sofa and a matching loveseat hugged the walls and a worn wicker coffee table sat in the middle of the room. I thought of ways I'd redecorate when I had a chance, with more modern island-style furnishings. The small kitchen had a seventies vibe with old beige linoleum, white painted cabinetry and a blue tile backsplash. There was no room for a table or chairs. A little old beige fridge stood awkwardly against the back wall next to the back door. In the backyard, a glass table and four chairs sat on the covered patio. The washer and dryer were also under the covered patio, which I thought was odd. But Duke told me that everyone in Hawaii kept their washers and dryers outside. A small grassy area bordered the patio and a few more palm trees stood along the back edge of the stone fence. Duke called the patio the *lanai*.

We went back inside through the kitchen to the living room and then down a short hallway to the two bedrooms. The main bedroom held a queen-sized bed with a faded floral bedspread and a big wicker dresser with a matching mirror. The other bedroom held a twin bed and a smaller dresser identical to the one in the master. One bathroom connected the bedrooms with the same beige linoleum. The sink and tub looked worn but clean.

Back in the kitchen, Duke brought out a handful of documents and had me sign in several places.

"Liz, this house is now yours, free and clear!" he announced when I was finished signing. Then he laughed. "Well, besides the property taxes, that is!" He handed me a binder full of documents.

"We had a professional cleaning company come in and clean the whole place, top to bottom." Duke opened the fridge and cupboards to show me. Everything was clean and empty.

"We boxed up all of your great-grandmother's clothes and belongings, in case you wanted to look through it all. The boxes are all in the spare bedroom closet."

I was looking forward to going through those boxes. I nodded. "I never got the chance to meet my great-grandmother."

Duke gave me a sad smile. "I know, family issues."

I nodded.

"Maybe you can get to know her a little by living here now," he suggested. "Now, the electricity and water and cable are all on in my name, so you'll need to change those over to your name in the next week." Back to business, Duke handed me a piece of paper with information on all the utility companies.

A knock on the front door interrupted us. An older lady stood on the front porch, smiling at us through the screen door. "*Aloha!*" she called out.

"Liz, this is Ruth, your next door neighbor," Duke introduced us as we stepped outside.

Ruth was an older native Hawaiian woman in her sixties. She had warm bright eyes and long black and graying hair pulled back in a bun.

"*E komo mai!* Welcome to the island and the neighborhood!" She hugged me and kissed my cheek.

"Thank you!" I wasn't used to hugging and kissing strangers, but I tried not to show it.

"I knew your great-grandmother for many years. She was a wonderful woman," Ruth told me. "She will be missed."

"What was she like?" I asked, intrigued.

"She loved telling stories!" Ruth laughed. "She was a singer, got to be pretty famous in the '50s. She wrote a few Hawaiian songs. Spoke fluent Hawaiian. And she taught Hawaiian language and *hula* classes later in life."

"Wow. She sounds awesome."

"She was! She respected and loved the ancient Hawaiian ways and worked tirelessly to preserve them."

I thought of my mother and grandmother, Hawaiian women who wanted nothing to do with the Hawaiian ways. I didn't understand how anyone could reject their heritage like that. I planned on learning whatever I could about my ancestors.

Before leaving, Ruth offered to help me with whatever I needed while getting settled in. We made plans to go grocery shopping together later in the day.

Duke left soon after with the offer to call him if I ever needed anything. Alone at last, I walked around the house again, examining everything more carefully now. Pictures of my great-grandmother were scattered throughout the house. She had been an attractive woman with long flowing dark hair, a smile that lit up her whole face and eyes that sparkled mischievously. I was surprised to find a picture of me as a little girl. I wondered how she got the picture and wished again that I could have known my great-grandmother. It was a real shame that my parents hadn't ever tried to bring me to Hawaii to meet her while she was still alive. She was family, after all.

My next priority was a walk to the beach. It only took me ten minutes to walk several blocks to a beach access point. Before I knew it, I was looking at the most gorgeous white sandy beach I had ever seen. The ocean was an amazing aqua blue. I took off my flip flops and squished my toes in the soft, warm sand. It felt wonderful between my toes. I walked down to the water's edge and let the small waves wash over my feet as I took it all in.

I was surprised by how warm the water was. The California ocean was never this warm.

I spent the next couple of hours walking all the way down to one end of the beach and then back. People were out with their kids or their dogs, playing in the sand and the water, surfing and body boarding, laughing and having a good time.

I had to get back for my grocery shopping date with Ruth. And I really needed to find a used car. I appreciated Duke's quick tour of the island, but I couldn't wait to get out there and explore it on my own.

True to her word, Ruth drove me to a nearby grocery store. I felt like I was in a whole new world full of foods that I'd never seen before. There were aisles of interesting-looking Asian foods and some kind of raw fish called *poke*. Ruth explained that *poke* was a local favorite. She explained that it was cubed *ahi sashimi*, otherwise known as yellowfin tuna, marinated with sea salt, soy sauce, sesame oil, seaweed and chopped chili pepper. She got a sample for me from the guy behind the meat counter. I took a small bite and grimaced. I had tried and liked fancy sushi rolls before but this *poke* was basically just raw fish. I wasn't sure about it. Ruth laughed and said I'd get used to it.

Back home with my groceries all put away, and a little shell shocked at the price of food in Hawaii, I dug out my laptop from my bag and got to searching for a car on Craigslist. As I scanned the ads, I munched on local-style roast *Huli-huli* chicken that I'd bought at the store. This chicken was exceptionally moist and sweet. Delicious! I licked my fingers. I clicked on a couple of ads and was happy to see prices below Kelly Blue Book low values. I emailed a couple of people, asking if I could test drive their cars in the next day or two.

Next, I got the boxes out of the closet in the guest room and started going through my great-grandmother's stuff. One box held various Hawaiian print dresses and several wood-carved jewelry boxes full of necklaces, earrings and brooches featuring colorful Hawaiian flowers. Another box contained old Hawaiian records and music books, old Hawaiian maps and some vintage Hawaiian postcards from various people to my great-grandmother. And an ukulele. I took the ukulele out and strummed it, thinking of my great-grandmother playing it.

Suddenly feeling exhausted, I noticed that it had gotten dark outside. Yawning, I put everything back in the box. I intended to go back through it all again another day. My great-grandmother didn't seem like such a stranger anymore. Even though I had never met her, I felt like I had gotten to know her a little today.

I headed to the master bedroom with my luggage and congratulated myself on a successful first day in Hawaii. I threw on an old T-shirt and went to the bathroom to brush my teeth. I studied myself in the mirror as I brushed. Not bad. At least I had nice eyes, kind of like my great-grandmother's eyes actually. I rinsed and put my toothbrush away. Finally, I took my blond wig off and hung it on a stand. Maybe I should get a brunette wig now. I'd definitely look more like my great-grandmother if I was brunette.

Looking at my reflection in the mirror again, I caressed the smooth contour of my bald head. Even though it had been twelve years since I'd lost my hair, I still didn't recognize the bald girl in the mirror as myself. I shook my head and turned off the light.

Back in the bedroom, I climbed into my great-grandmother's surprisingly comfortable bed. As I began drifting off to sleep, I wondered what she would think of me if she had ever had the chance to meet me. Would she like me? Or would she think I was a freak of nature?

Chapter 6

The next day, Ruth drove me around again. I test drove two cars and decided to buy a blue Hyundai Tucson. At the local bank, I signed up for a new checking and savings account and got a cashier's check to pay for the car.

I bought a guide book at a local bookstore and explored the island. I drove on the elevated highway running along and tunneling through the majestic Koolua Mountains, the 3,000-foot-tall, dramatic, knife-edge mountain range separating the windward side from the rest of the island. I headed out to the west side of the island until the road stopped at a rugged, rocky beach. I also went north along the eastside of the island, where winding roads on the coast took me past little towns with advertisements for shave ice and shrimp.

On my first trip to the North Shore, where the famous surfing competitions take place every year, I noticed a bunch of cars parked on the side of the road across from a breathtakingly beautiful beach. I decided to investigate. After finding a tight spot to park my car and then waiting for a long line of cars to pass, I ran across the street to the beach. A few surfers were out catching waves while sun bathers lounged on towels, watching. A little further down the beach a group of tourists circled around something. As I approached, several people stepped away from the circle and I saw two big sea turtles napping on the sand near the water. Several other big turtles bobbed up and down in the waves.

I had never seen such turtles. They were huge! Each turtle probably measured four feet in diameter or more. Ropes lay in the sand around the turtles to keep anyone from getting too close. An official-looking young woman in shorts and a T-shirt with a state ID name tag made sure no one stepped over the ropes. The turtles opened their eyes and slowly swiveled their heads around. I wondered what they thought of us humans standing around gawking at them.

The young woman patiently answered people's questions. Listening in, I learned that these sea turtles were on the endangered list and this beach was their favorite spot on the island to sun bathe.

I hung out for a while, listening to the turtle lady, taking in the surreal beauty of the beach and admiring the majesty of the sea turtles before I decided to move on. I was starving, and I'd been told I had to try some garlic shrimp in the North Shore. I found a parking lot where several food trucks were parked selling "local grindz," and I dug into the most delicious garlic shrimp ever. My mind returned to the sea turtles I had just seen. I had never given turtles a second thought before, but after seeing these gorgeous sea creatures up close and personal today, I had to admit that I wanted to learn more about them. I vowed to return to that same beach to check out the turtles again soon.

* * *

A few days later, I went to my first job interview at the Honolulu Yacht Club, and I was offered the job of controller within an hour of the interview. I figured it would be the perfect job to have in Hawaii so I took it without a second thought.

The yacht club was stuck in the '70s still. Everything was old fashioned and out dated. My tiny office was at the back of an old dilapidated building and my chipped desk sat in between rusting old file cabinets. But I could always step outside and gaze at the beautiful blue ocean and feel the cool breezes if it got too claustrophobic for me inside. I got to work cleaning up old files and getting the old manual processes automated electronically. I offered suggestions for fiscal improvements around the club, which made my boss happy.

Before I knew it, six months had passed since I'd moved to Hawaii. I'd kept mostly to myself settling into a routine of working hard during the week and exploring the islands on my own on the weekends with the occasional casual chat with Ruth. But I was starting to think it was time for me to get out and make friends. And meet men!

Chapter 7

"Hey, Liz!"

I jumped and looked up from my desk, surprised to see Jean, the front office receptionist standing there. She was a local lady in her fifties who had worked at the yacht club for twenty years. I had been so absorbed in what I'd been doing that I hadn't heard her come into my office.

"Oh! Hey, Jean," I stuttered and immediately minimized the screen I had up—an online chat room. Thank god my computer faced the back of the office and no one could see what I was doing! I was chatting online with a guy I had just met through a dating website.

"You wanna go get some *ono* grindz with us?" Jean asked.

"No, no, I've gotta get this report finished."

Jean frowned. "You work too hard!" She always told me this. Her job allowed her to hang out in the front office and chat with yacht club guests all day long. "Can we bring something back for you?"

"No, no. Thanks though. I brought a lunch today."

Jean left and I got back to Brad, who was only twenty-five. Three years younger than me! I didn't usually go for younger guys, but there was something special about Brad. He was the perfect height at 5'9", six inches taller than me, and he had dark, unruly, curly hair. I imagined running my fingers through it. He had a great smile and green eyes, like me. The perfect package.

Brad had contacted me a few days ago through the online personals website right after I'd posted my personal ad. His personal ad title was *Passionate and Intense*, which were qualities I also possessed. Brad stated in his ad that he believed in karma. I had always loved the idea of karma; that people got what they deserved.

We hit it off right away in emails and then moved to the online chat room. Now we were chatting online and emailing each other constantly. It was impossible for me to concentrate on anything else anymore, I was having so much fun flirting with and getting to know Brad!

Brad owned a scuba diving company on Maui and worked as a scuba instructor and tour guide. I was bummed that he didn't live on the same island as me. But I was willing to relocate. Inter-island flights were cheap. We could fly back and forth to see each other every other weekend in the meantime.

Back in the chat room, Brad was telling me about his last relationships.

My last two serious relationships were with accountants! he typed. *But they were too traditional. I'm a very passionate and sensual man.*

This made me smile. *Maybe you should look for women in other fields, say sales or real estate!* I teased.

It's not that, silly! I'm attracted to analytical types, like accountants. But I need wildness too....

I broke up with a guy I was dating because he was way too conservative in the bedroom.

Tell me more. :) typed Brad.

He refused to do certain things....

Well, I will do anything for my woman, Brad replied. *Nothing is taboo in the bedroom. NOTHING!*

Oohh! You're getting me all hot and bothered at work! I teased. *Stop that!*

Brad replied, *I'm glad I can get you hot and bothered so easily!*

I teased him by typing, *I was getting hot and bothered thinking about you last night!*

So was I! This is going to be a great relationship! I like that you're able to express yourself so freely with me! I've been looking for someone exactly like you—an accountant who has a wild side!

My eyes widened. Brad thought we were starting a relationship and that I was exactly what he had been looking for!

Brad continued typing, *I want to hear your voice. Call me tonight, will you? 555-567-4291.*

I'd like to hear your voice, too! I'll definitely call you later!

Great! I've got to go now. TTYL! Brad signed off the instant messenger.

I sat there afterward, rereading all of our online conversations as well as all of our emails from the past couple of days. I couldn't believe how much Brad and I had in common. Brad had converted to the Mormon religion when he had married his now ex-wife, who was Mormon, and I had been raised in the Mormon religion. I had left the religion in my early twenties, and Brad had left it when caught his wife cheating on him. We were both from California; Brad was from Northern California, and I was from Southern. Brad had moved to Hawaii a year before me. If not for this online dating website, we never would have met.

Sighing, I shut down the instant message program. I needed to get back to work. But thoughts of Brad kept popping into my mind. His smile. His hair. He had posted ten pictures of himself on the dating website, and I loved each one of them! He was so gorgeous! I couldn't stop looking at his pictures and wondered what his voice would sound like.

The day dragged on, and I barely got anything done at work. I felt guilty for ignoring my work, but when five o'clock rolled around, I couldn't get out of there fast enough. After I made my daily trek to the gym to get in a good workout, I stopped on the way home to pick up a green smoothie for dinner. Debating when I ought to call Brad—I didn't want to appear too eager to call him, after all—I decided to wait another hour.

After an hour and a half had passed, I nervously dialed his number. My heart pounded in my chest, and I waited on pins and needles as the phone rang. I cleared my throat and fidgeted. But the phone just kept ringing. Finally, his voice came on the line and my heart sped up in excitement. But no! It was just his voicemail. Both disappointment and relief flooded through me as I listened to his greeting. His voice was very deep and manly, and I instantly liked it. He sounded sexy! As his greeting ended, I hung up without leaving a message. Instead, I sent him a text message.

Tried to call, but you didn't answer! I got to hear your voice first! Sadly, you'll have to keep waiting to hear mine! After rereading my text, I hit send. That ought to make him smile.

Brad texted me back thirty minutes later. *Sorry! My good buddy dropped by for a surprise visit. We'll talk tomorrow night.*

What a bummer. I frowned and texted him back, *Okay, till tomorrow* and went to bed disappointed. Tomorrow was sooooo far away.

* * *

The next morning, in line at Starbucks, I checked my phone and saw a new message. Figuring someone from work had called while I was in the shower, I dialed my voicemail.

Brad's deep voice filled my ears. "I thought I'd call you first thing this morning, expecting and hoping to get your voicemail. And now I've heard your voice, too! So I guess we're even!"

I burst out laughing and several people turned and looked at me. But I didn't care. Brad was so cute, getting me back like that.

I got my coffee and smiled all the way to work. As soon as I entered my office, I immediately logged onto my computer and started up the instant messenger Brad and I had been using.

Morning, sunshine! Brad typed as soon as I had finished logging on.

You got me pretty good this morning! I typed. *I burst out laughing at Starbucks and everyone looked at me like I was crazy!*

I thought you'd like that! Brad replied. *I want to see you this weekend! Do you have a couch I could crash on?*

I raised my eyebrows at this. I hadn't been expecting to meet him for another couple of weeks. *Wow! That's soon! We only met online on Monday! We haven't even talked on the phone yet!*

We'll talk on the phone tonight! I want to get you before any other guy does!

I laughed. Brad was the only guy I was interested in, by far! But I didn't want to go too fast with him. That always seemed be my big mistake with guys. *You're making me nervous now!*

Brad continued, *You're too cute! I don't want to make you nervous. But if we don't get together this weekend, we'll have to wait a month to meet each other. I'll be going to the mainland for business during the next month.*

Now I frowned. I didn't want to rush things with Brad, but I also didn't want to wait for a whole month to meet him. *A month is a long time to wait ... but I don't want to go too fast with you....*

I don't want to go too fast either. No worries ... maybe it's better if we wait a month if you're uncomfortable with meeting this weekend, Brad returned

My resolve weakened. I was an impatient woman.

Brad continued, *I'm so excited to meet you! And I think you'll be pleased by how well this weekend goes for us!*

I gave in. *Okay! Let's go for it!* I had a good feeling about Brad.

Great! You will make yourself available to me all weekend!

Oh, I will, huh? I typed back, smiling and thinking of all the ways I could make myself available to him.

Yes, you will! Brad replied. *I really think this is right for us. We'll talk tonight and you'll see! Is it okay if I call around nine?*

I replied that it was good for me and then spent the rest of the day waiting in anticipation.

At 8:30 that night, my phone rang. I was surprised to see Brad's name on the caller ID.

"Hello?" I tried to sound confident, sexy and sweet all at the same time.

"Hello!" Brad replied in that deep and sexy voice "We finally speak!"

"Yes, it's about time!"

"I'm surprised; your voice is so sweet! I thought it would be deeper for some reason!"

I blushed. "Well, your voice is much deeper than I had imagined! It's very sexy!" I laughed nervously.

"Oh, you like it, huh?" He deepened his voice even more.

I laughed again.

"Sorry about last night; my friend came by to tell me that he and his wife are having a baby! It's their first."

"Oh, that's great news!"

"So where are you right now?" Brad asked.

"I'm lying on my bed. Where are you?"

"I'm lying back on my sofa."

I pictured him spread out on a leather sofa. "Long day?" I asked.

"Yeah, this week we're training tourists from the Midwest who are out here on a company holiday. How about you?"

"No, it's slow at work this week, which is how I'm able to talk to you all day long. How can you spare time to talk to me when you're so busy at work this week?"

Brad laughed. "Multi-tasking!"

I laughed.

"I'm really glad I met you this week," Brad said.

"Me, too!" I admitted. "I've been smiling a lot more since meeting you!"

"You make me smile a lot, too. You make me really happy," Brad said. "So, are we still on for this weekend?"

"I think so ..." I answered, still uncertain and hesitant. "I don't want to rush into anything physical. I thought our current set up was perfect because we live on separate islands and can't possibly go too fast!"

Brad laughed. "We don't have to do anything this weekend. We'll just hang out and have fun. If something happens and it feels right, we'll go with it. If we decide we just want to be friends, that's good, too. No pressure. No expectations."

"Okay," I agreed, still a bit hesitant.

"It's been a long time since I've been intimate with a woman," Brad admitted. "I don't sleep around, and I only want to be intimate with one woman, so it's serious for me when I get intimate."

I liked what Brad was telling me but I had gotten my hopes up only to be burned in the past.

"No pressure at all, Liz," Brad continued. "I can sleep on your sofa or even the floor if need be. Can I book the airplane tickets?"

Brad seemed to be everything I was looking for in a man and he said all the right things. "Yes," I told him. "Make the plans!"

"Great. So," he asked sheepishly, "what do you wear to bed?"

"A T-shirt," I said. "Why? What do you wear?"

"I sleep naked...."

This of course made me imagine him naked. Trouble!

"But I can wear underwear to bed while I'm there with you," he added.

Now I was picturing him in little tighty whities. I wasn't so sure I would be able to control myself in either case.

"Brad, I need to tell you something about myself before you meet me." I paused. and bit my lip.

"What is it, Liz?" Brad asked. "You know you can tell me anything. It won't change the way I feel about you."

Here goes nothing. "Well, when I was a teenager, I developed a rare disorder called Alopecia. Have you ever heard of it?"

"No, what is it?"

"Well, it's an auto-immune disorder, a hair loss disorder and it affects people differently. Some people get thinner hair, some people get bald spots, and some people completely lose all of their hair all over their bodies. When I was sixteen, my hairdresser noticed a little bald spot on the back of my head. My dermatologist gave me a cream to put on the spot and my hair grew back. A year later though, my hair thinned out visibly. My dermatologist gave me a different cream this time and my hair grew back again. Another year went by and my hair started falling out again. But this time it kept falling out faster than before. My dermatologist gave me a whole new cream to try but it didn't work. This was in March of my senior year in high school. Within a month, all the hair on my head was gone. A few months later, all the hair all over my body was gone, too."

"Oh God, I'm so sorry that happened to you, Liz!" Brad sounded genuinely concerned. "That had to be very traumatic!"

"It was. I almost didn't graduate from high school because I stopped going for a month. I wallowed around at home, feeling sorry for myself until my mom finally convinced me that life had to go on, with or without my hair. She took me wig shopping for the first time. My first wig was terrible; a big curly crazy thing!" I laughed. "Wigs have improved a lot since then. Now strangers will tell me how much they love my hair and ask me if it's my natural color or if I get it colored at a salon."

"What do you tell them?"

"I always admit that it's a wig! It's kind of fun!"

"I never would have guessed that you wear wigs!" Brad admitted. "Your pictures are gorgeous! Your hair looks gorgeous!"

"Thanks!" I grinned and blushed at his compliment. "I still have eyelashes for some reason, thank God! And I got tattooed eyebrows in my early twenties. And at least one good thing has come out of it; I never have to shave!"

"That must be nice!" Brad agreed, and then he asked sheepishly, "Soooo, do you have any hair *down there?*"

"I do have a few hairs down there, but very few." I grinned even bigger.

"Ohhh, nice!" He sounded pleased.

I blushed again.

"Liz, thank you for sharing that with me!" Brad said. "I want you to know that I do not care if you have hair or not. No one is perfect. We all have our flaws."

I sighed in relief. I was so glad to get that over with. I always hated having to tell guys about my hair loss. That was probably the number one reason I didn't go out often. Too much work. Too much risk of rejection. I went on, "I've grown pretty accustomed to it over the years. I like to think that I am fairly well adjusted. But I still have insecurities."

We stayed up talking on the phone for another hour. By the time we said our goodbyes, I was more excited than ever to get to see Brad in a few days.

Of course, the rest of the week went by agonizingly slow.

Chapter 8

Can you believe that we'll be sitting next to each other tonight?

Brad texted me first thing Friday morning. I don't think I'd slept a wink the night before.

I'll have butterflies! he texted. *It will be so good to finally see you, Liz!*

His message made me smile like a fool. I'd never dated a guy who said such cute things all the time and I loved it. I sent him a text agreeing with him about the butterflies.

We talked on instant messenger off and on during the day, but for once we were both actually busy with work. When it was time to pick up Brad from the airport, I sped all the way, singing along to the songs on the radio, feeling high on life. I got there early enough to park my car and get to the baggage area before his arrival. Then I waited anxiously, pacing back and forth, feeling more and more nervous about seeing him in person.

As people filed into the baggage claim area from the terminal, I looked for Brad and tried to appear calm and confident. I watched as moms and dads with little toddlers, young couples in love, and elderly couples made their way to the baggage carousels. Every time a man similar in height and build walked through the door, my hopes would go up and then crash when I realized it wasn't him.

Then I saw him, and I forgot to breathe for a moment. Dear God, he was even more gorgeous in person. He wore tan shorts and a white button-down shirt and flip flops. He grinned when he spotted me. I smiled back and tried to focus on breathing again. My face grew red hot from nerves.

Brad approached me and immediately hugged me, as if we were old friends. "Hello!" he whispered warmly in my ear as he held me close for a minute.

"Hi!" I said back, feeling more nervous than ever in his embrace.

He pulled back to look at me. "What's up?" he asked, feeling my tension.

"I'm so nervous!" I blurted out before I could stop myself.

He laughed. "Don't be nervous! Come on, let's go." He grabbed my hand, and we headed for the parking garage. His easygoing attitude helped me relax a bit.

We decided to eat at a local steakhouse in Waikiki. As I made my way through rush-hour traffic, I started asking Brad questions to get him to do all the talking. I asked about his childhood, his family and his job. He told me funny stories about growing up with two brothers and his dreams of buying a home in Hawaii someday.

At the restaurant, as we were led to a booth by the hostess, Brad suggested we sit side by side instead of across from each other. So we snuggled in close to each other in the booth. Brad casually put his hand on my leg, and my heart raced at his touch.

"I definitely need a drink!" I said. He grinned and agreed.

We ordered beers and toasted to finding each other. As we sipped at our beers, Brad showed me the various scars he had gotten over the years growing up and shared the stories about how he had gotten each one.

Suddenly turning serious, Brad looked at me and asked, "Can I kiss you?"

I smiled. Of course he could kiss me. I had been dreaming of it since the first time I saw his picture. "Absolutely!"

Brad leaned in, and I met him halfway. The butterflies in my stomach went crazy the moment our lips touched. His lips were soft and full. He started off with small, light pecks but soon the kiss deepened. I kept my eyes open at first but soon I couldn't help but surrender to the kiss. I grabbed hold of his shoulder, and Brad wrapped his other arm around me. I forgot that we were in a crowded restaurant and other people might be watching us.

Eventually we pulled apart, grinning like fools at each other. Things were going so well; I almost couldn't believe it! Our waitress must have been watching and waiting for our kiss to end, because she arrived just then with a conspirator's smile and winked at me as she asked if we were ready to order. We decided to share a steak.

Brad kept brushing my leg with his leg, putting his hand on my leg, grasping and squeezing my hand from time to time as we ate. He kept glancing over at me and smiling that sexy smile of his.

When we finished eating, Brad paid the bill. I offered to help but he wouldn't hear of it. Then he offered to drive us back to my place, since he'd only had the one beer at the beginning of dinner and I'd had two. I was relieved I wouldn't have to concentrate on driving anymore. As Brad drove, he put his free hand on my leg. The closer we got to my house, the higher his hand moved up my thigh. A part of me wanted to move his hand back down in an effort to keep things from going too fast, but another part of me was enjoying his touch way too much to stop it.

When we got to my place, I gave him a little tour and worked on trying to cool off.

"What's all this?" Brad asked, pointing to some art books and pencils lying on the coffee table.

"Oh, I like to draw in my spare time." I brushed it off. I hadn't drawn much since high school. But moving to Hawaii had inspired me to pick it up again.

Brad picked up one of the books. "May I?"

"Oh yeah, sure."

Brad thumbed through the pages. "Nice work; you've got talent."

"Thanks!" I lit up. "When I was younger, I wanted to be a famous artist someday. But I ended up going for the more practical route—accounting."

Brad nodded.

"Would you like anything to drink?" I asked.

"No, I'm fine." Brad put the book down and pulled me close. Then he ran his fingers through my hair. "So, this is a wig, huh? I would never have guessed it. It looks like real hair." He grinned at me. "You look really beautiful in person. Your pictures don't do you justice!"

I blushed. "Thank you!"

"I bet you look beautiful without the wig."

"Ha!" I laughed nervously. "You won't be finding out any time soon."

"I'll get you to take it off for me before the end of this weekend!" Brad predicted boldly.

"Oh, you think so, huh?" I teased him.

"Yep." Brad smiled.

"Well, if you behave well, maybe, just maybe, I'll give you a five-second peek!" I tried to tickle Brad, but he pulled me close and started kissing me. Slowly at first, like our first kiss at the restaurant. Then deeper and more passionately. Soon we were falling onto the sofa together, arms around each other, kissing, caressing.

So much for going slow. I shivered as he pulled my shirt off over my head and then he practically ripped his own shirt off. I stared. He had a smooth hairless chest and nicely defined abs. I trailed kisses across his chest and down his stomach. I looked up into his eyes. He looked back at me and smiled.

Am I really going to do this? My body was on fire from his touch. I was having a lot of intense feelings for him. I was pretty sure he felt the same.

Who was I kidding? I had never had self-control when it came to men. I ignored the voice in my head telling me to stop what I was doing, that I didn't really know Brad and gave in to my hormones. I started undoing the button on his shorts and quickly realized that he wasn't wearing any underwear. I laughed. "Going commando, huh?"

"I also shaved down there for you ..." he hinted slyly.

"Ooohhh, this I have to see!" I said as I unzipped. Indeed, there was not a hair to be found!

In between kisses, we got the rest of our clothes off. He slowly looked me up and down and I blushed. He grinned and then started toward my bedroom. I stood there for a moment, thoroughly enjoying watching his bare ass as he sauntered off. He turned, laughed and motioned for me to follow him.

"I'm coming, I'm coming!" I said, laughing.

"Not yet," Brad said, "but you will be!"

* * *

I slowly woke up the next morning, happily surprised to still be in Brad's arms. I lay there for a while as he continued to sleep and marveled at my luck in finding him. He was perfect for me. I was excited about the day ahead. And the rest of the weekend. And possibly the rest of my life!

Don't get ahead of yourself, Liz! I reminded myself of the times I had gotten my hopes up about guys in the past.

"Good morning, sweetheart," Brad said sleepily, pulling me out of my thoughts.

In no time, we were kissing and caressing each other again, unable to keep our hands off each other.

When we finally dragged ourselves out of bed a while later, we decided to go eat breakfast at a local pancake place. We threw on swimsuits, shorts and T-shirts with the plan to go snorkeling at Hanauma Bay, a popular tourist attraction, afterward. I put on extra wig tape to ensure my wig didn't fall off in the water.

"How are you two this morning?" our server asked, smiling as he sat us at a table in the back of the restaurant.

"Great!" replied Brad cheerfully. "And how are you?"

I had to laugh at how friendly and outgoing Brad was. I was definitely more quiet and reserved. We each ordered coffee, and Brad ordered the meat lovers' breakfast skillet while I ordered the ham and cheese omelet. When our coffee arrived, we both put in tons of cream and sugar and then laughed at the fact that we took our coffee the same way.

As we waited for our food, Brad talked about his career as an investment adviser before moving to Hawaii. He'd made a lot of money but he hated it. One day he just decided to quit and go do the one thing he loved—scuba diving. Which brought him to Hawaii. And to me!

I shared my big pet peeve about Hawaii. "The cost of living is sky high here compared to most of the mainland, so you would think that pay scales here would be higher, too, in line with the increase in the cost of living, like in San Francisco or New York, you know?"

Brad nodded.

"But no! I'm actually making a little less here in Hawaii than I would be making in California. It sucks!" I pouted. "But as everyone says, that's the cost of living in paradise."

"It doesn't have to be," Brad offered. "You should renegotiate your salary now that you've proven yourself."

"Yeah...." I wondered if my boss would go for that.

"Do it, Liz!" Brad encouraged me. "You've got nothing to lose. What's the worst that could happen? Your boss says no?"

"I guess...." I pondered what my boss might say. He was the most laidback boss I had ever had. He approved all vacations without a second thought. And he had just given sick pay to a part-time person who didn't qualify for sick pay, simply because the person asked for it. The more I thought about it, the more I realized that he probably would give me a raise if I asked.

"I'll do it first thing Monday," I decided just as our food arrived.

After eating, we headed toward the famous Hanauma Bay. I had never snorkeled before, and I was nervous about my wig coming off. Not to mention, I had always been afraid of deep water.

"Are you okay?" Brad asked

"Huh?" I asked and then realized I was clenching and unclenching my fists.

I laughed and released my grip. "Sorry, I've never snorkeled before, and I'm a bit nervous!"

"Why?"

"I have this stupid fear of deep water." I looked over at him and decided to 'fess up. "My grandparents owned a houseboat when I was young, and they used to take my parents and I on trips to the lake each summer. But I remember kicking and screaming whenever my grandmother tried to get me to play in a lake with the rest of the family. And then one time when I was a teenager at a summer camp, some boys threw me in a lake as a prank."

"That's awful! What happened? Did you nearly drown then?"

"No, I know how to swim. I took swim lessons and diving lessons growing up."

Brad arched an eyebrow.

"I love swimming in pools. It's the deep, scary, fish-filled lakes—and oceans—that get me!"

Brad laughed.

"And oceans have sharks!" I added with emphasis.

"There won't be any sharks at Hanauma Bay!" Brad assured me. "I'll take care of you." He squeezed my hand. "No need to worry!"

I tried to calm my nerves as we drove. Brad was an expert at diving and snorkeling so he would be the best possible teacher for me. And I lived in Hawaii now. How could I not try snorkeling, at least once? We stopped at a Costco on the way, and Brad bought my first snorkeling gear for me. I was getting a little excited. This would be fun!

We parked at Hanauma Bay and then we had to watch a video about protecting the reef and the fish before being allowed access to the bay. The video actually got me even more excited me about snorkeling. As we walked down a hill to the bay after the video, I admired the stunning turquoise ocean, the water so clear you could see the coral underneath. The palm trees lining the beach waved gently in the wind.

People had already claimed space on the sand near the water, but we found a nice spot halfway down the beach where there was a gap in the coral. We laid our things out. Brad showed me how to spit inside the goggles to help keep them clear while under water. He helped me put them on and tugged the straps to tighten them for me. When I said I was ready, we went to the water's edge and then put our flippers on.

The water felt cold at first, so I took little baby steps, trying to get used to it. Once we were waist deep, Brad asked if I was ready. I nodded and put the mouthpiece in my mouth and bit gently down on it as Brad instructed. I tried breathing through my mouth and felt comfortable, but when I tried to put my face in the water, I started hyperventilating and couldn't stay under. I was determined to overcome my fear so I went under again and tried to calm my breathing.

Brad was patient with me. When I was finally able to keep my face underwater, he suggested that I hold his hands and try floating on my stomach. As soon as I started floating, I hyperventilated again. But I worked on my breathing again and suddenly I realized I was okay floating there in the water. I made the thumbs up signal to Brad. He grinned and gave me thumbs up, too. Still holding onto one of my hands, he started swimming around and pointing out things with his free hand.

My eyes widened as I was finally able to see what lay just below the surface of the water. I wanted to say "wow!" but I remembered that I had the snorkel in my mouth. Tons of different fish darted to and fro. A school of yellow fish swam together, several black and white fish hung out nearby and a blue fish sped by below me. My goggles made it look like the coral was within reach but it was a few feet below me. I saw pink starfish and eels and an octopus down on the ocean floor.

After a while, Brad signaled that we ought to head back to shore. I reluctantly agreed.

"I'm so proud of you!" Brad said as soon as he got his snorkel mask off.

"I know! I can't believe I finally did it!" I admitted giddily, shocked at how far I had come in the last few hours. My wig hadn't shifted or slid around at all in the water either.

"You took to it pretty quickly once we got you to float."

"Oh my god! It was so much fun! I can't stop thinking about it—about all the fish and coral and everything. I totally want to go back out again."

Brad laughed. "We'll go again, don't worry!"

We lay in the sun for a while, warming ourselves back up and then we hit the water again a little later. The second time in the water, I explored the bay on my own, meeting up with Brad every now and then. I felt like an old pro at snorkeling now.

I was so worn out on the drive home, I could barely move. But after a long hot shower followed by a nice dinner at a cozy little restaurant in Kailua, I somehow found renewed energy with Brad later.

I was so happy with how things were going, so comfortable with Brad that I took my wig off for bed that night. Brad smiled, kissed my bald head and then softly massaged my head as I lay falling asleep in his arms. I had never been this intimate with a man before, but it was something I had always wanted. I was amazed at my numerous breakthroughs with Brad. He was the best thing that had ever happened to me!

* * *

As I awoke the next morning, I realized it was our last morning together. I snuggled up to Brad, relishing being so close to him. I didn't want to let go of him. He must have felt the same; we snuggled for a long time. Eventually Brad suggested we head to the North Shore to check out the big surf and watch the surfers. So we put on our swimsuits, shorts and T-shirts again and headed off. We picked up breakfast burritos at a local joint and ate as we drove. We talked about religion, politics and music and found that we agreed on everything.

It was another perfect Hawaiian day. The beaches in the North Shore were bustling with swimmers, surfers and sun bathers and tourists. Brad pulled into the parking lot at Waimea Bay and miraculously found a newly empty spot. We walked down to a spot in the sand out of reach of the giant waves and laid our towels out. We plopped down right next to each other and just sat watching the waves and the surfers. Brad eventually relaxed back and put his head in my lap, so I started playing with his hair. I was as content as could be as we sat there at the beach together.

"I like you," Brad suddenly said.

"I like you too," I told him. "I'm having so much fun with you this weekend, I don't want you to leave."

"I don't want to leave either. But I've got this thing called a job. And they expect me to show up tomorrow," Brad teased.

"The nerve of those people, expecting you to show up!" I teased back.

"So let's just take the next week to think about whether we really want to see each other again. After all, we do fight an awful lot," Brad joked.

"Yeah, I'm not sure if we can get along." I had never gotten along so well with anyone before. I was totally falling for Brad. I wanted to spend the next weekend with him. And the next weekend after that and the next and the next....

After tiring of the beach, we headed off to a Mexican restaurant for a late lunch. All I could think about was how Brad needed to get back to the airport for his flight home soon. I did not want to drop him off. We both ordered margaritas and when our drinks arrived, Brad proposed a toast. "To our finding each other."

"To our finding each other!" I agreed happily, and we clinked glasses. Then Brad leaned in for a kiss.

Brad suggested we try to fit in a few more things after lunch, but time was running out on our little weekend together, so we reluctantly headed to the airport instead. At the airport terminal, we hugged and kissed and said our goodbyes. I watched as he walked into the airport and then sadly got back in my car and drove home.

I waited and waited to get a message from Brad letting me know that he had returned home and missed me already. But I got nothing. Finally, around nine, I got onto instant messenger to see if he was there and he was. I typed him a quick message. *Hey! Was your trip home good?*

Brad replied, *It was, thanks.*

I waited for more but Brad didn't type anything else. That was all he was going to say? I waited longer, debating what else to say. Finally, I typed, *I had so much fun with you this weekend! I miss you already!*

Brad typed back, *I feel similarly.*

I frowned. That was it? He seemed a bit distant. Maybe he was just tired. I didn't want to worry over nothing so I typed a goodnight to him, logged off and then went to bed.

It was time to get back to the real world. I needed to wake up early the next morning for work and it was going to be a busy week. Financial statements for the prior month were due. Plus, I was going to ask my boss for a raise!

Chapter 9

Hey, wild one! Brad typed on instant messenger first thing the next morning.

Hey! I typed back. *I just talked to my boss about a raise, and he said he would talk to the treasurer and get back to me! He smiled and said it was an easy request!*

That sounds encouraging! Brad typed back.

I know, huh? I replied. *It's all thanks to your encouragement!*

Ahhhh.... was all Brad typed back.

I sat for a minute, debating whether or not to tell him what I wanted to tell him. I was an upfront and honest person, and I had advertised myself that way in the online personals. Brad must have liked that about me, otherwise he wouldn't have contacted me. So I went for it.

I've decided to close my online personal ad because I'm only interested in seeing you. You are caviar, and all the rest of the guys out there are hot dogs! I typed, thinking I was pretty funny.

Did you expect to find someone so fast? he typed in reply.

I squinted at the screen. Huh?

He added, *Because I signed up for a year, and I'm mostly on this thing to make more friends and contacts.*

I frowned. That wasn't the response I had expected from Brad. Just a day ago, he had toasted to us finding each other.

Brad continued typing, *I'm not planning on meeting anyone else besides you, but I'm keeping my profile up to make more friends. You should keep your profile up and change your message to say that you are looking for friends.*

Okay.... I typed, uncertain of his response.

I still want to see you and only you, I just think we should keep our options open, Brad typed.

Okay.... I typed again. I was a little shocked at his mention of keeping our options open.

He went on, *I got burned by a girl I fell for recently. She seemed to be everything that I wanted and so I asked her to move in with me. And then she totally changed. She was just using me. So I get a little suspicious when girls try to talk about next steps like closing our personal ads after one weekend.*

I'm really sorry about that. Some girls are bad news. But that's not me, I really like you. I was a little hurt that he would be suspicious of me.

Brad continued, *I really like you, too. I still want to see just you. But since we live on different islands, you should go out with guys on Oahu and have fun when I'm not there. I'm not the jealous type at all. Just let me know if you find someone you'd rather be with. If you get intimate with another man, I can't be intimate with you anymore. I only want to be with one person. But I'd be happy for you if you found someone better suited for you than me.*

I was having a hard time breathing. This wasn't making sense. The man I had just spent a wonderfully romantic weekend with, the best weekend of my life, the man who I thought I had connected with on every level, the man I had made love with over and over again, the man I had opened up to and allowed into the most secret parts of my life, the man who had called me sweetheart and toasted to us finding each other—this man was now telling me that he was okay with me hooking up with someone else. Just last week, he had been desperate to meet me as soon as possible so that no other men could get to me before him!

I felt nauseous. Brad obviously didn't have the same feelings for me as I had for him. Sadly, I had moved too fast—again! Would I never learn? I should have listened to that voice in my head telling me to slow down that first night with Brad. I had been so sure that Brad was different. But I had been wrong. Again.

I couldn't help but wonder if it had something to do with me being bald. Maybe Brad decided that he preferred a normal woman with hair. I couldn't blame him for that. I wished I were a normal woman with hair.

Feeling utterly depressed, I typed a message to Brad telling him that my boss was calling me into a meeting, and I logged off the instant messenger.

Then I sat at my desk in stunned disbelief for a few minutes.

I tried to shake it off, forget about Brad and concentrate on work. I absolutely had to get some work done. But I couldn't stop thinking about the whole crazy situation. I told myself that maybe he needed some time to see that he could trust me. Or maybe he was so overwhelmed by his strong feelings for me that he was scared and this was his way of dealing with it. All I knew for sure was that I didn't want to lose what I had just found with Brad.

I thought back to the men I had fallen for in the past. It seemed like all of them had been nothing but trouble. Shad had claimed to be divorced but it turned out he had still been very much married. Derrick had appeared to be clean, stylish and in great shape when I first met him. But once we moved in together, he turned out to be lazy, dirty and fat. And I had learned, quite by accident, that Mike enjoyed getting dressed up in women's underwear from time to time!

Was there not one decent man for me on this planet?

I got through the rest of the day in a sort of sad, stunned, broken state, going over and over everything in my mind again and again, trying to make sense of it. I stayed out of the online chat room.

Brad called me later that night after work.

"What's up? Where were you all day?" he asked right away.

"Well," I hesitated. "After what you said this morning, I decided that I must have misread you this weekend. And so I decided to step back and reevaluate everything—"

Brad cut me off, "You didn't misread anything, and you don't need to reevaluate anything! Everything is the same as it was this weekend!"

I wrinkled my brow in confusion. Earlier, he had been telling me to date other guys and now he was reassuring me that everything was still great between us. That sounded nice. And it was so good to hear his voice. I just wanted to keep listening to him talk. I didn't want to lose him. "Okay," I said hesitantly.

"I've got to get going," he said. What? He was confusing me again. He just called me. We were just getting started with our conversation. And now he had to go? "I've got to do some stuff before I head to bed. But I'll talk to you tomorrow, okay?"

"Okay," I said hesitantly again.

"Goodnight." Brad hung up.

I felt slightly better after talking to Brad, but it would have been nice if he had wanted to talk a little longer. At least he was saying that we were good though.

Unfortunately, the next day Brad seemed distant again. I tried to be relaxed, calm and patient, but those had never been my best attributes.

Jean approached me Wednesday morning. "Girl, what is wrong with you this week?"

I wasn't good at hiding my emotions. I filled Jean in on the whole Brad thing.

"Well," Jean said, after giving it some thought. "If he told you that everything is good, I think you should just back off and give him space. Guys like to have a challenge. Play a little hard to get! See what happens."

I nodded. I didn't like it, but what choice did I have?

"When my boyfriend first asked for my number, he didn't call me for six weeks," Jean told me. "You just gotta sit back and wait for guys to make their move. They don't like to feel pressured or smothered. They like the chase."

Jean's advice made sense. So I tried not to bother Brad. If he contacted me on instant messenger during the day, I would reply back but keep it casual. I didn't initiate any conversations with Brad myself anymore. Brad remained distant. I couldn't help but worry that Brad might think my distance meant I didn't like him anymore. Because that was exactly how I was taking his distance.

By Thursday, I was crazy with frustration and confusion. If Brad really felt the same, then why wasn't he flirting and talking with me this week like he had last week? I wanted to understand what was going on.

I decided to do what Brad had told me to do on Monday—go out with other guys. Before Brad came along, I had been chatting with several other guys on the online personals. And a couple of the guys were asking to meet me now. So I set up dates for the weekend. While I was online communicating with the other guys, I noticed that Brad was still actively using the personals website every day himself. The damned site posted how long it had been since people had last logged on. Brad's was "within 24 hours."

Damn him! He was giving more attention to the online personals than to me. I tried not to think about it. I tried to tell myself that he was just looking for friends. But I didn't believe it.

Within hours, I had dates for both Friday night and Saturday night.

I tried not to think about Brad on my dates, but Brad was the only thing I could think about! Brad, Brad, Brad! Brad was so much better looking and funnier than these other guys. I felt so much more at ease with Brad than these guys. Going out with other men only confirmed what I had already been feeling—I didn't want to date other men, I only wanted to continue what Brad and I had started.

I couldn't hold back the tears as I drove home over the Koolau Mountain from my second date Saturday night. My heart was heavy. I felt like an empty shell. It was raining, and I found myself wondering if Brad would care, if anyone would care, if my car slid off the road in the rain and tumbled down the mountain, exploding in a ball of fire and killing me instantly. I let my tears cloud my vision, willing something bad to happen to me. But somehow I made it home in one piece.

Sunday morning, I woke up utterly depressed. I logged onto the online chat room, hoping that by some miracle Brad would see me there and be his old flirty self. I hadn't logged onto the chat room since Friday. Brad must miss me by now, right? I'd given him enough space, hadn't I?

In fact, Brad was online and he said hi to me right away. We chatted about the weather and other small, meaningless things, and then Brad signed off, saying that he was going to go get breakfast. I tried to stay positive with him online, but once he was gone the tears came instantly. He was still being distant with me. For the millionth time, I wondered how things could start off so great and then just change overnight for no apparent reason.

After agonizing all day Sunday over what I ought to do, I decided I couldn't go on like this. I wrote Brad an email. I admitted to him that I had really fallen for him that first week, but that he was a different person this week. I basically told him off. After reading it over and over and over and debating whether to send it or not, I finally sent it. I waited the rest of the day, hoping to hear something back. Hoping that at least he would apologize for leading me on and hurting me. If he finally just made a clean break and let me go, told me that I was right, that he was distancing himself and that things weren't going to work out, then I could move on. But Brad had no response at all.

Fine, so be it. I was done with him either way.

Chapter 10

I dragged my sorry self into work on Monday morning to find an official letter waiting for me on my desk. I wondered if it was concerning my request to get a raise. At least there would be something good happening in my miserable life. I ripped the envelope open and took out the letter inside.

My heart dropped as I read the letter. My boss stated that I had been hired at an already higher than average rate and he was not prepared to give me a raise. Furthermore, he said, he considered my request for a raise to be an act of insubordination. Tears flooded my eyes. I couldn't even finish reading the last few lines of the letter.

Insubordination? Was he kidding? The week before, when I'd asked him for the raise, I'd shown him research from the Internet, proving that people in my same position were making a little more than I was. He had acted as if it would be no problem to get the treasurer to approve my raise. And now he was leaving this insane letter on my desk accusing me of insubordination? Why couldn't he have just told me no when I'd asked for the raise last week? And how was my asking for a small raise an act of insubordination? Did he even understand what insubordination was?

I shredded the letter in anger. The nerve! What a self-centered, egotistical asshole! He was always off golfing or out to lunch instead of actually working at the club. His salary was almost double what I was earning. He had some balls accusing me of being insubordinate for asking for a small raise! If anyone was doing anything wrong here it was him, not me!

I stifled a scream. This was all Brad's fault! He had given me the idea to ask for a raise. *"What's the worst that can happen?"* he'd said. Well, this letter was pretty bad.

I couldn't believe the direction my life was suddenly taking. First Brad and now my boss. Was all of this some kind of sick practical joke? Everyone seemed to be acting one way with me one week and then the complete opposite the next week! What the hell was going on? Why did everyone have to play games? Couldn't people just be up front and honest with each other? Treat each other with respect?

I wished I'd never asked my boss for a raise. Or sent that stupid email to Brad on Sunday. I should've just called him and talked to him. Scratch that! I wished I had never even met Brad!

I tried to compose myself and behave as normal as possible, even though I was raging inside. Luckily my boss didn't work on Mondays. Or Tuesdays. So I wouldn't see him until Wednesday. Maybe by then I'd be over it.

Not likely.

I was seething inside as I sat at my desk and worked. Anger always made me feel better. Stronger. In control. I embraced the anger. And the anger grew.

I kept bouncing back and forth between my anger at Brad and my anger at my boss. Going over every little detail in each case. But nothing made any sense no matter how many times I went over it.

Around two, I realized with surprise that I had missed lunch. And I didn't even feel hungry. I had always turned to food during troubling times. Especially chocolate. But I couldn't care less about food now. Not even chocolate.

On my way home from work, I blasted my *Nine Inch Nails* CD and sang along to my favorite song: "Head like a hole! Black as your soul! I'd rather die than give you control!" It fueled my anger and made me feel better.

On Tuesday, I got an ingenious idea. I set up a new personal ad on the online dating website where Brad and I had met and tailored it to get his attention. I posted a picture of some random girl I had once known a while ago and named her Katie. And then I waited.

Within the hour, Brad contacted Katie by email. Ha! I was right! I knew he would take the bait! I was proud of myself for catching him. But I winced as I read his email to Katie. It was almost word for word what he had written me just a few weeks ago. He told Katie that she seemed like his ideal woman. He gave her his email address and asked that she write back soon.

Brad was just another player, and the truth hurt. Everything he had ever said had been a lie. I never meant anything to him at all. It was all just a game for him.

I felt sick for falling so hard for him. But at least I could see who he truly was now.

On Wednesday, I decided to mess with Brad. I wrote to him as Katie, flirting with him. Soon Brad was replying to Katie, asking if she wanted to chat on instant messenger with him, just as he had with me two weeks prior.

As soon as I signed onto instant messenger as Katie, Brad started talking and asking Katie to tell him all about herself. It was déjà vu.

I made up a bunch of stuff on the spot about my fake Katie character and typed out her story for Brad. *I've been living here for five years now. Came from San Francisco, born and raised. Work as a vice-president of business operations for a big hotel chain. Ended a three-year relationship last year. Took a break after that and now I'm ready to jump back in the dating pool!*

Brad typed back, *Send more pictures of yourself. I've been burned by people pretending to be someone else when they only put one picture up—it's easy to cut and paste from the Internet—sorry if I am a little cautious but I've learned to protect my privacy.*

I winced and typed back, *Seriously? People cut and paste pictures from the Internet???*

Brad replied, *Yes, and there are women from Russia or Japan, trying to get men to bring them to US. An ex even signed up once as someone else to ask questions about me.... weird people out there.*

I frowned. Brad probably had a history of treating women poorly and one of them had done what I was now doing. Getting back at him. I quickly typed, *Okay, now you're scaring me away from the online personals!!!*

I thought for a moment about how to proceed. *I can send you more pics tonight when I get home from work, okay?* I waited for another moment and added, *What about you? Are you really who you say you are?*

Brad replied, *I am the real deal through and through—doesn't get any better—but a successful man of honor and integrity who is handsome can be used by people ... just need to be careful at first.... hope you can appreciate that, Katie.*

I snorted. Brad was a bit cocky, wasn't he? A successful man of honor and integrity? As if!

Brad added, *The online dating thing hasn't been too successful for me by way of my being single still. I have met a couple women, just not taken it to the next level.*

I asked the million-dollar question, *When was your last relationship, may I be so bold as to ask?*

Define relationship.

I typed, *To the point where you are getting intimate with each other and spending the night at each other's places, I guess.*

Brad typed, *You can tell me who you are....*

I held my breath. Did he know it was me? Or did he think it was one of the other women he had treated poorly? I decided to act confused. I typed, *Huh???*

Brad typed, *"What's your cell number? I will call you.*

I typed back, *I am a little paranoid of giving out my cell number to strangers, which, let's face it, you are. Also, you just told me all about the bad side of this online thing and you said it's better to be careful.*

After getting no response, I typed, *What's your cell number? Maybe I'll call you!*

Brad typed, *Yeah, but until I hear your voice, I am uncomfortable talking to you more. No one asks when was the last time I spent the night at someone's house. Makes me a little uneasy.*

I was a little irritated. *Well, sorry, you asked me to define a relationship and that's how I define it.* I was finished trying to be Katie with Brad. It wasn't working the way I'd hoped. *We don't have to continue chatting. Have a nice day, Brad!*

Then Brad typed his cell phone number. *Call me and we can talk. There are certain individuals I know who like playing games. And there are weirdos. No reason to get defensive, Katie. I am just trying to protect myself and my privacy. Until I know someone; I won't divulge too much personal information.*

I said nothing back.

Brad continued, *Hey, well, I'm sorry if I offended you. I have met a couple of people online lately who would go to the level of creating multiple online personalities and pretending to be other people.*

He couldn't possibly be talking about me! I'd never done anything like this before in my life.

Brad typed, *Not sure why people would do those things, but it happens, so I am very cautious.*

I decided again that I should end this charade as Katie and tried to sign off. *I'm going to have to say goodbye. Sorry.*

Hey, I am for real. If you want to get to know a great guy, then call me.

I laughed. What a jackass! Brad seemed to have a seriously over-inflated ego. He bragged way too much about how great he was. Would such a "great guy" have treated me the way that Brad had treated me? No! Truly great guys treated women with respect. Truly great guys didn't talk about how great they were all the time.

Brad kept typing, *If you're who you say you are then great, but I've had people from Russia emailing me, Japanese women and even men who pretend to be women. If I am protective, it is only because I have a wonderful life and won't let just anyone into it. That should be a huge plus sign for you as that means I am not a player.*

Right! As if!

Brad typed more, *I think your picture is beautiful, but I have been scammed before. I still believe there are good people out there. Let's get over the hurdle of who we truly are then everything will be fine.*

I grunted in disgust! He was the scammer!

He added, *If that upsets you, then I am sorry.*

Brad opened up then. *I spoke to a woman for several months online who said she was from Newport Beach. Turned out she was from Russia and just wanted to come to America. My time is very valuable. Sorry you're giving up already....*

I typed, *I don't know, the other guys on this site are way more laid back than you. You are kind of freaking me out.*

Well, sorry. Best of luck to you. Take care. Wish you only the best, Katie.

I typed back, "*I'm sorry you've had bad experiences. Best of luck to you, too.*

I was ready to sign off, but apparently Brad was not quite so ready to give up on Katie. He typed, *Can I tell you why I am paranoid?*

I thought you already did!

Nope. Had a bad experience recently.

Well, I'm sorry to hear that.

Brad continued, *I met someone online. We met up. I thought everything was good. Then she went psycho, emailing me, telling me she fell in love with me, all after only a couple of days spent together.*

My heart raced. I knew he was talking about me now, and I could not believe that he was calling me psycho. He had totally led me on and yes, I fell for it! What did he expect would happen?

I typed, *Did she stalk you? Call you constantly or show up at your house or job and slit your tires or something?*

He typed, *Well, no.*

I was not going to put up with being labeled a psycho so I made up a story to illustrate what a true psycho was. *I know a guy who was stalked by a woman he went out with only a couple of times. She sent him threatening emails, broke his car windows, approached him when he was with another woman and screamed at him. All kinds of freaky shit! He actually had to resort to getting a restraining order!*

Brad typed back, *Well, hey, sorry it didn't work out. I will delete you from my messenger—didn't mean to scare you.*

I was ready to end the game. I couldn't believe I was even playing it to begin with! This wasn't me! *It was interesting talking to you! I hope you have better luck in the future, Brad!*

Brad typed, *Sure was.... wow.... bye.*

I left the conversation with relief. That had been rather upsetting! And what had I even gotten out of it anyway? Brad thought I was a psycho. Great.

I decided the last thing I wanted was for Brad to believe I was posing as Katie. I would need to leave Katie's personal ad up and keep it active. So later that night I signed onto the personals website and made a few changes to Katie's personal ad. I changed some wording around and added a few more pictures of the girl I had once known, just to ensure that Brad believed Katie was real.

The next day, Brad typed Katie a message on instant messenger. *I like your new ad better.*

I couldn't help it, I typed back to Brad. *Yeah—you influenced my changing it.*

Good.... don't say I never did anything for you! What is it about you that makes me keep sending you messages when you are clearly offended?

I don't know.

So what did you like about my profile?

I laughed; it was all about him, wasn't it? *Your profile made you out to be a wonderful, caring and kind man. Just what every woman wants, right?*

That's who I am.... many women prefer not have that man, instead settle for less.... don't quite get it.

I arched an eyebrow. He actually thought that he was the most kind and caring man out there! What an arrogant ass! Something was definitely wrong with this guy.

I had to ask him, *So, I've been curious—how did you handle that psycho girl you mentioned earlier?*

She is a very sweet woman, just came on too strong.

I laughed again. I came on too strong? You came on strong with me to begin with, you prick!

I typed back, *I hope you were kind to her at least.* I made up more stories. *My cousin recently fell hard for a guy, but after a few amazing dates the guy just blew her off out of the blue, and she was really hurt.*

Brad defended himself. *I didn't do anything. She sent me emails saying how she felt, then said she couldn't handle the stress, so I didn't have to do anything .... she made up her own mind. I liked her, but she was a little too emotionally unstable. Timing just wasn't right I guess. Timing is everything....*

Emotionally unstable? I had been pretty emotionally stable before Brad had come into my life!

Then Brad added, *Sometimes emotions can get in the way of reason and logic .... understandable.*

I told Brad, *I don't think timing is everything. It's definitely important, but I think chemistry, attraction, and connection play an even bigger part. Dating is hard! You think you've found someone and then somehow it all falls apart and you have to start all over again. Plus, women are definitely more emotional than men!*

They can be, agreed. Most men are pigs though, so it makes sense.

I burst out laughing! Brad was a total pig and yet he couldn't even see it!

I was done with him, so I made an excuse about having to go to a meeting and said goodbye. I changed my availability on instant messenger to *"away from desk."*

Brad typed, *Sorry about earlier. I am a good guy. Hopefully someday you'll realize this. Have a great day!*

I realized I was seeing Brad as he truly was—an arrogant, self-absorbed ass. I wondered how I could lead him on even more with my fake Katie.

Friday, as soon as I signed into instant messenger as Katie, Brad typed, *Good morning, wild one!*

I frowned. He used to call me that. I couldn't help but wonder if he was using the "wild one" term with Katie because he still thought that I was posing as Katie. But he probably just called all women by that little pet name.

I typed back, *Wild one???* as if I didn't understand why he was calling me that.

Yeah, why not? How are you this morning?

I decided to play it cool and brush him off. *Busy. You?*

About the same .... we're getting lots of business.

I continued my cool attitude. *Good luck!*

Thanks. Have a great day. If you want to chat later, just let me know.

I made no reply

Later on I thought of something and couldn't resist engaging with him again. *I've got a question for you. Why did you leave the kids and religion sections of your personal ad blank? And your astrological sign and political views are blank too....*

Brad replied, *Those are personal questions. I am especially protective of my information as some of my colleagues and neighbors have seen my profile.*

Do people make fun of you for doing the online dating thing?

Not at all—there is really no other option for me to meet people. I also didn't put my income as that is VERY personal. I don't divulge things like that to anyone, even a partner until it is necessary; if it ever becomes relevant. When I first started the online thing, I had my income on there and was very clearly being targeted by gold diggers. I want someone to like me for me not for my money. Once I met a girl and during the first phone call with her she asked how much money I made. I was shocked and sickened.

I agreed with him. *Yeah, I hate girls who can't rely on themselves for money. You know, go get a job and make your own damned money!*

Or women who need a man to be whole. Your partner should love you unconditionally and uplift and encourage you, not complete you as an individual. I want to SHARE my life with my partner, not get a life once I finally have a partner. Does that make sense?

I typed back, *Absolutely!* But at the same time, I think we all want that companionship that a partner in crime provides us. We're all searching for it. Online even! So we do in a sense need someone to make our lives more complete.

Brad admitted, *When I moved here, I made the decision that I am content being alone and single. I've dated a little here and there, but I will not settle just because there are slim pickings. If it is five or ten years before I meet 'her' then so be it.*

I realized that I had almost forgotten that I was talking to Brad as Katie, not myself. Brad must have thought that being with me would be settling. This would explain his strange retreat after our weekend together. But why couldn't he have just been more upfront about it? Why had he tried to pretend like he felt the same about me and that nothing had changed between us? And then quit talking to me! Did he actually think that he had been doing me a favor by not being up front and honest with me? He was probably just too chicken shit to deal with letting a woman go!

Brad continued, *I've settled in the past, vowed to never do it again.*

I just sat there staring at my computer.

Brad typed, *I'm sorry I was such an ass with you at first .... my bad.*

I finally typed back, *Well, apparently you had just been through a bad situation and were a little paranoid about it .... it happens.*

Brad typed, *Yeah, unfortunately.*

I was growing tired of pretending to be Katie. It was time to stop talking to Brad. I had my answers, and he seemed to believe that Katie was a real person. And it would be kind of fun if Katie ignored him now that he was interested in her. A little payback. I typed one last message. *I've got to get going, Brad. I'll talk to you later, okay?* I actually had no intention of talking to Brad again as Katie, but I wanted to lead him on and then leave him hanging just as he had with me.

Brad typed back, *Okay. Have fun, bye!*

I signed Katie off instant messenger as *"away from desk"* again and tried to get back to work. But after an hour of staring at my computer screen, I decided to play hooky and leave work early for the day. I made the rounds, letting everyone know that I was feeling sick and going home.

I walked out to my car. I felt broken by my experience with Brad. Pretending to be Katie and getting the truth out of Brad hadn't really helped me feel any better either, not like I thought it would. The problem was that I wasn't getting what I wanted—Brad. All I really wanted was what Brad had offered me with that first week—a relationship with him. But I knew damned well now that I was being stupid. I had fallen for the idea of Brad. Not the real Brad. I had to accept that he had used me. And that it was over. But I just couldn't stop thinking about it all.

The overcast, rainy day wasn't helping my mood. I wasn't paying much attention as I turned on the car on and then turned on my windshield wipers and backed out of my parking space at the club. When my car suddenly slammed into something hard, making a horrid crunching sound, I sucked in my breath and froze.

Finally, I turned around and peered out the back window. This was bad. "Shit!" I pounded my fists against the steering wheel. Could my life get any worse? I had run into a damn telephone pole! I turned the car off and got out to assess the damage.

I walked around to the back of the car. The left back bumper was totally crushed. How stupid could I be? I had been so distracted by my thoughts of Brad. This was all his fault! Damn him!

A few people from the yacht club came running outside to see what had happened. They circled around me.

"That was you? You crash your car? What you do, back into the pole?" One of my coworkers, Matt, a stocky maintenance man, stated the obvious.

"Yeah," I muttered. "I felt like backing into a pole today, you know, for the fun of it!" I groaned and massaged my forehead. I was getting a headache.

Jean put her arm around me. "Sorry, honey!" she said as she squeezed me in a half hug. "This sucks, huh?"

"Yeah."

"That's some serious damage! How fast were you going?" My boss joined the growing group of onlookers. Just what I needed, my asshole boss giving me a bad time! He would probably say that I had been insubordinate when I backed into the pole.

"I wasn't going that fast...." I trailed off. The damage was all to my car. The pole looked unscathed. I felt like an idiot.

"That's gonna cost you a lot to fix. You have insurance, right?" asked Matt.

"Of course." I rolled my eyes. "Oh god, that means my rates will go up now because of this!" It truly was just one thing after another lately.

"You know, you could say that you came out from the store one day and saw that someone had hit your car. A hit and run. Then your insurance rates won't go up." This suggestion came from my boss. Typical. He had no morals.

I couldn't help but consider his idea though. It was tempting.

"Yeah, the insurance companies are all crooks anyway! It won't matter!" Jean offered.

Everyone nodded in agreement.

I wanted to lie and get back at the universe for always picking on me. For always giving me the short end of the stick in life.

But I knew I couldn't do it. I hated lying.

It started raining harder, so everyone hurried back inside and I got back in my car. The sky turned dark from the storm. Or maybe it was just my mood. As I started my car back up, I put my *Blue October* CD into my CD player and forwarded to the song "Into the Ocean." The song spoke about lost love. The lyrics seemed to have been written just for me, just for today. I sang along:

> Let the waves up and take me down
> Let the hurricane set in motion .... yeah
> Let the rain of what I feel right now .... come down

I drove aimlessly listening to "Into the Ocean" over and over again.

I let my tears fall freely.

I pulled into an empty parking lot facing a deserted beach. I sat and watched the dark clouds, the rain pelting the ocean, and the violent waves crashing on the shore. I was filled with a sense of *deja vu*. I tried to hold onto it, understand it, but it slipped away.

Why did everything turn out so badly for me? I blamed my hair loss. If I hadn't lost my hair in my teens, maybe I would have had a different life now. A happy life, with a husband and maybe kids.

Sure, I was lucky to live in Hawaii now, but I was so lost and alone and confused. I had no good friends. And I had always been unlucky in love. What man wanted to be with a bald girl? I wouldn't want to be with a bald girl if I were a man!

I was useless. A waste of space. I had no place in the world.

Oblivious to the rain, I got out of my car and slowly walked down to the beach. I stopped in the sand just out of reach of the waves rushing up onto the shore. The wind whipped my soaking wet wig around my face but I didn't feel it. I felt empty. Numb. I had nothing, no one. Worst of all, I didn't see how things would ever get better. I had no hope.

I didn't want to think anymore. I was done thinking. Done caring. Done trying. I thought of the song I'd just been listening to. It ended with the words "*Into the ocean, end it all*" repeated over and over. I thought of ending it all, like the song said. I took another step toward the raging ocean and watched as a wave crashed at my feet, soaking my shoes. I looked back up, contemplating the end.

Chapter 11

Before I could take another step, something caught my eye. Something was out there in the water, bobbing up and down with the waves. I shielded my eyes from the rain with my hands and squinted, trying to see. Was it—a person? It was! The person went underwater for a few moments and then resurfaced, flailing their arms around in panic. I looked around the empty beach and parking lot for help, but there was no one else around to save them. Only me.

I looked back toward the person who was possibly drowning. I forgot all about my own problems. Should I try to help? Who was I kidding? I mean, hello! I had just barely conquered my fear of snorkeling a couple of weeks ago! Going for a casual swim in the calm shallow ocean waters on a beautiful sunny day with fins and goggles and someone there to hold my hand was one thing. Attempting to handle this scary, violent, stormy ocean all by myself was another thing altogether.

Instinct took over though and before I even fully realized what I was doing, I was running into the water, adrenaline pumping, determined to help. A giant wave that seemed to be twice my height came rolling up on me and even though I felt the old familiar fear, something deep inside of me propelled me forward. I held my breath and dove right into the wave. I was completely swallowed up in the force of it. I fought to stay calm. Kicking my legs, I rose to the surface and sucked in air before the next wave hit. I dove into the next wave, finding strength I never knew I had. I pushed on until I thought I might have made it to the spot where I had spotted the drowning person. I looked all around in every direction but I saw nothing. Was I too late?

I dove down and tried to look around but it was just too dark and murky. I couldn't see a thing.

When I surfaced again, I noticed I was getting pulled out farther from the shore. I tried to swim back toward the shore, but it felt like I was just swimming in place. A wave caught me by surprise, and I was underwater again, tumbling around and around. My wig was finally ripped off my head from the force. I tried to grab it but it was useless. It was gone. My lungs burned and I tried to get my bearings, but I couldn't figure out where the surface was. I swam in one direction but seemed to go nowhere so I started swimming in the opposite direction. My heart pounded furiously in my chest, my eyes were stinging from the salt water. I couldn't find the surface. Panic set in.

I didn't think I could hold my breath much longer. I might actually die out here! Ironically, I had just contemplated ending it all a few minutes ago. Be careful what you wish for, huh?

I couldn't help but picture Brad's face one last time. This was all his fault!

But I didn't want to die! Why had I ever thought that dying was the answer to my problems? I wanted to live! I thought of all the good in life. The people I had loved, the pets I had loved. I thought of all the beautiful music that moved me. And all the wonderfully delicious food. Books and movies that ignited my imagination and hope for humanity. I thought of how beautiful the world was. How beautiful Hawaii was.

Just as I realized that in my obsession over Brad, I had forgotten about all the good in the world, I felt something brush against my foot. I instinctively jerked away, frantically looking around, trying to see what scary sea creature was about to devour me. It was hard to see but there was something very large near my feet. It started slowly moving upward. A shark?

My fear turned to fascination as I realized it was a sea turtle. The turtle inched closer. It was a big one! It had to be bigger than five feet. Its shell was mostly light brown with radiating wavy olive markings. It looked like the turtle was smiling at me. How weird! I must be hallucinating now from lack of oxygen. The turtle was absolutely beautiful. I was blown away by it. I forgot about the fact that I was probably drowning and simply stared in awe at the turtle. Oddly, I felt peace and love and joy and hope.

I reached out to touch the turtle. As my hand felt the rough shell, I felt a little jolt and I heard one word like a whisper in my head. *Remember.*

Remember? Remember what?

The turtle turned then and began to swim away. Mesmerized, I started following it. And that was when I finally saw the surface of the ocean. Realizing that I couldn't hold my breath any longer, I pushed myself up and out of the water with my last ounce of energy.

Kicking my legs wildly, trying to keep my head above water, I gulped desperately for air and laughed. I wasn't dead!

"*A'ole!* I thought you drowned!"

Startled, I turned in the direction of the voice. A beautiful Hawaiian woman about my age sat on a surfboard nearby.

"I was about to jump in after you," she told me with a friendly smile. "But no need, yeah?"

I shook my head, unable to find my voice.

"Here." She paddled over to me. "Get on."

I struggled, weak from my ordeal, but with her help I managed to climb onto her board, which was bright pink with blue waves running along one edge.

"I'm Noe," she told me.

Noe had dark chocolate eyes, long lashes, full cheeks and a wide smile with full lips. Her long dark hair was tied back in a braid, and she rocked a hot blue string bikini. Her skin was a smooth creamy coffee color, just a bit darker than my own. Could Noe be the person I'd seen earlier? The person I'd thought had been drowning and needed saving? Who apparently didn't need saving after all! I suddenly noticed that it was no longer raining or even stormy. Blue sky peeked out from behind the clouds now.

"You okay?" she asked, taking in my fully dressed appearance.

"Yeah," I croaked. "I thought I saw someone out here drowning. I was trying to help."

Noe smiled. "Just me out here today." She looked around. "Good day to catch some waves."

I gave her a funny look, and she laughed.

"I know, I know! I'm a bit of an adrenaline junkie!"

I raised an eyebrow. *A bit?*

"So your name is...." Noe prompted me.

"Oh!" I stammered. "Sorry! Liz."

"Nice to meet you, Liz." Noe gave me a one-armed hug and kissed me on the cheek.

"Nice to meet you, too," I told her.

"You got cancer?" When I looked confused by her question, Noe nodded toward my head. I slapped my hand to my head and felt nothing but skin. I had completely forgotten about losing my wig in the ocean!

"Sorry!" she quickly apologized. "Sometimes I open my big mouth too much!"

"No, no, no. No worries," I reassured her. "I don't have cancer. I have Alopecia, a really rare hair loss disorder. I got it when I was sixteen."

Noe nodded her understanding. "Oh. I'm sorry. That must have been rough...."

I rolled my eyes. "To say the least." I remembered all the boys who teased me and the girls who whispered behind my back in class my senior year of high school. "I wear wigs," I explained. "I was wearing a wig but it came off in the ocean." I suddenly felt self-conscious. I had never been out in public without a wig before.

Noe could sense my insecurity. "Oh, well, you have a beautiful head!" she told me with a big smile.

I couldn't help but laugh.

"No really! It's like perfectly round and smooth. And your eyes are amazing! You should go without your wig!"

"Right!" I said. *As if!*

"You live around here?" Noe asked.

"Yeah, in Kailua."

"I live here, too. Never seen you around before...."

"I just inherited my great-grandmother's house. I moved over from California almost a year ago." I was amazed at how much I was opening up to this woman. But I felt comfortable with her. Almost like we were old friends.

"Oh! Who was your great-grandmother?"

"Puanani Kekoa."

"No way!" Noe got excited. "She taught me *hula* as a little girl."

"Really? That's so cool," I admitted, a little jealously. "I never got to meet her."

"Oh, I'm sorry to hear that. She was the sweetest." Noe looked a little nostalgic. She studied my face. "You know, I can see the resemblance now. You look a little like her."

"I do?"

"Yeah." Noe continued to study me. "I think it's your eyes."

I made a mental note to go home and look through my great-grandmother's pictures again.

"Hey! You should come to my house tonight!" Noe told me. "A bunch of other folks who knew your great-grandmother will be there. They'll be so excited to meet you!"

"Oh, okay," I agreed.

"She used to talk about her great-granddaughter, you know?" Noe said.

"Really?"

"Oh yeah, she was so proud of you," Noe told me. "She wanted to get you to Hawaii, and it looks like she finally succeeded!"

"Yeah, although a little too late."

"Better late than never!" Noe grinned and then checked her waterproof watch. "Oh no! I gotta go run some errands before the party!" She turned back and started paddling back to shore. "The party's in two hours!"

I helped her paddle in. Once we got on land again, I remembered that I was the only one with a car, so I asked Noe if she needed a ride.

"No need. I rode my bike." She motioned to a bright pink bike leaning against a tree in the sand. It had a surfboard rack attached to it. Funny how I had completely missed that earlier.

As she secured her surfboard to the rack on her bike, Noe told me her phone number and address and instructed me to come by her house around six. Then she reached into a storage box on the back of her bike and pulled out a baseball cap.

"Just until you feel more confident about going around without anything on!" she said, winking at me as she put the cap on my head.

"Thanks!" I said, instantly feeling better with my new cover up.

She hugged me tightly, kissed my cheek, wrote her address down for me, and then got on her bike and rode off.

I sat in my car with a silly grin for a bit after Noe left. I couldn't believe what had just happened. What a weird day! I had tried to save a drowning person, nearly drowned myself, had a close encounter with a sea turtle and then survived to meet Noe, a new amazing friend. I was really excited to see her later at the party.

I felt like a new woman. I felt like I had been given a clean slate, a fresh start, a second chance. And I wasn't going to waste it.

Chapter 12

At six o'clock on the dot, I pulled up to an arched bamboo gate in front of a Spanish-style colonial house located right on the beach not far from my house. A stone fence surrounded the property. *Wow! Noe lives here?* I double checked the address, then entered the code Noe had given me and watched as the gate slid open. The center of the gate showcased an intricate iron turtle design. Interesting. I pulled my car into a curved driveway behind three other cars; a silver Toyota Prius, a white Volkswagen Passat and a teal Mini Cooper.

The arched bamboo front door matched the gate. A big round metal turtle-shaped knocker sat in the middle. As I knocked, I noticed several pairs of shoes off to the left of the porch. I followed the example and took my shoes off, sitting them next to the others.

Noe answered the door wearing a floor-length blue-and-white printed sarong tied around her neck like a halter dress. Her hair fell in soft waves all the way down to the small of her back. "Liz!" She hugged me again and then raised her eyebrows as she ran her fingers through my new wig.

"I have extras at home," I explained.

"You look good!" she said. "Have you ever tried blonde or auburn?"

"Yeah, but recently I switched to brunette."

Noe nodded. "I'm so glad you came! Come in, come in." She motioned for me to follow her.

Noe's home was decorated in the subtle blues and greens of the ocean with bamboo flooring throughout. Art on the walls in the entryway depicted ancient Hawaiian women and men in colorful *hula* scenes. The living room had plush oversized beige sofas and chairs with lots of blue-and-green accent pillows. More Hawaiian art adorned the walls in here—beach, mountain and waterfall scenes. Open windows let the cool ocean breezes flow through.

Noe led me through her kitchen with gorgeous tan-and-teal granite countertops and stainless steel appliances. The entire back wall was open to her *lanai*, where a group of people sat talking and laughing around a long glass patio table under a covered awning. Hawaiian music was playing and waves crashed off in the distance.

Everyone stopped talking and turned toward us as soon as we stepped outside.

"Everyone, this is Liz!" Noe announced.

A chorus of friendly voices replied, "*Aloha*, Liz!"

"Liz, this is Fred and Kiana." Noe introduced me to the couple sitting closest to us. "They knew your great-grandmother very well."

The man got up and hugged me. "*E komo mai*. Welcome, Liz! My name is Fred."

"Hi, nice to meet you, Fred," I said, surprised by his name. I expected a Fred to be a middle-aged white guy from Iowa. This Fred was a tall and muscular native Hawaiian, who looked to be in his late fifties. He had deeply tanned skin, long dark brown hair pulled back in a ponytail and interesting Hawaiian tribal tattoos on his neck that continued down past the red Hawaiian floral *aloha* shirt he wore. I noticed he was barefoot. Wow! He had giant feet!

Fred chuckled and I blushed. Could he tell what I'd been thinking?

"I know what you're thinking!" he said with a wink. "My Hawaiian name is Alapa'i, which is a form of the Western name Alfred. I go by Fred to make it easier on everyone."

"Oh," I replied with a nervous giggle. "Nice to meet you, Fred," I repeated, this time with more enthusiasm.

"And this is my wife, Kiana." Fred put his arm around the woman who stood next to him. Kiana smiled up at him and then back at me. Kiana looked to be Hawaiian and in her fifties also. She wore a knee-length pink patterned sarong, wrapped around her body as a dress and tied at one shoulder. Her long, dark braided hair had touches of gray in it, and she had a white hibiscus flower tucked behind one ear. Hawaiian tribal band tattoos wrapped around her left arm and several smaller tattoos adorned her fingers, hands and wrists. Kiana was also barefoot but her feet were much smaller and daintier than Fred's and her toenails were painted pink like her sarong.

Kiana hugged me, too. "Welcome, Liz!" She pulled back and studied me. "You do resemble your great-grandmother!" She smiled and hugged me close again. "I am so glad you have finally returned to the islands!"

"Returned?" I asked, confused, looking at Fred and Kiana. "I've never been here before. Not that I remember anyway."

Fred and Kiana shared a look.

I remembered my encounter with the turtle earlier in the day. I had been sure I heard a voice saying, *"Remember."* Was I was supposed to remember an earlier trip to the islands? Had my parents brought me here when I was a baby or something?

Noe interrupted before Fred and Kiana could respond. "And this is Lily and her husband Kai."

We took turns hugging and kissing cheeks. Lily was radiant in a white sundress. Kai wore tan shorts and a blue T-shirt. They looked to be in their thirties.

"Lily is our daughter," Kiana explained.

"Nice to meet you, Liz!" Lily said. "I learned *hula* from your great-grandmother." She looked toward her mother. "And Momma took lessons from her when she was a young girl, too!"

"Maybe you can teach me some *hula*," I suggested to both Lily and Kiana.

"We'd love to!" they both agreed.

"And last but not least!" Noe announced as the last guest at the far end of the table stood. "This is John."

John looked to be in his twenties and was a tall, thin white guy. He was grinning from ear to ear. "Welcome, Liz!" He sauntered over and gave me a big hug.

"John and Kai are kite boarding buddies," Lily explained the connection.

"Oh, what's kite boarding?" I asked

"It's part wakeboarding, part paragliding. We take a kite out with a surfboard and harness the power of the wind as we surf the waves," Kai explained.

"Yeah, you can get major air with the kite!" John added excitedly.

Lily laughed. "They like to show off and do jumps and stuff."

John volunteered to teach me sometime, promising that it would be the most exhilarating experience of my life.

"Oh, thanks. Maybe," I told him, one hundred percent sure that I would *not* be taking him up on his offer. Not in a million years! That sounded totally insane to me.

"Liz had an interesting day in the ocean today," Noe told the group as everyone returned to their places around the table. The chair at the head of the table was empty, so I hesitantly took it.

"Oh yeah?" John asked, his curiosity piqued.

Kiana offered me wine and I accepted.

I laughed nervously and took a sip of my wine, all eyes on me. "I thought I saw someone drowning." I could feel myself blushing. "I swam out to try to save them, and in the process I nearly drowned myself." I glanced at Noe, who grinned at me. Laughing, I added, "It turned out to be Noe. Surfing, not drowning."

"I was about to jump in to rescue her," Noe explained. "She'd been under so long!"

I tried to laugh it off. "Yeah, for a minute there, I wasn't sure I would make it."

"Did you see a light?" John asked with a wink.

"Something like that," I admitted. Everyone seemed eager to hear more, so I continued, "I saw this huge sea turtle. It swam right up to me, and I swear it looked me right in the eye...."

Fred smiled. "Ahhh! That was your *aumakua*, Liz! Your family's *aumakua* is the *honu*, the sea turtle."

I crinkled my brow in confusion. "Huh?"

Fred smiled and tried to explain. "Hawaiians believe in guardian spirits that take animal form."

"That could have been your great-grandmother trying to help you," Kiana said.

What? I looked around to get everyone's reaction and saw everyone nodding in agreement.

"Ho! That's so cool!" John said. "I've always wanted to have an encounter with my *aumakua*!"

"What's your *aumakua*?" I asked.

"The *mo'o*," John said matter-of-factly.

"The *mo'o*?" I repeated.

He explained, "The lizard!"

Everyone laughed.

"Did she speak to you?" Noe asked me.

"Uhh, I guess you could call it that," I confessed, blushing more. This was crazy talk, wasn't it? My dead great-grandmother appearing in the form of a turtle. Talking to me. And saving me?

"Well!" Kai demanded. "What did she say?"

"She told me to remember."

Everyone looked at me, waiting to hear more.

I winced. I might as well just confess. "Well, I had been contemplating ending it all." I paused and shrugged, looking around at the friendly, concerned faces. "I felt like I had come to the end of my rope, like I couldn't take it anymore." Embarrassed, I looked down at my hands.

Kiana reached for my hands. "We've all been there, Liz."

I looked back up at her and everyone else.

Everyone agreed.

"Well, what do you think she meant?" Noe asked. "When she told you to remember?"

"I don't know, that I should remember how good life can be?"

Noe nodded.

"Sometimes we have to go through a *hi'u wai*," Kiana said, "an experience that cleanses us, purifies and centers us, and reconnects us with ourselves. With life."

I nodded.

"This experience helps us get past all of our fears, concerns and problems and put the past behind us. We realize then that we truly want to be alive."

That pretty much summed up what I had experienced.

Kiana continued, "Hawaiians believe the ocean is a powerful, spiritual source of energy and healing. It is life. Today you connected with this life. You gained wisdom and insight."

I did feel more at peace with myself and more connected with life.

Fred proposed a toast. "To life!"

We all clinked our glasses together and drank.

"I know another way to help you appreciate life!" Noe said mischievously.

"Oh yeah?" I asked hesitantly.

"Oh yeah!" Noe nodded. "Rock climbing!"

My eyes bulged. Rock climbing?

Everyone agreed rock climbing was just what I needed next.

"You conquered the ocean today, girl!" Noe said. "And tomorrow you are going to conquer the mountain!"

Chapter 13

The next morning, lying lazily in bed, I recalled the strange and life-changing events of the day before. I thought about my great-grandmother. I tried to imagine her spirit as the turtle but the whole idea felt silly. Suddenly, remembering that Noe would be coming by at 10:00 to go rock climbing, I grabbed my phone from the bedside table and checked the time. 9:30! I needed to get going!

I was ready and waiting at 10:00, but Noe didn't show up until nearly 10:30.

"Morning, Liz!" Noe said, grinning as I opened the door. She gave me a big hug and kissed my cheek. "Howzit?"

"Good, good," I said, even though I was irritated that she was so late. I wanted to say "You're late!" but I held my tongue. Instead, I admitted, "I'm a bit nervous about this rock climbing thing."

Noe squeezed my shoulder reassuringly. "No need to worry." she said and winked. "You can handle it!" Noe had dressed in tan hiking pants and a blue T-shirt. I wore my gym gear, black nylon shorts and a gray cotton tank top.

"Should I be wearing pants?"

"Not necessarily. I like to protect my legs because I do more difficult climbs and tend to scratch my legs a lot. You should be fine today in shorts. But you do need water and snacks."

I nodded and patted my backpack, where I'd already packed a bottle of water and granola bars.

"You can borrow my climbing shoes and my spare harness, too. Let's *hele* on then!"

"*Hele* on?" I asked, not sure what she meant.

"Let's get going!" Noe clarified. Outside, she headed to the teal Mini Cooper I had seen last night parked in her driveway.

"Nice ride," I told her as we got into the car.

"Thanks!"

"How long have you been rock climbing?" I asked as Noe started driving.

"Oh," she thought about it, "going on ten years now."

"Wow! You must be really good at it!"

Noe grinned. "Not bad, not bad. Some people I know are better though. Naturals."

"Have you taught anyone else?"

"A couple friends." Noe smiled reassuringly. "No worries! You're in good hands, I promise! So! Tell me about yourself!"

I told Noe about my parents and my Mormon upbringing. "I quit going to church in college," I added and looked over at Noe for her reaction.

"I was raised Catholic," Noe admitted. "But I haven't been to church in years either!" She laughed. "Now I'm Buddhist."

"Buddhist, huh?" I pictured the always smiling Dali Lama in his orange gown. "I don't know much about Buddhism."

"Fred runs a weekly meditation group. You should come sometime. Check it out!"

"Uh-huh ..." I mumbled. Weekly meditation with a group sounded a lot like going to church every Sunday, which I had sworn never to do again.

Noe chuckled. "Go on then, tell me more! What do you do for a living?"

I told her that I was an accountant now, but that my first interest in life had been art. "I used to love to draw, but I thought I needed something more reliable as a career. So now I'm the controller over at the Waikiki Yacht Club."

"Okay. Well, what do you draw?" Noe asked.

"People. Faces, mostly," I said. "But really anything."

"Do you still draw?"

"Not much, but I've been getting back into it since moving to Hawaii."

"Good! You'll have to show me your stuff sometime." Noe glanced at me and I nodded. "What about love interests?"

"Oh god!" I rolled my eyes. "I've had nothing but bad luck in the romance department my entire life! I've pretty much given up on finding true love."

Noe looked over again, frowning. "Is that why you were at the beach yesterday, contemplating ending it all?"

"That's part of it."

"No man is worth it, girl!" she said, patting my knee. "There are plenty of other fish in the sea!"

I laughed. "I just keep falling for the wrong guys. And I seem to fall in love way too easily. There must be something wrong with me."

"Oh, girl! You're just a romantic!"

"Yeah...."

"You know, you might have had a really easy time with love in a prior life," Noe glanced at me, "so you just expect it to be easy as a result."

I narrowed my eyes. I had never given much thought to the idea of reincarnation. "Prior lives, huh?"

Noe laughed. "Anyway, there's a quote from an American Buddhist nun named Pema Chodron that I really like. *'It's only when we feel completely annihilated that we're able to truly open up finally and see what's been in front of us the whole time.'*"

I thought about it. "Yeah, I like that. My annihilation yesterday was an eye-opening experience for me, to say the least!" I laughed.

Noe laughed, too. "Hey, you joke but that's pretty special that you met your *aumakua*!"

"Yeah." That was definitely something I would remember for a long time although I still wasn't totally buying into the whole ancestors protecting you in animal form idea.

"Have you ever met your *aumakua*?" I asked and then wondered, "What is your *aumakua*?"

"The *mano*. The shark!" Noe said dramatically, grinning at me.

"Oh God, I hope you've never met your *aumakua* then!"

"Girl! Please!" Noe shrugged. "I swim with the sharks."

"What? You might be crazy!" I joked, laughing.

"I might," Noe agreed, laughing with me.

I asked her what she did for a living.

"I'm a Hawaiian history professor at UH."

"Oh, wow. That's cool." I was impressed. "I've never been interested in history before, but the Hawaiian Islands fascinate me for some reason. I've been trying to learn as much as possible since moving here."

"Anything you want to know, I'm your girl," Noe said. "Have you been to the Bishop Museum yet?" She looked at me expectantly.

"No, not yet."

"I'm taking you then!" Noe decided. "It'll be an all-day thing with me. I'll bore you to death with facts!"

"No, that sounds great!" I studied Noe as she drove. "A Hawaiian history professor who rock climbs, surfs in storms, and swims with sharks! You are one of a kind!"

Noe laughed, and we fell into a comfortable silence then as she drove. I admired the changing views along the way. We drove up through the middle of the island, past the Dole plantation and through pineapple fields and coffee fields. Then down to the North Shore along the coast. Past an airfield where people were skydiving overhead. Tall mountains rose up along the left side of the road and rocky wild beaches lined the right.

"Here we are!" Noe announced as she made a U-turn and then parked on the mountain side of the road. "Mokuleia."

"This place is gorgeous!" I gushed as we got out of the car. "Untamed and majestic."

Across the street, a few brave surfers were out tackling the violent waves. One guy surfed wave after wave with little effort, staying up on his board no matter how rough the waves got. He was tall and had chin-length, dark wavy hair and looked Hawaiian. I couldn't take my eyes off him.

Noe noticed who I was watching. "That's Aaron Aiona, world surf champion in the late '90s."

"Looks like he's still got it," I commented. "How old is he now then, thirties?"

"Mid-thirties, yeah."

We watched Aaron avoid a wipeout that another surfer crashed in. "He's running for mayor of Honolulu now," Noe added.

"Oh." I wasn't interested in politics. Politicians were usually power-hungry, greedy men who only pretended to want to help the common man.

"Yeah, his father owns one of the biggest construction companies on the island. Aiona Builders." Noe opened the trunk of her car and gathered our gear. "Here, will you carry the shoes and harnesses in your pack and I'll carry the rope?"

"Okay." I shoved the shoes and harness in my pack and put it on. It was heavier now but manageable.

"Oh, and a couple extra bottles of water." Noe added more to my pack.

Noe pointed to a path leading through thick grass to the mountain. It looked formidable. "Let's get going!" she said with a grin. "We've got a thirty-minute hike up to the climbing spot."

We started off on flat ground on a small, hidden pathway through overgrown brush, most likely cut by previous hikers. Noe talked excitedly as we made our way. "Rock climbing is a lot of fun. Sure, it's challenging but it's rewarding and it's a lot easier than you think. It's all about knowing what your body is capable of and trusting yourself. Climbing requires creativity and balance! And when you're up there connecting with the rock, figuring out where to put your hand or foot next, you tend to be able to think more clearly. I've solved many of life's problems while climbing!"

"Okay, well, you make it sound interesting at least," I told her, still unsure of what I was in for.

Noe laughed.

Soon the trail became steep and rocky. I started breathing harder and harder from the effort of moving upward. At least there was a cool breeze off the ocean and nice shade from the trees bordering the path.

After hiking partway up the mountain and climbing over various sized rocks and boulders, I was sweating and needed water.

"Hey, Noe, can we take a breather for a sec?" I asked, desperately panting.

"Yeah, absolutely!" Noe said, apparently not out of breath at all. "There's a resting spot with amazing views just a couple more minutes up the mountain."

"Okay," I agreed reluctantly and pushed myself on more.

Not too much later, I saw a large flat rock up ahead. I followed Noe up over some smaller rocks surrounding it until we were both standing on the top and I breathed a sigh of relief.

Noe had been right about the view. I greedily guzzled my water and stared out at the sparkling blue ocean. I turned back toward the mountain we were hiking up and decided we must be halfway there.

"Oh, look!" Noe excitedly exclaimed, pointing to a spot out on the ocean. "Whales!"

I looked toward the spot where Noe was pointing, but only saw a big splash in the water. A few seconds later, a whale surfaced nearby, jumping out of the water and splashing back down under again.

"Wow!" I shouted. "I've never seen a whale in real life before!"

Noe laughed.

We stood watching the whales play for a few more minutes.

"Well," Noe finally said, "shall we continue on? We're almost there."

"Yeah, let's go." Seeing the whales had rejuvenated me.

A few minutes later, Noe stopped to point out a plant growing on the side of the trail. "This is the famous naupaka plant."

A strong sense of déjà vu came over me as I stared at the flower. All the petals on the lower half of each flower were gone, as if someone had plucked them off.

"There are two types of naupaka plants," Noe explained. "One type grows up in the mountains. And the other type grows down by the ocean."

"How odd," I commented distractedly, trying to understand the *déjà vu*.

"There's a legend," Noe explained, "about ancient Hawaiian lovers, a princess and a commoner."

This caught my attention. I turned and looked at Noe.

"They fell in love," Noe went on, "but it was *kapu* for royal Hawaiians to marry commoners. They were forced apart, and the princess ended up dying alone up in the mountains and the commoner died alone down by the sea."

I frowned.

"The flowers started growing this way, with only half their petals, after their deaths."

"How sad." Something about the legend really got to me. I felt like I might burst into tears.

"Yes," Noe nodded. "But the legend says that the two lovers will be reunited one day and when they are, the flowers will grow with all of their petals again." Noe smiled at me. "Ready?"

So there was hope.

Noe turned and headed back up the mountain again. "Let's go!"

I was still lost in the legend for a moment, but when I realized Noe had disappeared from sight I hurried up the trail trying to catch her. After another fifteen minutes, I finally stepped out of an opening in the trees to a ledge that ran across the entire side of the rocky mountain. Ropes ran down to the ground through metal rings at the top in multiple spots. Several people were in various stages of climbing and others were tied into the ropes down on the ground.

Noe spotted people she knew and shouted out greetings to them. "Come on, Liz! I'll introduce you and you can watch a few people climb to see how it's done."

"Hey, Pat, Jill, Ryan." Noe made introductions as we approached. "This is Liz."

Everyone shouted out greetings.

"Liz is a newbie! I'm teaching her how to climb today."

"Great!" Jill said. "I'm about to go up, so you can watch me. I'll explain what I'm doing as I go." Jill was threading the end of a rope through some loops on the harness she wore. She then retraced the end of the rope through a knot she had made. She looked to be securely tied in to the rope through her harness.

"This is my double eight knot." Jill pointed to the intricate knot she had tied in the rope. "It keeps you from falling!"

Pat was also tied into the rope, but at the other end of it. "I'm going to belay Jill," he explained. "I keep the rope tight, and then let out or take up slack in the rope when she needs it. If she slips, I can keep her from falling too much with this belay device." He pointed to the metal contraption on his belt that the rope was threaded through. "It locks up tight when someone falls so they don't fall very far, a foot or so, depending on how tight you keep the rope."

"You should take a fall, Jill, so that Liz can see what happens!" Ryan joked.

"That's a great idea!" Jill said excitedly.

"Oh, you don't have to do that," I protested, appalled at the idea of someone falling just to show me what it looked like.

"It's no big deal, you'll see!" Jill insisted.

"Okay, let's double check each other," Pat said to Jill. "I'm double backed here, here and here." He pointed to the three buckles on his belt where he had doubled the belt strap back through. "The carabiner is though the belay loop, the belay is locked and my break hand is down." He tugged on the rope, running from his belay device to the ground and the rope stuck.

"Okay." Jill nodded her head, pleased with what Pat had told her. "I'm double backed here, here and here." She pointed to her three belt buckles that had the belt straps doubled back through them. "My rope is running through two points on the harness, and here's my double eight and my stopper knot." Jill showed him her knots.

"Good!" Pat was happy.

"On belay," Jill announced.

"Belay is on," Pat confirmed.

"Okay. Climbing." Jill turned around and faced the rocks, analyzing where to put her hands and feet.

"Climb on." Pat gave her the go ahead and then explained to me, "That was our safety check. We do a safety check every time before we start climbing to make sure that each step is followed and each knot is tied correctly. We don't want any accidents."

I nodded and smiled. Safety was good!

We watched Jill as she started up the rock. She tested her handholds as she went, and then found good placement for her feet.

"See this handhold here?" Jill paused to point out a small piece of rock jutting out from the cliff.

"This is a great hold. See?" Jill showed me how to grasp the hold.

"And see this foothold?" Jill motioned toward the small piece of rock that stuck out near her left knee. "I can put my left foot here and get myself higher. When in doubt, figure out how to get your feet higher and higher so that you can find better handholds."

She moved steadily up the route and made it look easy. Suddenly she called out, "Falling."

Pat reacted lightning fast by tightening the rope with his belay device right as Jill pushed herself off the rock. She didn't fall much before the rope caught her.

Jill threw her hands up and grinned down at me. "See? Falling is a piece of cake!"

"Yeah, sure," I agreed. That hadn't looked too bad.

Jill deftly maneuvered herself back onto the rock. She finished the route, using all kinds of positions, from standing on her tiptoes on small juts to straddling the sides of the rock walls. She hung on to what looked to be miniscule handholds and somehow her feet seemed to stick to the rock wherever she put them, no matter how flat or smooth the rock appeared to be. I was impressed.

Meanwhile, Pat continuously pulled the loosening rope through his belay device, keeping Jill tightly roped into him.

When Jill reached the top of the rock, she called, "Take."

Pat replied, "Got."

"Ready to lower," Jill called out.

"Lowering," Pat replied, flicking back a lever on his belay device. He started working the rope back through the belay device, allowing Jill to slowly lower back down to the ground.

"That was amazing!" I said as Jill landed safely and then unhooked herself from the harness.

Jill laughed. "Thanks!"

"How long have you been climbing?" I asked.

"Oh, gosh, since I was a kid. I love it!"

"I can tell."

I watched as Pat climbed next, then Noe, and then Ryan. Each person had different ways of climbing the same route.

After everyone else had taken a turn, Noe turned to me. "Ready to give it a go yourself now?"

"Uh, sure," I said, half excited and half nervous.

Noe reached into her bag and pulled out another climbing harness for me. "Put this on." She guided me as I put my legs through the two straps of the harness. "Then pull it up over your waist and tighten it up here by pulling the strap as tight as you can."

I followed Noe's instructions and made sure the harness was as tight as possible and that each of the three straps were backed through the buckles two times just as the others had done it. Noe showed me how to tie the initial eight-shaped knot near one end of the rope, thread that end up through a loop in my harness and then double back through the eight-shaped knot again. Finally, Noe showed me how to tie a second safety knot above the double eight knot.

After Noe was finished getting me tied in, she looped the other end of the rope through her belay device then secured her belay device to a loop on her harness and locked it tight. We doubled checked everything.

"Okay, Liz!" Noe grinned. "Are you ready?"

"Yeah, let's give it a go!" I said, feeling anxious as I turned to face the rock.

I wasn't sure where to begin. After analyzing the rock for a minute, I noticed a small spot for my right foot and a hold for my left hand. So I started with that. And then I analyzed the rock for my next move and decided that I had to stretch to get my left foot up off the ground and onto a higher ledge. It worked and I felt stable on the rock. I grinned triumphantly back down at Noe.

"I think you're a natural, Liz!" Noe said. "I didn't have to give you any hints on how to start. You figured it out on your own! Nice job!"

"Thanks! This is already more fun than I thought it would be!" I admitted and then turned back to the rock to analyze my next move. I saw more potentially good handholds a little higher up so I tested one and then grabbed hold of it and pulled myself up, feeling around for good foot placement as I went.

"Good, Liz, but try to use your feet more to move yourself up, instead of pulling yourself up with your arms. You'll wear out faster if you're mostly using your arms."

"Oh, that makes sense." I immediately started looking for better foot placements. But my arms were getting tired fast.

"Oh, man, you were right!" I admitted after making a few more moves up the rock wall. "My arms are suddenly feeling super weak."

"That's normal when you first start climbing," Noe reassured me. "You can always rest whenever you're in the middle of a climb by straightening out your arms on a hold and leaning back. Like this." Noe demonstrated for me. "Try it."

I followed Noe's instructions and felt instant relief. "Oh! That's nice!" I relaxed and let out a deep breath.

Noe laughed. "You're doing great, Liz! I know you can get to the top of this route today!"

"Okay." As I rested, I looked around at my surroundings. I was probably fifteen feet up off the ground, and I had a great view of the mountain range we had hiked up. The cars parked on the street below looked tiny from way up here. And the ocean spread out beyond. It was really quite a magnificent spot to be in!

After a few minutes, I decided it was time to try again so I turned back to analyze the rock. But I immediately felt stumped. I didn't see any handholds or foot placements in reach. The rock wall had gotten quite flat and smooth in this section. I reached for what looked like a handhold up above me, but I couldn't quite reach it. After a few minutes, I looked down at Noe. "I'm stuck...."

"No problem. You're at a spot where you need to use a special technique called stemming. See how you are in a big crack between two rock walls that come together?" Noe asked.

I studied my location. "Yeah...."

"Put your left foot on the left wall and your right foot on the right wall. The opposing pressure will keep you up," Noe explained.

I looked at the rock wall and then back down at her skeptically.

"Try it!" Noe laughed.

I didn't think I could trust my feet that way. But as I tested my weight, I was surprised to find that my feet held to the rock and I felt secure.

"Wow!" I shouted down to Noe. "I never would have thought of that!"

"There are lots of tricky moves in rock climbing!" Noe explained. "I'll teach you everything!"

"Okay! I'm in!" I agreed wholeheartedly. "This is amazing!"

"I know, yeah?" Noe laughed. "Now that you've conquered stemming, keep moving up the wall that way, moving your feet higher and higher, until you get to the next good handhold. You can also push back on one side of the wall with one of your hands to give yourself even better leverage. Think creatively about how to move upward. It's not all just footholds and handholds, you know?"

"Yeah, okay." I turned back to the rock and moved upward again, this time thinking more creatively. At one point, I even put my back up against one side of the wall with my feet against the other side of the wall and scooted myself up inch by inch. I nearly fell at one point, but saved myself and Noe applauded. When I finally made it all the way to the top of the route, where the rope ran through the big metal hook, I shouted out triumphantly, "Woohoo!" It took me longer than anyone else, but it was so exciting to make it!

I called out, "Ready to lower," and tried to relax back in my harness. It was a little nerve racking to just let go and swing there in the air after clinging to the rock for so long. But as Noe slowly lowered me, I realized that the ride down was almost as fun as the climb up.

"Thank you so much for bringing me here today and introducing me to this rock climbing stuff. I love it!" I said as soon as I was back down on the ground.

"My pleasure." Noe hugged me. "You are a natural at it. Now I have one more person to go climbing with."

"Great!"

Noe laughed. "Next time, I'll teach you how to belay."

"What about now?" I asked, ready for more.

Noe laughed again. "You're going to be pretty sore tomorrow from what you just did." She started packing up the gear.

"Oh, okay," I agreed, reluctantly. "Well, when can we climb again?"

"Next weekend?"

"Sweet!"

Noe laughed again at my enthusiasm. I couldn't help but laugh, too. I never imagined myself as a rock climber. But stranger things had been happening lately.

"Now come on!" Noe said, throwing her pack on. "We've got a *luau* to get ready for."

Chapter 14

It was nearing sunset by the time I arrived at Fred and Kiana's house for the *luau* in celebration of Fred's birthday. The day had cooled off and the sky was turning brilliant shades of red and orange. Tall palms surrounded Fred's white plantation-style home. Tons of cars were parked in his driveway and on the side of the street around his house. Popular guy! I found a spot to park down the block and then walked back up to Fred's house. Kiana answered the big red door as soon as I knocked and welcomed me with a smile, hug and kiss. She looked beautiful in her red floral sarong. Tonight, a red Hibiscus flower was tucked in her hair. She took my hand and led me on a tour of their home, which was surprisingly modern. Dark woods, straight lines and various shades of reds graced each room. People bustled about in the black-and-white kitchen with last-minute preparations. I offered to help, but Kiana shooed me out to the backyard and told me to relax, enjoy the scenery and mingle.

The backyard was a tropical paradise. The large, covered *lanai* was paved with large flat stones. A natural stone pool surrounded by lush palms and a black lava rock waterfall sat to the left of the *lanai*. Perfectly manicured green grass stretched all the way to the bushes bordering the far end of the yard from the beach. People stood around in circles, talking and laughing. As I walked through the crowd toward the beach, I realized the bushes were the naupaka flowers Noe had mentioned earlier. I picked a flower and studied the few petals and had the same strange sense of *deja vu* again.

I noticed Fred sitting cross-legged down on the beach then. He looked as if he might be meditating. Curious, I walked nearby, watching him out of the corner of my eye. His eyes seemed to be closed and his arms rested on his lap. He looked peaceful, almost asleep. I continued on past him, stopping at the edge of the ocean. I let the little waves break over my feet as I admired the views that Fred was lucky enough to have right outside his back door. The cool ocean water felt nice on my tired feet.

"So how was rock climbing today?" Fred asked, surprising me and making me jump.

"Oh!" I looked behind me. Fred had snuck up on me. I laughed. "You surprised me! I expected you to be sitting back there meditating still."

"Sorry. I thought you heard me."

"No worries," I said. "Today was awesome! I had no idea I would enjoy rock climbing so much."

"Great!" Fred clapped his big hands together. "I'm glad to hear it. Although I figured you would take to it."

I raised an eyebrow. How could he have known?

"How did you know I was meditating?" Fred asked.

"Noe told me you run a meditation group. You were either asleep or meditating!"

Fred laughed and nodded. "Have you ever meditated before?"

"No." I gazed out to the ocean. Sitting cross legged in silence with a bunch of other people? I was a fidgety person by nature and I didn't think I would last five minutes. "I might be up for giving it a try," I said, turning back to Fred. "I've been stepping out of my comfort zone lately and it's been...." I searched for the right word, "liberating."

"Ah yes!" Fred grinned at my choice of word. "Well, if you enjoyed rock climbing, then you'll appreciate meditation. Rock climbing forces you to stay present, in the moment, as you figure your way through the route. Meditation helps you practice staying present, which will help you in rock climbing as well as in everyday life."

"Do you rock climb, too?" I asked.

"I do, I do." Fred smiled but then it turned into a frown. "Not as much as I used to though."

"Oh!" I remembered it was his birthday. "Happy birthday!"

"Thank you, Liz!" Fred laughed. "Would you walk with me for a minute? My legs are stiff from sitting."

"Of course."

We set off down the beach together. Finally, Fred broke the silence. "Do you know much about Buddhism?"

"Well, I've seen those fat, laughing Buddha statues."

Fred laughed. "Well, that's a good place to start, I suppose! Buddhists believe that our purpose in life is to awaken ourselves, to become enlightened. And the path to awakening is through the mind. Taming the mind. Meditation helps us do that."

"Oh, okay."

Fred continued, "Our minds tend to go off on their own, telling us stories about whatever may be happening to us, actually building up our problems until a small matter becomes monumental to us."

I looked over at Fred, surprised. "That's exactly what I do," I said, seeing it clearly now for the first time.

"That's what everyone does, to one extent or another," Fred explained.

"Oh, I do it really, really well!" I assured him.

Fred chuckled. "Your mind, or your ego, tries to help you deal with the unpleasant things that happen to you by getting you to either withdraw and escape by drinking, gambling or taking drugs or by getting you to act out in anger."

"I do the anger thing," I admitted.

Fred nodded. "People think that there will be less pain if they can avoid their feelings or if they can act out on their feelings. But that actually only makes the pain worse."

I thought about what Fred was saying. It made sense. My mind was constantly making things worse. Always thinking, thinking, thinking! Always over analyzing everything. Making small things big. Putting blame on everyone else. Making me feel superior. Making me feel right. Which really only left me alone after everything was said and done.

I bit my lip and shook my head. "I don't know why I couldn't see this before. My mind takes over, a lot, and I get angry, a lot, and even though I always think anger will make me feel better, it really just makes everything worse." I frowned. "I haven't been very happy."

Fred gave me a knowing look. "It's ironic the way our minds try to help us by talking us into shutting down and closing ourselves off from others. When the truth is, we cannot find happiness until we let others in. Until we learn to stay open."

Wow. I nodded again.

Fred stopped and grasped my hands. "I can see you are still an open person, Liz. Nothing has ever completely shut you down or closed you off. You've remained open in spite of it all. That is difficult for many people."

I could feel myself blushing now.

Fred continued, "We can help you open up even more, Liz. Being unconditionally open is scary, we feel vulnerable whenever we are completely open. Even you, as open as you are right now, still have walls up. Am I right?"

I nodded. I thought about how quickly I lost my temper whenever I felt like I wasn't being treated fairly. My gut reaction was always to shut down, put up walls, separate myself from everyone else. Just like Fred was saying.

"Meditation will help you take back control of your mind. And Buddhist teachings will help you find a different way of coping. We can help you work on staying with that uncomfortable feeling whenever something negative happens to you instead of acting out on it. That takes bravery. Moving toward what you have habitually avoided takes bravery. And I think you are very brave, Liz."

I smiled.

"Being willing to do this alleviates suffering. Both your own suffering as well as the suffering of others."

"I'd sure like to suffer less," I half joked.

Fred smiled. "The key is to learn how to be okay in resting happily in uncertainty; not knowing, not acting like you know, and not needing to know."

"I like that idea," I admitted. What if I gave up on needing to know? I could see how my life would get easier if I wasn't always making up stories in my head about what people around me might be saying or thinking or doing.

"This is where true freedom is found. In just letting go."

I nodded, almost feeling the freedom Fred was promising me.

"We better head back to the house," Fred said.

It was nearly dark when we returned and *tiki* torches lit up the yard now. Classic Hawaiian music was playing in the background, and I could smell the delicious scent of barbeque. My stomach growled in response.

Fred glanced at me and chuckled. "You've worked up quite an appetite today, I bet!" he teased me.

"Yeah, rock climbing is a lot of work," I admitted, still surprised by how much fun I'd had.

"Well, come on, I'll introduce you around and then we can eat!" Fred put his arm around me.

"Okay," I agreed, feeling a little shy.

Fred led me to the small group of people mingling with Kiana and Noe.

Kiana smiled as we approached. "I didn't have a chance to ask you earlier—how was rock climbing?"

"Pretty awesome, I must say!" I gushed.

Noe laughed. "She's totally hooked!"

"That's great! We're all into rock climbing around here, so you'll always be able to find someone to go with you, whenever you want to go," Kiana told me.

"Sweet!" I looked around at everyone.

"Hey, Liz! Howzit?" Kai approached and hugged me. Lily was right behind him with more hugs.

"Great!" I replied "How about you guys?"

"Ho! *Pau hana* time! I'm ready fo' plenny *ono* grinds!" Kai said, rubbing his stomach and laughing.

I giggled. Kai was definitely a local boy. Hearing the local Hawaiian pidgin always made me smile. "Yeah, me too!"

"We've been at the beach all day," Lily told me. "Kai and John didn't want to leave!"

"Hey!" John defended himself. "There were killer winds today!"

"It was an epic kite boarding day," Kai agreed.

Fred introduced me to the people I didn't know yet, his brothers, cousins and nieces and nephews. Everyone was so friendly. I was hugged over and over again.

Suddenly, the sound of drums began and everyone turned toward two big, handsome Hawaiian men wearing nothing but little red loincloths. They were beating a tribal rhythm on two big long drums. Several female *hula* dancers danced their way out to the middle of the lawn then. They wore red bikini tops and grass skirts. White flower *leis* hung around their necks. I spotted Kiana amongst the *hula* dancers. She moved gracefully, and I was suddenly overcome with emotions I didn't understand until I remembered that my great-grandmother had taught her the *hula*.

One of the drummers started chanting something in native Hawaiian. When he was finished, the *hula* dancers responded with a similar chant, their feet moving left to right and their hips swaying back and forth to the beat of the drums.

I wondered what the chant was about.

"It's a welcoming song," Fred said, reading my mind again.

Fred translated the lyrics for me:

Aloha ka leo—The voice of love

O kahi manu—Of one special bird

E hea mai—As it calls to me

Lua ole ka mele—The song of this bird

Ona manu—Is not like

Ma`a mau no—That of any other

Hauoli au—I am pleased

I lohe mai—In hearing

Ke kona aloha e ho`oipo—The invitation to love

Eia ka pane—Here is the answer

Ka e o—The response

Ho`olauna kaua a pili no—Let the two of us get to know one another

When the *hula* ended, the drummers and dancers bowed and exited to happy applause from the audience. Fred then took center stage. He held a vintage ukulele. Someone brought a chair out for him and once he was sitting comfortably, he began to play.

It was Israel Kamakawiwo'ole's version of "Somewhere Over the Rainbow." Tears come to my eyes. I wasn't sure why, but this song really got to me every time I heard it. And today the lyrics in the song were especially meaningful, having just met this wonderful group of people who seemed to be taking me in as one of their own.

The colors of the rainbow so pretty in the sky

Are also on the faces of people passing by

I see friends shaking hands

Saying, "How do you do?"

They're really saying, "I ... I love you"

As Fred finished the song, everyone applauded again. I quickly wiped the tears away, hoping no one had noticed. But then I realized I wasn't the only one wiping at tears and I couldn't help but smile.

"*Mahalo* everyone, for coming to my birthday *luau*!" Fred said. "Let's not waste any more time!" Everyone cheered in agreement. "Let the feast begin!" He motioned toward the other end of the yard, where elaborate tables were set up low to the ground with white tablecloths and centerpieces of green ferns and pink and purple orchids, hibiscus and birds of paradise. Floor mats sat in place of chairs.

Two big Hawaiian men carried a giant roasted pig from an underground pit in a nearby corner of the yard. They placed it in the center of the table and began to carve it up. It smelled absolutely delicious, and I couldn't wait to dig in. There were many platters of other types of food on the table already.

Noe came up and grabbed me by the arm. "Sit by me." She led me to a place near the middle of the table and we seated ourselves on the mats. Noe then explained all the food on the table.

"We've got *poke*, *lomi lomi* salmon (salmon with tomatoes and onions), chicken *lau lau* (chicken with spinach, onion and garlic), Hawaiian purple sweet potato, *haupia* (coconut pudding), salads, rice, *taro* rolls, and *poi*, the traditional Hawaiian food!"

"Woo, boy," Kai announced across the table from us. He looked up and down the table at all the food. "We goin' pound tonight!"

Everyone laughed.

"Dig in!" Fred announced from his position at the head of the table.

Everyone began talking excitedly and serving themselves. The sounds of people talking were soon replaced by the sounds of forks and knives hitting plates.

"Dis is primo, cuz!" Kai announced to the whole table with a full mouth. Everyone laughed, nodding and mumbling their agreement.

Before I knew it, I was stuffed. I groaned in satisfaction and Noe laughed. "First *luau*, huh?"

I nodded.

Fred tapped a knife against his glass, calling for everyone's attention again. "We have a special after dinner treat for you now. Please follow me!" He winked in my direction and then turned and headed toward the beach. Everyone followed.

The drummers were on the beach now, setting the mood for a dramatic performance. Several men in red loincloths were wrapping knives in cloth and then lighting them with fire from nearby *tiki* torches.

Everyone cheered and clapped as the dancers started twirling and throwing their fire knives up in the air. They skillfully caught the lit knives and continued twirling them around, behind their backs and between their legs. They did cartwheels and flips with the flaming knives and not one of them ever dropped a knife.

"Isn't it beautiful?" Fred asked, startling me for the second time that day.

"Yes, its mesmerizing!" I agreed. I hadn't noticed Fred next to me. "But a bit scary too!" The fire knives flew through the night sky, leaving beautiful red glowing trails in their wake. I wondered what would happen if one of the men dropped a fire knife, or worse, fumbled trying to catch it.

Fred chuckled.

We watched the fire dancers in silence until the show ended with the fire dancers throwing their fire knives back and forth to each other until eventually only one man held all the fire knives. Everyone cheered.

Fred led everyone back up to the *lanai* again where the tables were now set with decadent trays of desserts. Coconut cakes, banana breads, macadamia nut tarts, and fresh tropical fruits with chocolate dipping sauces sat beckoning.

"Oh no!" I joked. "Just what I need! More food!"

Noe laughed. "I think you can handle it after your hard work today!"

After devouring the desserts, Noe rubbed her stomach. "I'm so full, I don't know if I can get up!"

"Fo' real! Da kine wen max out on dis partay!" Kai groaned. "And I wen eat too much food."

Everyone laughed and agreed.

"Brahs, I tink I goin' fo' *hele* on," Kai said, getting up and yawning. "I goin' moe moe awready."

"Yah, me too, brah," John agreed, also getting up. "See ya all latahz den."

"Latahz!" everyone chimed in together. Hugs and goodbyes were exchanged.

"Liz!" Fred caught me as I was walking out the door, "I wanted to invite you to join me tomorrow morning at ten for a personal meditation session."

"Oh, okay," I agreed, yawning. "I must warn you though, I am a bit fidgety."

Fred smiled. "That's okay, Liz! So am I," he reassured me.

"Okay," I said, yawning again.

Fred gave me a big hug. "Go home and get some rest. You'll probably be sore tomorrow, so wear comfortable clothes, stuff you can stretch in. We'll do some yoga first. The stretching will help with your sore muscles."

"Okay." I said. I waved goodbye and then walked down the block to my car. It had been an amazing day. I'd really enjoyed meeting everyone else in Fred's family, and I was already feeling as if these people were my new family. But I was exhausted!

When I got home, I fell asleep almost as soon as my head hit my pillow. I dreamed of Aaron. He had longer, wilder hair in my dream and he was practically naked, wearing only a white loincloth. His chest was sculpted and hairy and I had the urge to reach out and touch it. I was so close to him, so close I could smell his delicious manly scent. He handed me a naupaka flower, but it was different than the naupaka flowers I had seen. It had all of its petals. Puzzled, I looked up at him, searched his eyes. He held my gaze and slowly leaned down to kiss me. Right as his lips were about to touch mine, I awoke with a start, my heart pounding.

Something had woken me, a sound in the room maybe and I sensed something, some presence. I lay there holding my breath, listening, trying to see in the dark. I finally took a deep breath and could have sworn I smelled fresh flowers. But I didn't have any flowers in the house. I reached over and turned on my bedside lamp. Everything was just as it should be. No monsters were hiding in any corners. I got up and wandered around the house, turning on lights and making sure I was alone.

It must have all been in my head. Satisfied that all was well, I got back into bed again. I remembered my dream then, of Aaron in his loincloth and laughed. Talk about my brain making things up! That had been some crazy dream. Something unidentified nagged at me though and I had a hard time falling back asleep.

Chapter 15

I woke up late again. I felt rested despite the strange dream about Aaron and my scare in the middle of the night. But as I tried to get out of bed, various muscles screamed in agony, reminding me of my rock-climbing adventure. I had never been so sore! But I was eager to get to Fred's house to try meditation, so I popped a couple Advil, took a quick shower and left.

Fred welcomed me with the customary hug and kiss on the cheek. He wore dark blue board shorts and a light blue, loose-fitting T-shirt with a Hawaiian motif on the front. He led me into a big sunny room at the back his house. "Our meditation room," Fred said. Sheer white drapes framed the three floor-to-ceiling windows that were open. A large meditating Buddha statue sat in the middle of the room along the back wall. The statue's face looked serene with closed eyes and a peaceful smile. Its hands rested gently in its lap, one folded on top of the other. Plush red-and-orange floor cushions and rolled-up yoga mats sat stacked in the corner near Buddha statue. Serene artwork hung on the side walls. One painting depicted a sandy beach with gentle waves, one was a photo of a bamboo forest and another photo showed green sea turtles swimming underwater.

"It's nice," I said. "Peaceful."

"*Mahalo*!" Kiana joined us then. She wore seafoam green yoga pants and a white tank top. My own gray sweats and black tank top were grungy in comparison.

"Kiana will lead us in a few yoga moves to loosen up our bodies before we sit for meditation," Fred explained.

Kiana smiled at me. "You've done yoga before, haven't you?"

"Yes, I was good at balancing and holding the poses," I boasted. "But it's been a while," I admitted, in case they expected me to be a pro.

"Great!" Kiana grabbed two yoga mats and handed me one. "We'll get you back on track!"

"I have to share something with you before we get started," I said, nervously. "Have you ever heard of Alopecia?"

Kiana and Fred both shook their heads.

I explained my rare disorder. They were surprised.

"They say that Alopecia is caused by stress," I said. "I always thought they were only blaming stress because they had no idea what actually causes it."

"Well, our bodies do react strangely to stress sometimes," Fred said, nodding his head.

"Right. So I'm trying to have an open mind now."

Fred grinned.

"Maybe my hair will grow back again if I can learn to stress less?"

"Anything is possible," Fred said. "Meditation helps you learn how to quiet your mind, which can help reduce the self-inflicted stress we cause ourselves."

Kiana nodded. "Yoga can be a stress reliever, too. I'd love to work with you to help you with your stress."

"Thank you for sharing that with us, Liz." Fred gave me a hug.

Kiana hugged me next. "Let's get started!" She rolled out her mat at the front of the room. Fred rolled his mat out a few feet back, facing Kiana. I followed Fred's lead. I noticed the floor-to-ceiling mirrors along the wall at the front of the room for the first time.

"Okay," Kiana began. "Let's start with Child's Pose." She knelt on her mat and sat on her heels with her legs slightly separated. Fred and I followed. "Exhale," she instructed. She stretched forward on the mat, reaching her arms out in front of her and laying her torso on her knees. She placed her forehead on the floor. "Allow the pelvis and hips to settle down onto the heels. Feel the deep folding of the thighs. Feel the elongation of the back body and the broadness of the back body."

We moved into sun salutations next.

Kiana continued coaching. "Nice and smooth, nice and slow, lift the back ribs a little taller, lift the outer armpits a bit higher. Stretch up through the elbows. From there, take a simple little side bend to your left. Lift the right ribs up off the hip. The right armpit off of the ribs. Good. One more inhalation. Back to center. Lift up through the midline once again. And from there, take that nice little side bend to the right, unsticking, ungluing the left side body. Good. Root down through the left thighbone, through the left hip, through the left sitting bone. And peel open the left side body."

The way Kiana explained the moves helped me push myself deeper into each position. I could feel my muscles loosening and warming up with the stretches. I breathed in deeply, really noticing my breath. Kiana smiled encouragingly at me as I followed along.

"Okay, bring the hands back down to Runner's pose. Slide your front foot back into Plank position. Lower down to Upper Dog. Move up into Downward Dog. Float the right heel into the sky. Swing it through to

Runner's pose. Now drop your back heel down. Come up into Warrior One position. Hold for one breath. Good."

We ran through all the warrior poses. I admired the way Kiana smoothly maneuvered her body through each pose. I tried to move as gracefully as she did. We held each pose for several breaths. I was feeling strong and powerful. I used to love doing yoga. Why had I ever stopped?

"Okay, let's do one Triangle pose. Bring the hands back down to Runner's pose. Slide your front foot back into Plank position. Lower down to Upper Dog. Move up into Downward Dog. Float the right heel into the sky. Swing it through to Runner's pose. Now drop your back heel down. Come up into Warrior One position again. Hold it for a breath. Then move into Warrior Two. Hold it for a breath. Straighten your front leg. Reach forward with your left hand, bring the left hand down and to the outside of the right foot and twist to the right. Raise the right arm up to the ceiling and gaze up to the fingertips. Hold it for three breaths."

This pose was more difficult for me. It hurt a bit and I struggled to maintain it.

"Good. Now the other side." Kiana coached us through the Triangle Twist on the left side.

"Let's wrap this up!" Kiana said. "Inhale and come up to standing. Turn the feet parallel. Step or hop the feet hip width apart. Inhale and sweep the arms up overhead. Exhale. Forward fold. Couple of breaths. Bend the knees. Extend the arms up overhead. On the exhale straighten the legs." Kiana brought her hands together at her heart and bowed. "Namaste."

Fred and I both repeated Kiana's gesture.

"Excellent, Kiana, as always!" Fred praised. "*Mahalo*!"

"Yes, Kiana! That felt great!" I added.

Kiana beamed. "My pleasure!"

Fred took over. "Let's move on to our meditation." Fred rolled up his yoga mat and put it back. "Now, Liz, we mostly practice mindfulness meditation. This means that we focus on our breath as we sit and when thoughts come into our minds, we quietly let them go by and get back to focusing on our breath again."

"Okay," I said. "Focus on the breath. Got it." I had been doing that as I had worked on my yoga poses.

"Thoughts are kind of like clouds in the sky," he continued. "They come and they go. They are always shifting, never permanent."

"Or you could say that thoughts are like waves on the beach," I suggested.

"Right, Liz!" Fred grinned. "So, in meditation, when you are paying close attention to your breath, you'll start to see just how often your mind takes over, without you even being aware of it, and starts its own commentary or judgments about the past, present or future."

I nodded again.

Fred continued. "When you notice that your mind has taken over, bring it back to observing your breath."

"Okay," I agreed. It sounded simple enough.

"You'll do that over and over and over again. But never give up! There is no such thing as bad meditation," Fred told me. "The whole point is to keep practicing. Our minds need to be exercised just as our bodies need exercise. Meditation is mind exercise. We strengthen our ability to let thoughts go through meditation."

"Got it," I said.

"Great! After practicing meditation, you'll find that you'll be able to observe life more and more without always getting caught in the commentary going on in your head."

"Perfection is not the goal," Kiana added. "Nobody is perfect. We each have little setbacks now and then, and that's no big deal. In fact, the whole lesson to be learned in meditation is that everything in life is no big deal. The good stuff is no big deal, and the bad stuff is no big deal."

"Oh, yeah?" I asked. "Even the good stuff is no big deal?"

Kiana smiled. "It's only when we make a big deal out of things that we have problems. For instance, something good happens to us and we make a big deal of it and begin to act cocky. But maybe we lose that good thing, and we make a big deal of that and begin to feel depressed. See how it goes both ways?"

"Ahhh." A little lightbulb had just gone off in my head. This was what I did; I made a big deal out of everything, good and bad! "Yes! I see."

"It is only by always striving to stay in the middle and not make a big deal out of anything that we find true happiness," Kiana added.

"True happiness would be great!" I said.

"But true happiness is not the destination, Liz. It is your state of mind on the journey," Kiana corrected me.

"Absolutely right, Kiana!" Fred agreed. "Now, the mindfulness meditation we will be practicing here can also be practiced outside of your formal meditation, in your daily life whenever you catch yourself making a big deal out of anything."

"Okay," I said, thinking it ought to be easy to catch myself making a big deal out of things now that I understood why it was a problem.

Fred picked up two cushions and plopped them down in front of the Buddha statue. He sat cross legged on his and looked up at me, patting the cushion next to him. "Come," he said. "Sit!"

I sat cross legged on my cushion. Kiana joined us with her own cushion.

"Now," Fred explained, "you want to sit up straight and tall, keep your spine straight. And rest your arms in front of you on your legs, with your right hand on top of your left hand." He showed me the proper position and I copied him. "That's right."

"Now close your eyes," Fred told me.

I closed my eyes.

"And just concentrate on your breath. In and out. In and out." It sounded like Fred was moving around as he spoke, but I resisted the temptation to look and kept my eyes shut.

I concentrated on my breath. In and out. In and out.

The deep and resonant tone of a gong suddenly rang out, and I couldn't help but open my eyes. Fred had just struck a beautiful traditional bronze gong on a modern black frame. I hadn't even noticed the gong earlier. Fred grinned at me as he sat again on his cushion. "We set the gong at the beginning and end of each meditation session," he explained. "Now, close your eyes, Liz!" he teased as he repositioned himself in his cross legged sitting position.

I closed my eyes again and listened to the sound of the gong slowly fading into nothingness. Somewhere outside, a car horn honked. It became so quiet in the meditation room that I could hear the wind rustling the trees outside.

Fred suddenly spoke up again, "And if you find your thoughts taking over, Liz, remember to just bring yourself back to focusing on your breath again."

I nodded in understanding and continued to focus on my breathing, remembering Fred's suggestion that thoughts were a lot like clouds, drifting across the sky, always coming and going, never being fixed or permanent. I liked thinking of my thoughts that way. Light and airy and fluffy. I imagined blowing away the thoughts that bothered me. But I liked my own idea of thoughts as waves on the beach too. I pictured the waves on my favorite beach, the one nearest my home in Kailua. Rolling in, and rolling back out. The waves were usually so gentle and predictable in Kailua. Except for that stormy day last week. I can't believe I almost drowned that day. Boy, that had turned out to be a life-changing experience. What if I had never gone to that beach that day? What if I had never stood out on the sand in the rain, wishing I had never met Brad, wishing everything could end? I never would have met Noe. I never would have become friends with her and met Fred and Kiana and the rest of their friends. It was because of Brad that I was here now, making awesome new friends, learning to rock climb and learning how to meditate. I should thank Brad! I smiled to myself, thinking of thanking Brad. Ha!

My eyes flew open in shock. Learning how to meditate! Oh crap! I realized that I had let my thoughts completely take over mere seconds after starting the meditation. I turned my head to look at Fred but he was still sitting next to me with his eyes closed. It looked like he might be grinning a little though.

I resolved to get back to focusing on my breath again as Fred had instructed me to do. So I repositioned myself, closed my eyes again and concentrated on my breathing again. In and out. In and out.

Boy, my back was sure hurting. Right in the middle, it was really starting to ache. I tried to ignore it but it seemed to be getting worse and worse. I tried to slowly and quietly stretch as I sat in my cross legged position on the cushion. My arms were starting to feel a little sore too. I pushed my shoulders up and back in another little stretch. I had been using muscles yesterday that I had never really used before, reaching and grabbing and tiptoeing on the rock. It had been so much fun! I couldn't wait to get back on the rock again. I was determined to get stronger and better. *I'm going to be a rock climber! I never would have imagined it in my wildest dreams!* It had seemed like such a dangerous and adventurous sport. Not something for a boring person like me to try. But it wasn't as dangerous as I had thought. And I was starting to see that I wasn't as boring as I had once believed. Actually, nothing in life was turning out to be the way I once believed! I had wasted my life living under these false beliefs. Beliefs that had only held me back. Nothing was going to hold me back anymore.

The tone of the gong rang out again and startled me out of my train of thought. My eyes flew open again. Oh no! I had lost concentration on my breath again.

Fred was standing by the gong. "How was your first experience meditating?"

"I got lost in my thoughts the whole time!" I admitted.

"But you caught yourself, didn't you?" he asked, smiling, somehow knowing.

I nodded.

"You must have meditated in a previous life." Fred grinned.

I laughed but I couldn't help wondering. I asked Fred, "Can you teach me about that, the whole idea of reincarnation, I mean?"

"What do you already know?"

"Well, I know that lots of cultures believe in reincarnation."

"Yes, almost every culture has at one time or another believed in reincarnation."

"And I know some people claim to remember their past lives."

"That's right! The Buddha was able to remember all of his past lives. Many Buddhist saints, scholars and meditators have been able to remember their past lives as well."

I raised my eyebrows. "What about you guys?"

"I remember some things vaguely," Fred said.

"Me too." Kiana nodded.

"Like what?" I was curious.

"Well, we know we've lived in Hawaii for many lifetimes," Fred said, looking at Kiana.

They shared a look.

"Scientists have just begun to study the whole idea of rebirth," Fred told me. "Professor Ian Stevenson of the University of Virginia is well known for studying people who seem to remember their past lives. Of the 1700 cases he investigated, 47 of those could not be explained by anything other than past lives."

"Interesting." I nodded.

"Yes, you should read about his findings."

"I've always been scared of deep water for some reason. My parents said I would never get in the water when we went to the beach, and they swore that I had no reason to be afraid of the water. I never had a near-drowning experience. So I can't help wondering where that fear of deep water came from."

"It is possible, Liz, that you had that traumatic experience in a previous life," Kiana said. "And the effects of that experience have stayed with you as you've continued on into each of your new lives."

"Whoa!" I tried to imagine such a thing. "That's heavy."

Fred agreed with a nod. "What if you could confront your fear and move on by remembering and accepting the traumatic experience from your prior life?"

"How can I remember something from a prior life?" That sounded nearly impossible. I still didn't even know if I believed in reincarnation.

"My memories of my past lives usually come to me in dreams, and sometimes in meditative states, when I am most open."

"I've had some interesting dreams since moving to Hawaii ..." I said.

"That's probably because you lived here in a past life and returning has triggered the memories."

I blew out a big breath. Wow. That actually made sense. And I liked the idea that I had lived in Hawaii in a prior life.

"Maybe your traumatic experience occurred here in Hawaii," Fred suggested, nodding his head.

I thought about that. "Do you think...." I started and stalled, feeling ridiculous.

Fred tilted his head, waiting patiently for me to finish.

"Can you help me try to remember?" I finally blurted.

"Oh, definitely!" Fred said. "I'd love to help. We can begin working on it in our meditation sessions."

"Really?" I was excited. "When can we get started?"

"Does Wednesday night work for you?"

***

As I drove home, I thought about the possibility of a prior life in Hawaii! Was such a thing even possible?

I suddenly spotted a skinny black-and-white dog walking down the side of the road. I was afraid he might get hit by another car so I pulled over, put my flashers on and got out. The dog stopped a few feet away, stared at me and then turned around and started walking away. I knelt down and patted my knee. "Come here, cutie!" I called. The dog stopped and looked me over again. "I'm friendly!" I told him. "Let me help you!" I patted my knee again and made kissing sounds. Finally, the dog trotted over and sniffed at me. His fur was matted and dirty and he smelled bad, but he was the cutest dog I'd ever seen. He had no identification, collar or tags.

"Oh, you poor thing!" I patted his head, and he licked my hand. "You look like you haven't eaten in a month!"

The dog barked in agreement and then licked my hand again.

I knew I had to at least feed him.

"Come on then." I led him to my car and opened the back door for him. He jumped right in and laid down on the backseat, wagging his tail. I was already in love.

I figured I could alert the Humane Society to see if anyone came looking for the little guy. But in the meantime, I would take care of him. I stopped at the store on the way home and picked up dog food, dog shampoo and a leash and collar. I'd always wanted to get a dog, and I was hoping no one would claim this cute, skinny little dog. He was meant to be mine. I knew it in my gut.

At home, when I put food down for him, he gobbled it up and then licked the bowl.

"Wow! You were hungry, weren't you?"

He barked.

I put a bowl of water out for him too and he lapped it up until it was gone.

"Thirsty too, huh?"

I bathed him next and after I rinsed him off and patted him dry with a towel, he ran around the house, shaking himself off and rolling around on my rugs.

The dog followed me around the house for the rest of the day. And when I got into bed, he jumped up and snuggled right next to me. I stroked his clean soft fur.

"We have to find a name for you...."

I thought of some dog names I'd heard since moving to Hawaii. ""How about Kai?"

He just stared at me.

"Kiki?"

He seemed to give me a dirty look at that one.

"Koko?"

He nudged my arm with his head, barked, then closed his eyes.

"Koko it is!"

I fell asleep with Koko at my side.

Chapter 16

Monday morning, as I sat at my desk reading emails and twisting and stretching in my chair to relieve my sore muscles, Peter, the club treasurer, knocked and opened my door.

"Good morning, Liz." He poked his head in. "May I come in?"

I motioned for him to enter, and he sat in the chair opposite my desk and adjusted his expensive tailored suit. "How are you?"

"I'm great, Peter," I said. "How are you?"

"Wonderful!" He smiled, revealing perfectly straight white teeth.

Peter was in his fifties. He was probably over six feet tall and had close-cropped graying hair. He was a handsome man but old enough to be my father. We worked together each month to coordinate presenting the financial statements to the board. He was always friendly with me and easy to work with.

"What brings you into the club so early on a Monday morning?" I asked, curious. I usually saw Peter around the club in the late afternoons, after work hours.

"I stopped by this morning to chat with you!" Peter said.

"Oh?" I was curious.

"I heard you asked for a raise," he added.

I narrowed my eyes. Where was he going with this?

"But Ken refused to give you one."

I nodded warily.

"And he wrote you up for being insubordinate."

I rolled my eyes. I couldn't help it.

Peter laughed. "I need a controller. And I want to hire you."

My eyes widened. "Really?"

Peter was the owner and CEO of Ali'i Properties, the largest real estate development, investment, and management firm on the islands.

Peter nodded. "I've seen your work, seen you in action." He winked and then leaned forward. "I've wanted you for a while now."

I raised my eyebrows at his choice of words.

"Ken's an idiot." Peter sat back and folded his arms.

I nodded my agreement.

"I can give you twice what Ken is paying you."

I was speechless.

"It will be more work, longer hours," he warned me. "And you'll have to work with me a lot more than you do now!" He chuckled.

"I see," I said, pretending to think it over. "When would you want me to start?"

"Give Ken your two weeks' notice today." Peter stood. He knew he had me.

We shook hands and as soon as Peter left my office, I emailed Ken my resignation notice.

Chapter 17

Fred and I started to meditate on Wednesdays and Sundays, and I practiced at home on my own a couple times a week, too. Each time I sat in meditation, I had a different experience. Sometimes I felt like I did well and was making breakthroughs, and sometimes I felt like I was just wasting my time and getting nowhere. I couldn't remember anything at all related to possible past lives. But I took Fred's advice to heart and tried not to make a big deal out of any of it.

Fred taught me all about the Buddha, who was first known as Siddhartha Gautama, born into a wealthy royal family over 2,500 years ago in what is known today as Nepal. As a prince, Siddhartha was provided with anything he could ever want or need but he wasn't allowed to have knowledge of religious teachings, and he was shielded from real life in the villages. Siddhartha was curious though and so he snuck into the village to see for himself what life was like there. He was confronted with sick and dying people for the first time and became depressed. He left his life as a prince behind and took a vow of poverty, hoping to attain enlightenment.

Siddhartha mastered the teachings of the various teachers he studied under, but was never fully satisfied with their practices. Finally, after nearly drowning in a river from starvation, he found the Middle Way, a path of moderation away from the extremes of self-indulgence and self-mortification. He was finally awakened to the true nature and cause of suffering, along with the steps necessary to eliminate suffering. He was enlightened. He immediately began teaching others what he had learned and soon became known as the Buddha.

Fred was teaching me what the Buddha had learned. The Four Noble Truths: life means suffering, the origin of suffering is attachment, the end of suffering is attainable, and the end of suffering is found through letting go. Everything was making sense—I could see how my unhappiness in my life came from my attachments. It had always been easy for me to become attached to people or things or events and incredibly hard for me to let go.

I wanted that to change. I didn't want to become so attached to anything anymore.

Kiana and I practiced yoga a couple times a week, and Noe and I went rock climbing at least once a week, usually on Saturdays. I was pushing myself and getting better at yoga and climbing. I loved that I was always sore in new places. That meant I was getting stronger.

I finished my last two weeks at the yacht club on autopilot. I closed down my online personals profile and Katie's as well. Instead of spending my days chatting with guys in the online personals, I was now spending every spare moment searching online for more information on Buddhism, meditation, reincarnation, yoga and rock climbing.

* * *

The Sunday before I started my new job, I told Fred and Kiana all about my experience with Brad.

"We all make mistakes," Fred said, after hearing my story. "No one is perfect. It's more about what you do next than what you did last."

I nodded. Fred always had such wise words.

"Things are constantly going to fall apart on you," Fred went on. "That's just life. A cycle of falling apart and coming together. Trying to avoid the falling apart, trying to keep everything together all the time—that is what makes us suffer. That's what in Buddhism is called *Samsara*, a hopeless cycle that goes around and around endlessly. It's when you accept life as it is, no matter what happens, that you find a way out of *Samsara*. Just let go. Let go of everything. Let go of all of your ideas and all of your beliefs. Let go of anything or anyone that you find yourself holding onto. Let it all go. And you'll find peace and happiness like never before."

I nodded. I was seeing the truth in everything Fred said.

Kiana jumped in, "The point isn't to overcome the problems or pass the tests in life. The point is to notice everything as it happens to you and to let there be room for all of it. This is where true happiness comes from. You want to have the ability to turn quickly when life suddenly throws you a curve in the road as opposed to skidding to a halt or crashing on the side of the road when you can't handle the curve. Does that make sense?"

I nodded again. I hadn't allowed room for anything in my life before. Or handled the curves in the road very well. But I was starting to feel like I could do better now.

Fred reached for my hands. He searched my eyes. "I want to stress that whenever we think that something is going to be either good or bad, we don't really know. Letting there be room for not knowing is the most important thing of all."

"I get it. I was so depressed after Brad. But here I am, in a much better place now." I smiled at Fred and Kiana. "I wish I had learned about Buddhism a long time ago," I said with a sigh. "I feel like my religious upbringing actually screwed me up. All the guilt, all the rules that make no sense, all the high expectations. It's impossible to live that way."

"People search for sources of love and peace in many ways," Kiana said. "And many people find love and peace inside the walls of religion."

"I don't see how anyone can find peace that way. Religions persuade people that every little thing in the Bible is fact and that they'll go to hell if they don't follow what the Bible says. The Bible is just a collection of stories that people wrote a long, long time ago."

"Well, actually, Liz," Kiana interrupted my rant, "the Bible has many good messages. Messages that are not that different from the Buddha's teachings." She smiled. "One could say that Jesus was an inspirational prophet who had achieved enlightenment, much like Buddha had, and Jesus wanted to help others achieve enlightenment just as Buddha did."

I had never considered such an idea. But I instantly liked it.

"The problem," I said, "is organized religions have rewritten the Bible and interpreted it to suit their purposes. I highly doubt that the Bible is the same today as it was back when it was first written."

"You're right," Kiana agreed.

"And people tend to pick and choose what they do or don't want to take away from the Bible," I added.

Kiana nodded. "True. The Bible is full of parables and hidden meaning and religions have preached to us what they believe the parables mean. But if you read the Bible again with an open mind, forgetting what all the various religions over the ages have preached, you will see that Jesus's teachings are very similar to the Buddha's teachings."

"Any method that helps people get closer to God and fulfill their true potential, find peace and happiness, is a good method. That's why there are so many religions out there," Fred explained. "Everyone requires different tools."

"Well, Okay." I understood for many people the only way to find peace, comfort and security was through religion. Even though religion did not work for me, I could see how it was wrong for me to assume that they were wrong and I was right. That was just as bad as them assuming that I was wrong and they were right.

That was the problem, I suddenly realized; everyone on earth always thinking that they were right and everyone else was wrong and all the conflicts, arguments, hate and war that came from it.

"I just wish the whole world would become more open-minded," I said with a big sigh.

"Someday." Fred smiled.

I hoped Fred was right. What a wonderful world it would be if everyone was open-minded and accepting of everyone else. I could almost picture it. Heaven on earth.

"Will you do something for me, Liz?" Kiana asked.

"I guess so...."

"Try reading through the Bible again, this time with an open mind. See if you can spot the same messages the Buddha taught."

I had studied the Bible from cover to cover, over and over again growing up in the Mormon religion. When I finally decided to leave that church, I had thrown my Bible away. I never wanted to open a Bible again.

Kiana smiled at me. I knew she expected me to do this.

"Okay," I agreed reluctantly.

"Good!" Kiana said in triumph. "I know you'll be surprised by what you find!" She hugged me.

Kiana gave me a Bible before I left that day, successfully curbing my excuse of not having a Bible or having time to get a Bible. But when I got home, I threw it on my sofa table and that's where it stayed, collecting dust.

Chapter 18

My first thought as I drove up to the high-rise building with reflective blue glass called Harbor Court was "I have arrived!" My second thought as I drove into the parking garage and parked my Hyundai Tucson between a BMW and a Mercedes was "I do not belong here!"

My anxiety increased as I rode the elevator up to the twentieth floor offices of Ali'i Properties. The doors slid open to a minimalist and modern lobby where a young, petite Asian girl in a form-fitting black dress and shiny black sky-high heels welcomed me. Her lips were painted a dark red, and she wore heavy eyeshadow and mascara. Large gold hoop earrings and a matching necklace and bracelets sparkled as she spoke. She led me down a hall to my new office and then asked if I needed anything. Water? Coffee? I shook my head no and she headed back to her desk in the lobby.

I took in my new surroundings. A giant mahogany desk sat in front of a floor-to-ceiling window with an ocean view. I sat in the plush chocolate leather chair and twirled around in it. I had three computer screens and my own mini-bar. I grinned. What more could a girl ask for?

"Good morning!" Peter entered my office as I was rummaging through the mini-bar. "It's a little early to start drinking!" he joked.

I blushed. "I wasn't...."

"How about coffee instead?" He handed me a steaming Starbucks cup. "Caramel Macchiato? Am I right?"

"Yes!" How did he know? I hadn't dared to stop and get a coffee on my way to work this morning, fearing I'd be late. I happily took a sip.

"You like your office?" Peter asked.

"What's not to like?"

"Come on! Let me introduce you around." Peter took me up and down the halls, introducing me to the team. Lahela, a sweet, plump Hawaiian woman in a silk floral floor length dress, was the Human Resources Manager. Elena, a sexy Latino woman in sexy black slacks and a low-cut gray silk blouse, was the Accounts Payable Manager. Marissa, an older Hawaiian woman with graying hair in a gray knee-length skirt and white button-up blouse, was the Accounts Receivable Manager. And Scott and Stephanie, two *haoles* like me, were the two Property Accountants. Scott was wearing crisp blue slacks and a white button up with a red-and-white polka dot tie and Stephanie wore gray slacks and a red silk blouse.

Everyone seemed nice and happy to meet me, but I felt out of place in my casual cream-colored chinos and blue, short-sleeved cotton blouse. This look had worked the yacht club, but I was going to have to step it up a notch now. I was going to have to do some shopping. I usually avoided shopping malls. The thought made me shudder. The parking! The crowds!

Lahela led me back to her office then, where I went through an orientation and filled out paperwork. By then it was lunchtime, so everyone in the office walked over to the Plaza Club, a fancy member's only restaurant right down the street.

We were seated at a table next to windows with panoramic views of the city and the harbor. I watched as boats moved slowly across the sparking blue water.

"You should see this view at night," Peter said, smiling at me. "It's magical."

"I bet," I said, envisioning it at night.

"We should come for Pau Hana Friday," Elena suggested excitedly.

"It's great! You'll love it!" Scott nudged me. "Live music, drinks and *pupu* specials."

"Sounds fun," I agreed.

The menu listed an assortment of local Hawaiian dishes. I ordered the mango coconut iced tea and the ahi tuna melt. Peter ordered the Misoyaki butterfish. Elena got the warm spinach salad. Lahela asked for the Angus burger. Marissa opted for the clubhouse sandwich. Stephani ordered the clam chowder. And Scott ordered the kalbi short rib donburi, which was grilled short ribs, sushi rice, and baby bok choy with a fried egg on top. I laughed at his plate when it came.

"Hey, don't knock it until you try it!" he said as he stuffed his mouth with a big bite.

I enjoyed the delicious food and after lunch, as we walked back to the office, Lahela informed me of all the other wonderful places to eat downtown. I did a double take as a shirtless older gentleman behind the wheel of a shiny new BMW drove by. We passed an interesting lady dancing and singing to herself on one street corner and a disheveled man on another street corner was yelling at a lamp post.

Interesting people downtown.

"There are a lot of homeless people down here," Scott whispered as we passed a group of grungy-looking people sitting around a water fountain. I noticed various bags and blankets stacked around the group. One distraught woman stood and started yelling curses at the others.

"And druggies," Stephanie said under her breath.

"And *mahus*," Elena added.

"What are *mahus*?" I had to ask.

"Transvestite hookers," everyone answered simultaneously.

"Ohhhh." Maybe I would just bring my lunch every day rather than venture out onto the streets.

After lunch, Peter asked to speak with me in his office. He had a corner office twice as big as mine. Two desks sat together in an L-shape. A giant flat screen TV was mounted opposite the desk. He also had two floor-to-ceiling bookcases stuffed full of old books and a brown leather sofa. Various ancient-looking spears and knives hung on the wall behind the sofa.

"So, Liz!" He sat in his chair behind his desk and I sat on the sofa. "How is your first day going?"

"It's going great!" I said.

"Good, good."

"Thank you for this opportunity."

"You are welcome! I imagine it's quite a bit different than the yacht club, huh?"

"Uh, yeah," I said. "It's the exact opposite of the yacht club!"

He laughed. "Well, we've got a lot of big projects coming up and a lot of work to do."

I nodded.

"Our last controller left things in a bit of a mess, I'm afraid."

I nodded again. "Why did she leave?"

Peter frowned. "She and I didn't see eye to eye."

Oh. I decided not to inquire further. Peter seemed to be upset. She must have left him high and dry.

Peter shook it off and smiled. "But thank god I've got you now!"

I laughed.

"We might be working some late nights for a while until we get everything under control," he said, getting serious.

"Okay. No problem." I was confident I could get everything under control quicker than he thought.

Peter stood. "I'd like to show you our newest development project: Ward Palms." He motioned for me to follow him.

He took me to one of several glass-paneled conference rooms, where a large model of several high-rise glass buildings sat in the middle of the giant dark wood table. Marketing videos for the project were running on a flat screen TV mounted on the wall. The videos showed beautiful modern luxury condos with clean lines and floor-to-ceiling windows with views to die for all the way to Diamondhead. Native Hawaiians were featured throughout the videos, talking about the history of the area and the need to grow and change with this new sustainable living, working and shopping neighborhood.

"Beautiful, isn't it?" Peter asked.

I nodded. It all looked nice but I couldn't help feeling a little reserved about it. Ward Centers was already a well-established area with a movie theater and lots of nice shopping and dining choices. I guess adding condos to the area helped with the housing shortage on the island. But these condos seemed to be high end and over the top. Not very many people would be able to afford them. And they definitely weren't my style. Killer views aside, I'd prefer a nice cozy house on the beach, away from all the city lights and noise.

"We've been working with the Hawaii Community Development Authority to ensure we incorporate principles of sustainability and cultural respect that honor the rich genealogy of the land," Peter said proudly. "This area, Kaka'ako, used to be fish ponds and salt pans back in the day."

"Oh, I had no idea," I said.

"Now we are revitalizing the area into a colorful neighborhood set among green public open spaces and pedestrian friendly streets."

"That sounds great!" I liked the idea of more parks and pedestrian friendly areas.

"We've got both affordable housing as well as luxury condos," Peter explained. "And we're going to double the retail, dining and entertainment space."

"That's impressive," I said.

"Construction has begun on the main luxury condo here." Peter pointed to the model closest to the beach, the old parking lot directly across from the movie theater. "We're one hundred percent sold on the affordable units with a growing waiting list." He pointed to a building set several blocks back from the beach. Apparently affordable housing didn't come with a killer view like luxury housing did. "We're almost ninety percent sold on the luxury units."

I wondered what the difference in cost was for affordable units compared to luxury units.

"I'd like you to analyze the numbers and run some reports for me," Peter instructed. "I need balance sheets, income statements and work-in-progress reports. I've got a board meeting Friday. Can you get it all done by then?"

"Oh yeah, no problem," I told him confidently.

"Great!"

We headed back to my office, and Peter showed me where everything was on the server. After Peter left me to it, I did some research and found out that the luxury units sold for five times what the so-called affordable units cost. I didn't know anyone who could afford the affordable units, let alone the luxury units. Who makes that kind of money?

The rest of the week flew by. I was working twelve-hour days trying to make a good impression. On Friday night, we all went back to the Plaza Club for *pau hana*. This time, Peter insisted on driving us all to the club, so we all trekked down to the parking garage together. Peter led us to a giant black Hummer, and I almost laughed out loud at the fact that Peter drove something so unnecessary. Scott had to help lift me into the massive vehicle. But hey, all six of us fit!

The sun was beginning to set and the city lights twinkled as we walked into the club. I went directly to the panoramic windows to take in the breathtaking views. It was a magical sight. I felt lucky to be here.

Peter joined me. "Good first week, I hope?"

I smiled up at him. "Absolutely."

"Nice job on the reports, by the way. Thanks for getting them done so quickly."

"Yeah, no problem."

"The meeting went very well today." He winked at me.

"Oh good."

"So what do you think of those luxury condos?" Peter grinned and put an arm around me. "You interested in buying one?"

I could smell the scotch he was drinking on his breath. "Uh," I stammered, noticing his nose hairs for the first time. "I just inherited my great-grandmother's house in Kailua."

"Oh, we can sell that old shack for you," Peter said dismissively. "And I can give you a nice discount on the condo." He looked around to make sure no one else was nearby. Then he leaned in even closer and whispered. "I can give it to you at half price."

"Wow," I said, a little surprised. That was below cost. But I wasn't interested in living in a cold, modern box in the city. No matter what the price was. "Thanks for the offer," I said, not wanting to offend my new boss. "I'll think about it."

Peter nodded and finished his scotch in one gulp.

Feeling a little claustrophobic with his arm still around me, I lifted my near empty glass to my lips and drained it.

"Oh, let me get you another," Peter said, taking my glass.

"That's okay, I should get going," I said, deciding to split early. I was tired. And starting to feel uncomfortable.

Peter looked disappointed. He opened his mouth, and I knew that he was going to try to talk me out of it.

"Long week." I managed a big yawn before he could say anything.

Peter chuckled and nodded. "Well, you better get some rest then. We've got another big week next week."

Chapter 19

Saturday morning, I decided to take Koko down to the beach before Noe picked me up for climbing. Poor Koko had been home alone a lot, and it would do both of us some good to go play together down on the beach. I'd noticed dogs running around off their leashes on the beach, and I wasn't sure if Koko would be friendly with the other dogs, but we were about to find out.

We walked the two blocks to the beach with Koko on his leash but as soon as he saw other dogs running around down on the beach, he pulled at his leash with all his might, trying to get to them. As soon as we were down by the water, I let him go. He immediately took off, running toward a group of dogs who were sniffing at each other. As soon as I caught up to him, he took off running down the beach again.

I hadn't considered the possibility of him running away when I'd planned this little adventure. I panicked and started running after him, calling his name. He finally circled back around and started running toward me. When he got back to me, he darted out into the oncoming waves. He jumped and played in the water for a minute and then ran back to me again and shook himself off, getting me all wet in the process. I put my arms up in defense and laughed. He looked back at me innocently, his tongue hanging out of his mouth, tail wagging fiercely and then he rolled around in the sand.

I laughed again. I was going to have to give him a good bath now!

Suddenly I got knocked on my butt by a giant black shaggy thing that started desperately trying to lick my face once I was down. I shouted curses as I tried to fend off the crazy dog.

"Mahina! Mahina!" a man yelled at the dog as he ran toward us. "Come! Sit!"

He had to physically pull his dog off of me. As he scolded the dog, I tried to wipe the dog saliva from my face.

"I'm so sorry!" The man extended a hand to help me up. I took his hand and instantly felt a jolt of warmth that spread to my belly and down to my toes. Surprised, I looked up into the most golden brown eyes I had ever seen and did a double take. It was Aaron!

"Oh!" I laughed nervously, feeling my face grow hot from his touch. "It's okay!"

He tilted his head, studying me for a moment and then pulled me up with ease.

"Are you okay?" he asked, still gently holding my hand.

I nodded.

He looked down at our hands and then, as if finally realizing that I was a stranger, he let go. He ran his hands through his hair and I started wiping the sand from my legs and arms, trying to make sense of what had just happened between us. I was pretty sure he had felt it. too.

"She gets so excited sometimes, but I swear she has never jumped on anyone like that before." He shook his head. "I have no idea what got into her."

"She must sense that I've recently become a dog lover," I joked, nodding toward Koko, who was now sniffing Mahina.

"Is that right?" Aaron asked, amused.

"Yeah, I found Koko wandering on the side of the road and immediately knew I had to save him."

"That's nice of you. A lot of people would have driven right on by."

I shrugged.

"Hey, my name's Aaron."

"Liz."

"I haven't seen you around here before."

"No, I moved here recently."

I told him I was from California and about inheriting my great-grandmother's house in Kailua.

"What was your great-grandmother's name? I've lived in Kailua my whole life. I know everyone."

"Puanani Kekoa," I said.

"Oh yeah!" Aaron's face lit up at her name. "I knew her. We all took *hula* lessons from her growing up."

"You took *hula* lessons from her?" I asked, surprised.

"Yeah, why?" Aaron looked amused. "You don't think guys can do *hula*?"

I tried to backtrack. "No, no, that's not it!" I stammered. "I...."

"No worries!" Aaron laughed and did a little impromptu *hula* dance for me right there on the beach. He moved his hips around, waved his arms to and fro and stomped in the sand as he slapped his chest and shouted out something in Hawaiian.

I immediately pictured him half naked in nothing but a white loincloth and shark-tooth necklace. Just like my dream. Oh lord!

I felt my face flushing again. "Nice moves!"

"Thank you, thank you," he said, bowing.

"I never got to meet her," I confessed. "My great-grandmother."

He frowned then. "I'm sorry. She was a wonderful woman."

"Yeah, I've enjoyed meeting people who knew her and learning all about her since moving here."

Aaron smiled again. "I'll bet she's watching over you now that you've returned home to Hawaii."

"I have felt some sort of presence off and on," I admitted.

Aaron nodded as if that was perfectly normal. "We Hawaiians believe our ancestors return in animal form after they pass on."

"I've heard that," I told him. "I found out recently that my *aumakua* is a turtle."

Aaron nodded. "The *honu*. Also known as the navigator, able to find its way home time and time again."

I liked that. I felt like I was finally finding my way home lately.

"Mine's the *mano*." Aaron wiggled his eyebrows.

I thought of Noe. "Oh, the shark, yeah?"

"Yeah, yeah!"

"Have you ever seen a shark up close?"

"Several times. Actually a few weeks ago when I was surfing, a shark surfaced right near me and then went back under and swam away."

"Whoa! Did you freak out?"

Aaron laughed. "A little! I won't lie!"

I laughed. "I had a close encounter with my *aumakua* a few weeks ago, too."

Aaron's eyebrows shot up at this.

I didn't really want to explain what had happened to Aaron so I quickly changed the subject. "So, do you still do *hula*?" I asked.

Aaron shook his head. "No, not really, not anymore. Too busy. But I remember all the moves." He smiled wistfully. "I was pretty good at it. Could have participated in competitions. But my father had other plans for me."

"Oh?" I asked as though I hadn't already heard all about him from Noe.

"Yeah, the family business. Construction," he told me. "And my father hopes to get me into office."

I raised my eyebrows.

"I'm running for mayor."

"Oh. That must take a lot of money." I thought of all the TV and radio campaign ads and all the people standing on corners holding political signs every day leading up to elections.

Aaron chuckled. "It does! But we get lots of donations. People who believe in what we're trying to accomplish."

"That's good." I wasn't into politics. Or politicians. It was all fake in my opinion. Fake people. Fake promises.

"I hope you'll vote for me!" He grinned and winked at me.

I couldn't help but grin back. His eyes sparkled when he grinned like that. Too bad he was in politics. "Oh, yeah," I told him but I wasn't even registered to vote. And I didn't plan on registering any time soon! It was all rigged anyway, and I didn't want to have to serve on jury duty someday because of registering.

Mahina and Koko suddenly started barking and chasing each other into the waves.

Aaron laughed and nudged me. "Looks like Mahina has a new friend."

Koko decided it was a good time to take off running again. I called out to him but he ignored me and kept going.

"I'm sorry!" I apologized. "I've gotta go get him. It's his first time down here on the beach."

"No worries! It was nice to meet you, Liz!"

"Yeah, you, too." I started backing up.

"I hope we can run into each other again down here sometime!" Aaron called out.

I nodded and turned. And then I couldn't help it, I looked back. He was patting his dog's head and grinning at me. My heart did a little leap at the sight.

What was wrong with me? I was not interested in a relationship right now, especially not with a politician. I liked to be the quiet observer in the background, not the public person in the spotlight. And politicians were very much in the spotlight.

But I couldn't stop thinking about him for the rest of the day. About the way I had felt when he touched me. Warm and fuzzy inside all over. Almost in a familiar way. His grin was infectious and his eyes sparkled with mischief. And I kept picturing him in my dream, half naked in that loincloth!

* * *

Later that night, Koko and I were snuggling on the couch, channel surfing, when I came across a televised political debate between Aaron and his rival, the incumbent mayor, Duke Anderson. I had never watched a political debate before, but I wanted to see how Aaron did, so I put the remote down and listened in.

The two men were in the middle of a heated debate about the homeless problem in Honolulu.

"Low wages and over-priced housing have contributed to Hawaii having the third largest homeless population per capita in the country," the incumbent mayor, Duke, was saying. "I don't know how Mr. Aiona thinks he can help solve the homeless crisis, since Aiona Builders contributes to the problem."

Aaron almost laughed out loud. He covered up and made it sound like a cough.

Duke ignored this and went on. "Aiona Builders has a history of paying low wages. And it is the overdevelopment of our islands that has displaced so many of its long-time residents over the years. Tenement homes throughout Chinatown were razed in the '70s and '80s. In the '70s, Sand Island homes were bulldozed. Longtime Kalama valley residents were kicked out of their farms and homes for a planned dense development." Duke looked pointedly at Aaron. "Fisherman shacks and surf shacks used to dot the shores around the islands, but they were leveled all in the name of progress. And all the mainland transplants wanting to live in "paradise' raises property values sky high."

Aaron jumped in. "Aiona Builders has never and will never participate in any dense development projects," Aaron shot back. "We focus on the needs of the community. For instance, our big project right now is the new parking structure for the Kapiolani Women's Medical Center, which marks the first step of a fifteen-year master plan for the hospital. This new, seventeen-story, LEED-certified structure incorporates eco-friendly components such as roof-mounted photovoltaic panels and electric car-charging stations with a brushed concrete exterior to minimize cleaning requirements." Aaron looked at Duke and tilted his head. "The homeless have increased thirty percent over the last five years. On your watch, Duke. The current programs in place, The Honolulu Affordable Housing Preservation Initiative, HOME Investment Partnerships, and Pathways Project, are not doing anywhere near enough to help the homeless. And your recent move to kick the homeless groups out of certain parks and streets has only forced them to move to new parks and streets." Aaron paused and looked back at the audience. "But all of that aside, it's long past time to take bold new steps to solve the dilemma, instead of trying to point fingers and place blame."

Duke tried to defend his record. "We've eliminated the homeless from the main tourist areas, which is critical to our state's number one industry. And many of the homeless are from the mainland. We are currently working on a program where we send those people back to the mainland."

"You do realize that the homeless just move back into the tourist areas again sooner or later, don't you?" Aaron asked Duke in amazement. "You have only put a Band-Aid on the festering wound. And only eight percent of the homeless are transplants from the mainland. You won't make much of a dent in the homeless numbers if you are concentrating solely on sending the mainland transplants back to the mainland." He paused for effect. "Roughly ten percent of the homeless are veterans. We need to really step up our assistance of our veterans since Hawaii is home to such a large population of military people. And for many homeless people, including veterans, substance abuse occurs with mental illness. The problem is that the current programs for homeless people with mental illnesses do not accept people with substance abuse disorders, and current programs for homeless people with substance abuse problems do not treat people with mental illnesses. We need more centers and people who can help deal with these complicated homeless issues and finally help these people get out of the holes they got stuck in."

Aaron looked at Duke pointedly again. "And lastly, much of our homeless population is made up of long-term native Hawaiians who have fallen on bad times. We need to think outside of the box and do more for these displaced Hawaiians." Aaron turned back to the audience. "One idea that has been tossed around for years now is to build a native Hawaiian village once again along Sand Island water's edge. Put in more showers and toilets. Set up a recycled food program for redistribution of all the food that goes to waste. Help set up gardens for them." Aaron smiled at the camera, and I felt as if he was smiling at me through the TV. "I am more than willing to donate my time and money to help make this idea a reality, whether or not I am elected."

I had to admit that I was impressed with Aaron. He sounded like he actually knew what he was talking about and he had passion. I liked his ideas. I had to admit that I had underestimated him. The moderator took over at that point and started the two political opponents on a new hot topic—light rail. I lost interest and turned the channel.

I started thinking I should register to vote.

Chapter 20

"The Bishop Museum, otherwise known as the Hawai'i State Museum of Natural and Cultural History, was founded in 1889," Noe explained as we walked toward a regal-looking old stone building Sunday morning. "Home to the world's largest collection of Polynesian cultural artifacts and natural history specimens. It's the largest museum in Hawaii!"

Noe continued her history lesson as we entered the building. "The museum consists of two historical buildings—this one, Hawaiian Hall and Polynesian Hall. Both were constructed in the then popular Richardsonian Romanesque architectural style."

We entered the central gallery, a huge open room with wraparound balconies on several levels. Suspended up above us was a life-sized sperm whale model. Surrounding the whale were a life-sized shark, a sea turtle and some fish. Along the walls were hundreds, maybe thousands, of artifacts in Koa wood display cases. In the center of the gallery was a replica of an ancient Hawaiian hut.

"I used to be a tour guide here when I was in high school," Noe told me. "Stop me if I'm boring you too much with facts!"

"No, I love it!" I smiled.

"These Koa wood display cases are worth more than the original Bishop Museum buildings," Noe told me. "The museum is also home to the Hawaiian Royal regalia, including the Hawaiian royal crown and the consort's crown."

"Wow," I said, truly impressed. We passed some interactive booths with ancient Hawaiian tools that kids were playing with and then cases with ancient sculptures and jewelry. Photographs going back 100 years adorned the walls. Clothing worn by Hawaiians through the ages hung in glass cases. I was fascinated by all of it.

We stopped at a collection of photographs and letters. "Charles Reed Bishop built the museum in memory of his late wife, Princess Bernice Pauahi Bishop." Noe glanced at me. "She was the last legal heir of the Kamehameha Dynasty, which had ruled the Kingdom of Hawaii peacefully between 1810 and 1872."

Noe continued as we walked slowly from one exhibit to the next. "The museum was built on the original boys' campus of Kamehameha Schools, which was co-founded by Charles Bishop. A couple other buildings were added over the years. Castle Memorial Building was built in 1990. That's where all the major traveling exhibits that come to the Bishop Museum from institutions around the world are held. And the Richard T. Mamiya Science Adventure Center, which opened in November 2005, is designed as a learning center for children, and includes fun interactive exhibits focused on marine science and volcanology."

We approached a display featuring photographs and paintings of latter-day female Hawaiian royalty—the *ali'i wahine*. Princess Bernice Puahi Bishop, Queen Emma Kaleleonalani, Princess Ruth Ke'elikolani, and Queen Lili'uokalani. "These were the last few women who ruled over and led the Hawaiian Kingdom," Noe told me.

As I studied the photographs of Queen Lili'uokalani, I wondered what it had been like for her, the last ruling Queen of the Hawaiian Kingdom. She was a beautiful and elegant-looking woman. I read about how she inherited the throne from her brother, King Kalakaua, on January 29, 1891 and was then overthrown by wealthy American and European businessmen just two years later on January 17, 1893. She was imprisoned by the

Territorial Government in an upstairs bedroom of Iolani Palace for a year, where she spent time working on her memoirs and writing many songs, including the Queen's Prayer—*Ke Aloha o Ka Haku*.

What a terrible ordeal to have gone through. I felt sad for her and angry at the greedy men who took advantage of her.

"Do you think we can visit Iolani Palace sometime?" I asked Noe.

"Of course!" Noe said with a happy grin.

I read some words from Queen Lili'uokalani's memoirs, and I was struck by how eloquently she wrote. One paragraph in particular stood out:

"Those of foreign ancestry not in sympathy with the revolutionists, those whose daily comfort had been disturbed or whose business had been made unprofitable or ruined by the rich and powerful missionary party, appealed to me and my friends to restore the old order of things, that prosperity might again smile on the majority, instead of being locked up in the bank accounts of a very few."

She could easily have been writing about the issues today in modern Hawaii. Not much had changed in over a hundred years. The wealthy minority were still taking advantage of the majority.

"The queen supported Buddhist and Shinto priests in Hawai'i," Noe told me. "She was one of the first Native Hawaiians to attend a Vesak Day, Buddha's Birthday celebration, on May 19, 1901, at the Honwangji mission. Her attendance in the celebration helped Buddhism and Shintoism gain acceptance in Hawai'i."

"I had no idea," I said, impressed. "She accomplished a lot in her life."

Noe nodded. "She died in 1917 from complications from a stroke. She was seventy-nine. Lili'uokalani dictated in her will that all of her possessions and properties be sold and the money raised would go to the Queen

Lili'uokalani Children's Trust to help orphaned and indigent children. The Queen Lili'uokalani Trust Fund still exists today."

"What an amazing and inspiring woman," I said. "She never gave up."

When we came across a room of feathered capes, I froze, mesmerized.

"Ah." Noe noticed my interest. "The Hawaiian feather cape, or *ahu'ula*, was made for those of higher ranking in the Hawaiian society. They are usually associated with the *ali'i* class. Beautiful, yeah?"

The capes were beautiful. Each one was unique. Some were longer than others. Some were made of all yellow feathers and some were intricately patterned with red feathers woven in amongst the yellow feathers. But something about the capes was familiar to me. I wanted to reach out and touch one but of course I couldn't. They were roped off.

"Certain colors and patterns went into designing the capes, each meaning something different. Red was typically the color that represented higher status." Noe motioned toward the red cape, the one I was most interested in. "The olonā plant was used to make the netting for the cordage of the cloak. Harvesting and cultivating the olonā took a lot of time, and then turning the plant fibers into thousands of feet of cordage for the cloak tacked on even more time, making the whole process very lengthy. It could take years to make one cloak."

"Wow," I whispered.

"Hundreds and thousands of feathers were needed to make only one cloak but the birds were not allowed to be harmed in this process. Bird catchers would make careful use of the feathers and only remove a few at a time. This allowed the birds to continue to produce feathers in the future."

"It's a shame people today aren't as concerned with preserving nature," I commented.

Noe agreed.

We spent half the day in the museum. I could have stayed even longer, there were so many things I hadn't even seen yet, but I realized that I was starving. Noe promised we would come back again soon.

"No one has ever enjoyed the Bishop Museum as much as me before you!" Noe mentioned as we drove away. She turned the car radio to a local Hawaiian station. "I am a Queen" by Lilo of Kapena started playing. I turned the volume up. I loved this song and it was perfect after a day in the museum learning about queens. Noe smiled over at me and started singing along so I joined her.

"'Cause I am a queen

It's time that you finally see."

We laughed as the song ended.

"We deserve to be treated like queens!" I suddenly exclaimed.

"Absolutely!" Noe agreed. "But remember," she gave me a sideways look, "you have to act like a queen in order to be treated like one."

I thought about that.

"You know, I think that's been my problem," I said, frowning. "I've been playing the part of the servant, only too willing to please "The King" and do whatever is asked of me." I thought of Brad and what a fool I'd been with him.

Noe nodded. "Been there! Done that!"

"You have?" I asked, surprised. I imagined men worshiped Noe. She was a goddess.

"Oh yeah, when I was younger. There are all kinds of jerks out there."

I grimaced. "I online stalked the last guy I dated for about a week after we ended things. Well, after I ended things."

Noe laughed.

"I am so ashamed of that!" I admitted.

"Please, girl!" Noe patted my arm. "We all do stuff we regret!"

"What have you done that you regret?" I probed.

Noe rolled her eyes. "I stalked a surfer when I was younger." She laughed. "I went to every one of his competitions, and I even drove past his house a few times, trying to catch a glimpse of him."

My eyes widened. "No way! Did he ever catch on to you?"

"I'm pretty sure he knew! He smiled knowingly at me a few times, like he thought I was cute or something."

I laughed. "Well, there is no way that I will ever fall for another jerk again! I'm a queen now and all men must bow down before me!"

"That's my girl!" She smiled at me. "You *are* a queen!"

I didn't have a sister and never really had any close female friends, but I felt a close sisterly bond with Noe.

"You'll find someone much, much better! Now, let's go back to my place for lunch, my queen!"

As soon as we got back to her place, Noe opened a bottle of Merlot and poured two glasses. Sipping on wine, snacking on cheese and crackers and *poke*, which I was starting to actually like, Noe asked how I was liking my new job.

I told her about my new offices and everyone I worked with.

"That's great, Liz." Noe smiled. "You deserve it."

"It's a big step up from the yacht club," I said. "Did you know Ali'i Properties is rebuilding the Ward area?"

Noe frowned. "Yeah."

"What?" I asked.

"Well," Noe hesitated, "when they started digging about a year ago, they found historic Hawaiian burials at the site."

"Oh no." Now I was frowning.

"There are dozens of unmarked graves throughout the property, which is an unusually high number for such a site. Usually, only two or three unmarked graves are found at most construction sites." Noe paused to eat a cracker and then continued, "The State Historic Preservation Division has really dropped the ball on this project. Under state law, SHPD is tasked with protecting Hawaii's past. Its staff is supposed to review proposed projects for potential harm to historic sites and burials. If a site could be affected, SHPD is supposed to require the developer to hire an archaeologist to survey the property before any construction begins and make sure the survey is done right. That way, the developer can redesign the project while it's still being planned, as opposed to being built."

I nodded. "Makes sense."

"This never happened at Ward Village though. The Hawaii Community Development Authority gave the green light for the development plan without submitting it to SHPD. The developer, knowing that burials had been discovered in neighboring properties, contracted a private archaeologist anyway and sent its archaeological inventory survey report to SHPD for review. The survey reported back that there were at least eleven sets of human remains at Ward Village. With that information, the SHPD should have assumed that these burials were just the beginning."

"Yikes!" I said and finished my wine.

"This is our *kupuna* we're talking about," Noe went on. "Our ancestors. And it's also a rare find that could not only tell us how Hawaiians died, but lived. Archaeologists have been looking for at least a quarter-century for an old Hawaiian living surface—the top of the sand where people were making their houses, raising their families and digging holes to bury their dead. We could find out when Hawaiians lived there, what kind of houses they built, what kind of wood they burned, whether they were fishing with nets or building canoes and going out in deeper water."

"Well, what ever happened to the bones they found?" I wondered aloud.

"They relocated the bones to another area on the property and continued on with their building." Noe finished her glass of wine and poured more for us both.

I frowned and thought about all the ancient Hawaiian people buried throughout the islands from over the years; about the lives those people had lived. I wondered how I would feel if it was my *kupuna* being dug up and moved to enable big luxury high rises to be built.

I suddenly realized that it was my *kupuna*! My great-grandmother and her mother and father were buried at the Valley of the Temples, a peaceful cemetery/garden nestled up against the Koolau mountains. But I had no idea where any prior relatives had been buried. For all I knew, they were under Peter's luxury condos.

I wondered what Peter would say if I confronted him about the bones. And then I remembered Peter's somewhat drunken behavior with me Friday night. I hoped it wouldn't be awkward with him now at work.

That night, I had the strangest dream. Fred and Peter were fighting each other in ancient Hawaii. Fred was wearing the red *ali'i* cape I had seen in the museum. He looked strong and regal. Peter was sporting a Mohawk and he had a scar running down the side of his nose. He sneered at Fred. Each man had an army of skeletons fighting alongside them. Spears, knives and clubs shattered bones but the skeletons continued fighting. I woke up in a cold sweat. I wondered who would have triumphed. Peter? Or Fred?

Chapter 21

"Peter, can I ask you something?"

I had debated bringing up the buried bones with Peter all morning. But, whatever the outcome, I just had to know whether he cared or not.

"Sure, sure," Peter said. "Anything!"

We were sitting in his office, and we had just gone over some invoices Peter wanted to discuss with me. He seemed to be in good spirits today.

"I just heard about the bones uncovered last year during digging at the main site for Ward Village."

Peter narrowed his eyes and tightened his lips. "Yes, tragic." He started gathering all of his papers together.

I wasn't sure if Peter meant it was tragic that the bones had to be disturbed and moved because of his project or if it was tragic that his project had to be delayed because of all the trouble and expense of moving bones. Probably the latter.

"I imagine moving the bones would have been a difficult task. They were probably very fragile. They probably fell apart as they were moved, huh?"

Peter stopped what he was doing and looked at me. His eyes darkened.

I tried to change the subject. "That would have been interesting, to study the site. Were any artifacts found?"

Peter remained silent, staring at me. His left eye twitched. I noticed a faint white line running down the side of his nose suddenly. How odd that I had never noticed it before. Had it always been there?

I felt incredibly uncomfortable. I tried to make a quick exit.

I cleared my throat. "So, anyway, I'll make sure these invoices get processed as we discussed."

"Please see that you do," Peter said coldly. He continued to stare at me.

I forced a smile and then got up. I tripped on my way to his door. I practically ran back to my office. I sat at my desk, my hands shaking, wishing I hadn't mentioned the bones. I was starting to think that the only thing Peter really cared about was making money. What a disappointment.

Against my better judgment, I decided to venture out early for lunch. I needed to get out of the office for a bit. Clear my head, release the negativity. Move on.

As I walked down the street checking out my choices for food—sushi, Chinese, Japanese, Hawaiian plate lunch—I noticed a woman on the sidewalk several feet in front of me. She had dark hair down past her shoulder and was dressed normally enough in jeans and a T-shirt. But she was barefoot and she couldn't walk straight and kept tripping. I assumed she was one of the druggies I had been warned about. She twirled around and I sucked in my breath when I saw her old and ragged face. Her cheeks were sunken, she had dark circles under her eyes and her lips were dry and cracking.

I considered heading in a different direction in order to avoid her altogether, but then I decided I could just pass by quickly like everyone else was doing. She took a wild turn just as I was passing and crashed right into me. We both fell to the ground together in a heap.

Her eyes were completely glazed over, and she smelled truly awful. I held my breath and struggled to get back on my feet and away from her. But she reached out a gnarled hand and grabbed my arm, pulling me back down.

"Don't fucking touch me!" I yelled in panic as I tried to pull my arm away. But her grip was tight.

She inched closer to me, and I watched as her eyes went from a cloudy gray to a brilliant bright blue. "Be careful, dear." She spoke in a clear, strong voice, not at all what I had expected. "You are in danger!"

I got the chills. "What?" I croaked.

"You're on a dangerous path!" she went on. "Be wary of your enemies."

I yanked my arm away from her as hard as I could and finally freed myself. I turned to run. "Keep your friends close," she yelled after me. "You'll need them!"

Shaking, I turned to make sure she wasn't following me. I watched as her eyes glazed back over to a cloudy gray once again. And then she went back to stumbling drunkenly down the street in the opposite direction.

People on the sidewalk stared at me as I put my head down and headed back to the office. I'd lost my appetite.

I didn't see Peter for the rest of the day. He stayed locked away in his office with his door shut. I was sure he was purposefully avoiding me. But why?

* * *

I could hear dance music pumping as Noe drove into the municipal parking garage in Chinatown. It was Friday night, Halloween night, and Noe and I were headed to the annual Halloween block party on Nu'uanu Avenue. A couple of blocks of Nu'uanu were always shut down for block parties on each of the major holidays: New Year's Eve, St. Patrick's Day, Mardi Gras, Cinco de Mayo, the 4th of July, Halloween. If it was a holiday that involved drinking and partying, the party was in Chinatown! I hadn't been to one yet, but I'd heard all about the parties and was excited to finally see what all the fuss was about. And forget about work....

Peter had been cold and distant with me the rest of the week. I must have struck a nerve when I'd asked about the bones. I'd searched the records, trying to find information on the cost of moving the bones, figuring it must have cost Peter a lot of money, which was why he was so sensitive on the subject now. But I hadn't found anything.

They had to have moved the bones though, right?

As Noe and I walked from the parking garage toward Nu'uanu Avenue, I tried to put Peter and the mystery of the buried bones out of my mind and paid more attention to all of the creative costumes being worn tonight. I was impressed with the effort many people had gone to. A lot of people were dressed up as superheroes, vampires, or pirates. Of course there were plenty of sexy, cleavage-baring costumes. Some couples were dressed up as Tarzan and Jane, or Fred and Wilma Flintstone, or Frankenstein and the Bride of Frankenstein. One guy was dressed up as Where's Waldo! A bunch of guys dressed up as the Fruit of the Loom characters passed us by.

Noe was dressed up as a sexy Candy Corn Witch in a tight black tube top, a short orange ruffled skirt, thigh-high, orange-and-white striped stockings and black Mary Jane heels. The outfit was complete with a pointy orange candy corn hat with a white tip and black rim. She looked amazing, and everyone was checking her out as we walked by. I was more conservative in a Renaissance princess costume. I wore a long blue velvet gown with open sleeves. The skirt, neckline and upper part of the sleeves all had white satin insets. Gold trim in a V-shape lined the front bodice of the dress.

We paid the fee to get past security and into the party. It was difficult to move around; there were hundreds, maybe thousands of people here. Several stages with live DJs were set up down the street and a bunch of food and drink kiosks scattered throughout the area. We stopped and danced for a while with the masses in front of a stage with electronic music.

When Noe motioned for me to follow her to get drinks, I tried to keep up as she weaved her way through the massive crowd of people, but I quickly lost track of her.

Frustrated with losing Noe and all the people crowding me, I didn't notice when a man dressed as a knight stepped into me, nearly knocking me over and spilling some of his beer on me. I looked down at the mess on my dress and cursed.

"I'm so sorry! Are you okay?" The knight's voice was deep and sexy. And familiar. As I looked up into those beautiful brown eyes, my anger melted away instantly. "Liz!" Aaron grinned and put an arm around me. "We have to stop meeting this way!" His costume consisted of a black-and-gray tunic with attached sleeves, a gauntlet, cape, and cowl at his neck, big black boots and boot covers. And there was even a big red embroidered lion crest in the center of his tunic.

I couldn't believe that we had dressed up in similar costumes. "Oh, it's okay, I'm okay ..." I stammered. I felt my face heating up. "I'm sorry, I seem to have a sailor's mouth every time we run into each other!"

Aaron laughed and then suddenly swooped me out of the way as someone dressed up as Darth Vader did a crazy dance through the crowd.

"My knight in shining armor!" I said and then winced. I could not believe I had just said that!

But he happily played along, "My lady, I've come to save you from the perils of dancing alone." He spoke with a bad English accent and I laughed. He bowed and then held his hand out for me to take. "There are all kinds of weirdos out tonight!" he warned with a wink.

I took his hand and felt the same jolt of warmth I had felt on the beach a week ago when we had first met. I looked up at him to see if he felt it too. He was studying me. He squeezed my hand and then started moving his body to the sound of the music so I followed his lead. He grinned and encouraged me. The people dancing around us pushed us closer and closer to each other. Finally, Aaron put an arm around my waist and drew me in to him. He wore some kind of delicious musky cologne. I pressed my nose to his neck and inhaled deeply. I started feeling tingly and lightheaded.

A man in a business suit approached Aaron then, interrupting us, and whispered something in his ear.

"I've got some business to take care of, Liz," Aaron said. "You gonna hang here for a while?"

I nodded.

"Great!" He kissed my cheek and then grinned at me again. "I'll see you in a bit, yeah?"

I nodded again and watched as he disappeared into the crowd with the man. I could still feel his lips on my cheek where he had kissed me.

Suddenly Noe appeared out of nowhere, carrying two plastic cups filled to the rim with beer.

"Found you at last!' she shouted as she held one of the cups out for me to take. "What happened to you? I had to bribe the bartender to give me two drinks!"

"Oh." I smiled and took the beer from Noe. "I was just dancing with some guy but he took off right before you showed up!"

"Oh really!" Noe grinned. "Was he cute?"

I shrugged my shoulders. "So, so." I tried to casually sip my beer. I was determined not to make a big deal of anything anymore. I noticed Lily and Kai heading toward us then. I had to laugh when I saw their costumes. Lily was dressed as Madonna in a white tulle tutu and bustier complete with pearls around her neck and fingerless gloves. And Kai was dressed as a Michael Jackson in the red leather jacket and pants from his "Thriller" video. He stopped and did a classic Michael Jackson moonwalk for us. Everyone around us cheered and clapped.

We decided to get some food. After checking out all the food booths, we ended up with chicken kebabs. I kept an eye out for Aaron but he was nowhere to be found.

"I've got to find a bathroom," I said, after finishing my kebab and beer.

"Go into Indigo's and use theirs," Lily suggested. Indigos was one of the bars participating in the Halloween street party.

"Good idea. I'll be right back," I said and set off in that direction.

When I returned after the bathroom break, I didn't see Noe, Lily or Kai anywhere. *They ditched me!* But I told myself to relax, they must be somewhere nearby. I tried to remain calm as I started moving through the crowd, looking for them.

A hand lightly touched my shoulder and I swiveled around, thinking it was Noe, Lily or Kai or maybe even Aaron, but instead I found Brad standing there, smiling at me.

"Liz?" he asked, somewhat incredulously. "I can't believe it! You look great!" He moved in to give me a hug.

I just stood there, frozen in shock, my arms stuck at my sides, completely unable to respond. I couldn't breathe. I couldn't form any words.

I'd known there was a chance I might run into Brad again sometime, somewhere. But I thought I'd been ready for it. I'd hoped Brad could see how well I was doing, better now than before. I wanted him to see that I didn't need or want him anymore. I wanted to be in a position to reject him this time! But as I stood staring into those green eyes again, I realized I had never really expected this moment to actually happen.

"Long time no see, huh?" Brad was saying as he pulled out of the hug. "Wow!" He looked me up and down. "You look awesome! What have you been up to?"

I narrowed my eyes and studied him. Was he seriously acting as if we were just two old friends who hadn't seen each other in a while? He just stood there grinning.

"What are you doing here?" I finally managed to ask.

"Oh!" Brad laughed. "I've been here for a few days; I've been taking some of my customers from Maui on scuba tours of Oahu. They had the money and wanted me to personally show them around. So I said what the hell!"

I just nodded in response.

"We should go get drinks and catch up," he suggested, smiling wickedly at me. I finally noticed Brad was dressed up in a policeman costume.

I narrowed my eyes at Brad and furrowed my brow in irritation. What an arrogant, self-centered prick! I could feel my face grow red hot with anger.

As I opened my mouth to unleash an avalanche of cursing at Brad, a hairy, masculine arm went around my shoulder.

I turned in surprise to see Aaron. He looked at me questioningly. "Babe, is this guy bothering you?"

My anger melted away. I looked at Brad, who was studying Aaron. And then back at Aaron. The corner of his mouth inched up in a slight grin and he raised his eyebrows, waiting for me.

"No," I finally managed to get out. "This is just Brad. An old friend." I emphasized the word friend.

"Oh! Nice to meet you, Brad," Aaron said, grabbing Brad's hand and squeezing it. Hard. Brad winced and pulled his hand away quickly. Aaron acted like he hadn't noticed and went on. "I'm Aaron," he said. And then he added with emphasis, "Her boyfriend."

I glanced at Aaron out of the corner of my eye.

"Oh, lucky guy," Brad said cautiously.

"Indeed I am!" Aaron kissed my cheek and I felt all warm and tingly again. "Well, nice meeting you, Brad." Aaron slapped Brad on the back a bit harder than necessary. Brad winced again. "Take care now."

Brad slowly turned and started walking away, his shoulders slumped in defeat. He looked back at us once before disappearing into the crowd.

I couldn't help but smile. That was not how I expected my run in with Brad to go down. I had totally frozen when I'd first seen him! And then I had almost lost it. That would have been embarrassing. But Aaron had come in and saved the day.

"Thanks!" I said to Aaron. "How did you know I needed help with that guy?"

"I was trying to find you and then I saw that guy approach you. You looked like you were getting pretty mad at him."

I laughed it off. "Yeah. He's a jerk."

"He looked like a jerk." Aaron grinned at me. "You dated him?"

"Yeah, he turned out to be a player."

Aaron nodded seriously in agreement. "He looked like a player."

I laughed. "If you hadn't shown up just then, my sailor mouth was about to make another appearance."

Aaron laughed. "I like your sailor mouth."

Oh! My eyes popped. That was definitely flirting.

Aaron nudged me with his shoulder. "I told you there were weirdos out tonight!"

I laughed. "You did!" I tried to ignore the butterflies in my belly. "You know; I saw you on TV the other night."

"Oh yeah?" he moaned. "The camera really does put on ten pounds, doesn't it?"

I laughed again and punched him in the arm.

"I was really impressed with your arguments on the homeless problem," I told him, trying to be serious.

He frowned. "It's turned into a crisis." He shook his head. "It's pathetic how the people who are down on their luck are treated. It's number one on my list of things that I want to accomplish whether I get into office or not. Help turn these people's lives around."

"That's great." I looked him in the eyes. "Let me know if I can help in any way."

Aaron lit up. "You've got it!"

I suddenly spotted Noe waving at me from about twenty feet away. She gave me the thumbs up and a questioning look. I smiled and gave her the thumbs up back.

Aaron glanced in Noe's direction. "Your friend checking in?"

"Yeah."

He waved and gave Noe a thumbs up, too.

Noe laughed and then disappeared into the crowd.

"Alone at last!" Aaron joked.

I looked at the thousands of people crowded around us and laughed. "Right!"

Aaron bought us some local beers and we watched aerial dancers climb, twist and swing by wrapping and unwrapping their arms legs and torsos in long silk wraps hanging from trees. Oohs and aahs came from the audience each time the dancers let the silk unravel and dropped several feet.

"I could do that!" Aaron boasted.

"It looks fun!"

Next we got in line for malasadas, the popular Portuguese deep fried dough balls. As we munched on our hot cinnamon sugar treats, we headed towards the reggae music playing a little further down the block. We ran into Noe, Lily and Kai there. Introductions were made and we all danced together to the sounds of steels drums and bass guitars.

Bob Marley's song "Could You Be Loved" started playing and I got the chills. I couldn't help it, I started jumping up and down. Aaron copied me and we both broke out laughing.

"I love this song!" I yelled.

Around midnight, I started yawning. "Time to get Cinderella home?" Aaron stuck out his lower lip in a pout.

"Yeah, I'm not a big partier," I admitted, yawning again.

Aaron offered to drive me home. He led me to a blue pickup truck. Not what I had expected him to drive. I guess I was expecting a BMW or something. He opened the car door for me and made sure I was safely inside before shutting it. He played Bob Marley as we drove and told me about the publicity work he had done for his campaign earlier in the evening. He'd had some photo ops with musicians and then served as one of the judges for the costume contest. The guys dressed up as the Fruit of the Loom characters had won.

I'd forgotten that he was running for office. And then I realized that no longer seemed like such a bad thing.

Chapter 22

Saturday morning, as I sipped on my second coffee, I picked out my own climbing shoes and harness at the only rock climbing store on the island. Now that I was completely addicted to rock climbing, it was time for me to invest in my own climbing supplies and stop borrowing Noe's stuff.

"So...." Noe grinned as she handed me a blue carabiner to add to my collection. "How did last night go?"

"Fine, thanks!" I laughed.

"Aaron Aiona!" Noe exclaimed, impressed. She gave me a hip bump. "Did ya get lucky?"

I laughed. "Aaron was a perfect gentleman. He walked me to my door and kissed me on my cheek before saying good night."

"Ohhhh...." Noe sounded disappointed.

"And then he got my number," I added nonchalantly.

Noe high-fived me. "You go, girl!"

I splurged and added a beautiful electric blue climbing rope to my purchase. I couldn't wait to put it all to use.

Noe said she could only climb for a couple of hours today and then she had a school event to attend. But luckily Lily wanted to climb today too and was planning on joining us a bit later. So Noe and I drove separately out to the climbing site.

Noe and I climbed for a couple of hours and as soon as Lily showed up, Noe took off.

Lily wanted to know all the details about Aaron, so I filled her in.

"Hawaii's hottest and most eligible bachelor!" Lily teased. "And our girl Liz caught him!"

"Let's not get ahead of ourselves here!" I insisted, trying not to smile.

"New rope?" Lily pointed to my new blue rope running down the climb.

"Yeah!" I proudly showed off my new climbing shoes, harness and belay device too.

It was my first time climbing with Lily, and I discovered right away that Lily was different on belay than Noe. Noe always kept me on a tight belay, sometimes even helping to lift me up as I climbed. But Lily left the rope a little looser than Noe did. She insisted that I needed to rely less on the rope and more on my rock climbing skills. I struggled at first, mostly because I felt more fear than I normally did with Noe. But after I completed my first run with Lily, I realized that I actually did have skills! And now I felt more confident than ever. Lily and I completed four runs each and at the end of our last run, Lily got a text.

"It's Kai!" Lily rubbed her forehead. "His car broke down."

"It's okay, Lily," I told her. "You can go ahead and get going and I'll stay and clean up here."

"Are you sure?" Lily asked as she took her climbing harness off.

"Absolutely!" I told her confidently. "I'm an old pro at this now!"

Lily laughed. "I don't know about old, but you're definitely becoming a pro. You did really great today!"

I blushed. "Thanks for pushing me to do more than I thought I could."

"No worries! I knew you had it in you!"

"Be careful going back down now!" I warned as Lily tripped over a rock in her haste.

"I will, don't worry!" Lily agreed as she threw her backpack over her shoulders. "I'll see you later, okay?"

I agreed to see her later and then worked at getting my rope down and packing up my gear. The wind picked up and dark clouds formed in the distance.

I groaned. I hoped it didn't start raining on me. I started working faster at getting out of there.

The first fat raindrop hit my forehead right as I threw my pack over my shoulders.

Crap, crap, crap! I hurried toward the path that led back down the mountain. A few more raindrops fell. The path was going to get muddy and the rocks would get slippery in the rain. The rain picked up as I started my descent down the rocky path. I was trying to be careful but I was also trying to go as fast as I could at the same time. Suddenly, my right foot slid out from under me on a wet rock and I fell backward.

I yelped in pain as my ankle twisted and I landed on my butt. I tried to get back up but my ankle hurt like hell now. I cried out again in pain and frustration. I was injured and stuck alone on a mountain in the rain.

"Are you okay?"

I jumped. I'd thought I had been the last one left on the mountain. I turned and saw Aaron! What was he doing up here?

"Liz?" Aaron seemed surprised to see me, too. He tried to help me stand. "Do you climb?"

"I just started a few months ago. You climb too?"

"Yeah. I was climbing with a friend around the bend in the mountain, on Ambulance Chaser."

I was impressed. That was a 5-13 run. I couldn't even complete 5-9 runs yet.

"My friend had to take off, and I was cleaning up when it started raining."

"What a weird coincidence! Me, too," I said.

The rain was drenching us at this point. I tried to put weight on my bad ankle again, and I squealed with the pain.

"Your ankle might be sprained. Let me get you out of the rain and have a look at it."

I nodded.

He picked me up with ease and started back up the path. "I know of the perfect little cove for us to hide out in until it stops raining. I don't want to try to carry you all the way down the mountain in this downpour. It wouldn't be good if we both had sprained ankles. Or worse."

Back up on the climbing ledge, he headed far left toward a deep indentation in the rock wall and placed me gently down inside and then crawled in next to me. The outcropped rock protected us from the rain, for the most part.

He opened his pack and grabbed a couple small towels.

"Here," He handed me one of the towels. I thanked him and started patting my face dry. He dried his face with the other towel.

"Let me look at that ankle now." He took my foot gingerly and started examining it.

I shivered at his touch. In these close quarters he smelled wonderful, all wet and manly and musky.

"Cold?" he asked.

I blushed. Yeah, that was it—I was cold!

He grabbed a sweatshirt out of his pack and gave it to me.

I put it on, and he went back to examining my ankle.

"Hmmm." He frowned. "It's swelling already." He applied some pressure, and I yelped. "Not good."

He dug a bottle of aspirin from his bag and gave me a couple to take with water. "This will help get the swelling down," he said with a reassuring smile. Next, he dug an insulated lunch bag out of his bag. He grinned at me and my heart skipped a beat.

"To keep my snacks cold." He explained at my questioning look when he pulled a half melted ice pack out.

He lifted my leg so that it was resting on his backpack and then tenderly laid the ice pack on my ankle. The ice pack was still pretty cold. "Sorry! I know it's cold." He put an arm around me and held me close. "I'll keep you warm," he promised with a grin.

We sat snuggled up together in silence for a few minutes.

"How long have you been climbing?" I asked.

"Since high school."

"You must be pretty good by now then."

"So, so," he said with a grin. "How do you like it so far?"

"I love it!" I laughed. "I just bought all my own stuff this morning. I never knew I would get into rock climbing, otherwise I would have started a long time ago."

"Oh yeah? That's great! Maybe we can climb together sometime?"

"If you want to teach a beginner some basic moves, sure!"

"I'd love to!" he told me. "Once a month, I teach kids who are interested in learning."

"Oh, then you'd be a good teacher for me!" I joked.

He laughed and nudged me with his elbow playfully. I nudged him back.

I yawned then. "Were you as tired as me this morning?" I asked.

"Yeah, I had to get up early for a morning news interview."

"Oh no! You should have told me that last night."

"I forgot all about it until I got home and looked at my calendar," Aaron said. "That reminds me, I had the strangest dream last night."

"Yeah?"

"Yeah." He nodded. "You were in my dream."

"That's weird!"

"And in my dream, you were climbing a mountain—without ropes," Aaron added, arching an eyebrow.

"You are making that up!" I scoffed.

"No, seriously! I dreamed that last night." He looked at me sincerely.

"Ha." I laughed it off. "That would be cool. So...." I tried to change the subject. "What is up with this rainfall?" I laughed nervously.

Aaron studied the pouring rain. "It's not letting up," he said seriously. "We may have to stay here for the night."

"What?" I screeched.

"I'm kidding!"

I rolled my eyes.

We sat in silence again.

"Hey." I leaned toward him to kiss him on the cheek. "Thanks for rescuing—"

He cut me off, turning and cupping my face with his hands. And then he kissed me. On the lips! I had not expected that. The moment his lips touched mine, I was transported to some other place, some other time.

He pulled me closer and deepened the kiss. The warmth I had felt that fateful day on the beach when he had pulled me out of the sand was nothing compared to the warmth that flooded through my body now. We melted into each other. I couldn't get enough. He couldn't get enough. We were both starving for each other and hadn't even known it until now.

After some time had passed, we took a breath. Still holding tight to each other, our foreheads touching, Aaron mumbled, "Wow."

"Yeah," I agreed, letting out a sigh. "Wow."

He grinned and his beautiful brown eyes sparkled. He glanced away. "Hey, it's starting to let up now."

He was right. The rain had turned into a light sprinkle and blue sky showed through the clouds in spots. I wished for it to rain harder again. I really did not want my time with him to end yet.

Apparently neither did he. "Do you want to go get something to eat?"

I grinned and nodded.

"Let's test that ankle." He pulled away and gently lifted my leg from his bag and then looked at me to get my reaction.

"It feels okay," I confirmed.

He crawled out from our hideout and then held his hand out for me, pulling me up carefully. I put some weight on my bad ankle. It hurt a little but not nearly as bad as it had earlier. I smiled and stepped forward on it.

We slowly made our way back down the path, Aaron helping me the whole way. My mind was spinning. I wanted to kiss him again. We had amazing chemistry. I'd never felt like that before. My body ached for him.

Suddenly I remembered my pledge not to make a big deal out of anything, good or bad. I was determined to stick with that advice. I worked on staying in the present. I inhaled deeply and noticed the scent of the flowers on our path. I observed the way the plant leaves glistened after the fresh rainfall. Felt the warm humid air. Saw the dark rain clouds off in the distance now over the ocean. Remembered the feel of Aaron's lips on mine. Doh!

We made it safely to the bottom of the mountain and then I followed his blue truck to a Thai place about fifteen minutes away in Haleiwa. We ordered spicy cashew nut chicken with sticky rice and shared it with beers as we watched the sun set on the outside patio.

Aaron checked my ankle again after dinner. "I think it's just a mild sprain. Keep it elevated and keep icing it and taking ibuprofen until its back to normal."

"Okay," I said. "Thanks." I was feeling shy suddenly.

"Hopefully it will be better by next Friday," he said seriously.

"Why, what's Friday?" I asked, confused.

"Our first date, of course!" Aaron grinned.

I laughed.

He walked me to my car. "Thanks again." I said. "For saving me up on the mountain today, and for dinner."

He leaned in and kissed me softly on my lips. "My pleasure," he whispered against my mouth and then lingered for a moment peppering me with more soft kisses. "Drive safely."

"Okay," I whispered. I was dizzy and wobbly from his kisses but I managed to get in my car and wave goodbye. As I drove home, I tried to stay in the present again and not get lost in my head, daydreaming about Aaron and his lips. I realized suddenly that I hadn't told him about my hair loss yet. That was usually one of the first things I told people about myself. I hadn't even thought about it once with Aaron. And then I panicked. I must look a mess after getting soaked in the rain today! I pulled my visor mirror down expecting to see a monster staring back at me. But instead I was pleasantly surprised to see that I looked pretty normal.

Chapter 23

"What's wrong?" Peter asked with a frown Monday morning when he noticed me limping as I got my coffee in the break room.

"Oh!" I laughed it off. "I slipped and fell yesterday in the rain."

"Did you see a doctor?" he asked, concerned.

"Uh, yeah," I said cryptically as I put sugar and creamer in my coffee. "It's just a sprain."

He nodded. "Good. Can we go back to your office to discuss the financials?"

He led me back to my office and then shut the door behind him.

I was a bit uncomfortable with the fact that he had shut my door, but I sat down in my chair behind my desk and tried to act like it was no big deal. Peter sat in the chair on the other side of my desk. I pulled the statements up on my computer.

"So how are the quarterly numbers looking?" he asked.

"Well, I'm almost finished. So far it looks like this will be your best quarter yet." I turned my screen so that he could see it and filled him in on all the details.

"Good, good." Peter smiled for the first time. "Now, I need you to cut a $250,000 check from Ali'i Properties to Ali'i Holdings."

I narrowed my eyes. This was an odd request. We had an accounts payable clerk who cut checks. I never cut checks. Why would Peter come to me for this?

"Why?" I asked without thinking.

Peter stared at me for a moment, his eyes darkening again. "Because I told you to."

"Okay ..." I began, "but I need to put a description in the entry."

"Just put it as an intercompany transfer." He sounded like he couldn't believe I was questioning him.

"Okay ..." I said again hesitantly.

Peter forced a smile. I noticed the scar running along the side of his nose again. It seemed more noticeable now. "Thank you." He laid his hand over mine on the desk. "I'm so happy that you've come to work *for me.*"

I nodded and smiled back but my unease with Peter was rapidly growing. I wasn't feeling very happy to be working for him anymore. Alarms were going off in my head.

Peter left and locked himself behind closed doors in his office for the rest of the day.

But the next day Peter was back to his old self again, and I saw very little of him after that. The rest of the week went by without further incident.

I played around with the idea that I should be looking for a new job. But no, I needed to put in more than a couple of months here before moving on. I was stuck for the time being. I was just going to have to tread lightly around Peter going forward.

All thoughts of work ceased as soon as Aaron picked me up Friday night. He looked gorgeous in his gray slacks and white *aloha* shirt. I had splurged on a new navy blue maxi dress with spaghetti straps and side slit for our date.

His eyes popped. "You look beautiful," he whispered as he kissed my cheek.

I blushed. "Thanks! You look quite nice yourself!" My blush deepened as he grinned at my compliment.

He drove to Alan Wong's, a fancy restaurant in Honolulu I'd heard about but never thought I'd get to try. We sat in plush chairs and looked over menus with no prices. Yikes!

We ordered a bottle of wine to begin.

"I suggest we get the Prix Fixed Dinners," Aaron said. "You get a little of everything that way."

I was up for that. I nodded.

Chilled tomato soup and grilled mozzarella were placed in front of us. As I tasted each, I was amazed by how delicious the food was. Next we were given ahi avocado salsa stacks, which popped with flavor in my mouth. Then came the butter-poached cold lobster and after that ginger-crusted *onaga*. I was starting to feel spoiled and full when finally, the last course of kalbi-style short ribs was delivered to us.

"Room for dessert?" Aaron asked knowingly with a grin as I pushed my half-eaten plate of ribs away.

I rolled my eyes as *haupia* sorbet in a chocolate shell with tropical fruits was placed in front of us.

"You don't want to miss this!" he said as he dug into his.

He was right. It was heaven!

"I can barely walk after all that food," I whispered as we left the restaurant.

Aaron laughed and rubbed his belly. "It was worth it though, yeah?"

"Oh yeah!" I laughed. "I might not need to eat at all tomorrow though!"

"Aaron!" An Asian man approached us as we were about to exit the restaurant.

"Ray!" Aaron grinned and hugged the man. They exchanged pleasantries and Aaron introduced me. "Liz, Ray and I are old friends. We went to high school and college together."

"Yeah," Ray laughed. "We used to get into all sorts of trouble."

"Oh really?" I raised my eyebrows.

"Remember that one time we streaked across the football field our senior year at Punahou?" Ray threw his head back and laughed.

"You streaked? Naked?" I asked, surprised.

Aaron nodded and laughed. "It was a dare!"

Ray filled in the details. "It was during half time of the playoffs between Punahou and Saint Louis. We got a standing ovation!"

"Good times," Aaron said wistfully. "What about that time we made everyone think a ghost was haunting the theatre?"

"Oh boy!" Ray slapped Aaron on the back. "Mrs. Hinano almost had a heart attack when you started playing that ghostly recording during rehearsals for our graduation *hula*."

"You guys did *hula* together in high school?" I asked.

"Yeah, yeah," Ray said. "We each got a professional recording of our *hula* performances for graduation. Hey, you two want to go get a drink at the bar? Chat for a bit?"

We ordered another bottle of wine at the bar and sat and talked for about an hour before saying our goodbyes. As I stood to leave, I realized I was feeling a little bit tipsy from all the wine.

"I want to see that recording of your hula performances," I said, giggling as we exited the restaurant.

Aaron chuckled. "Oh yeah?" He paused and thought about it and then added, "Well, do you want to come back to my place now and watch it?"

I raised my eyebrows. "Back to your place, huh?"

"Hey, strictly for video watching!" Aaron playfully wagged a finger at me.

"Of course!" I nodded seriously. "Wait! Are you okay to drive? Because I'm definitely not!"

"I'm okay to drive, Liz," Aaron assured me.

"Okay, good." I giggled again.

Aaron drove us back to Kailua and up into the prestigious Lani Kai beach neighborhood. He parked in the brick paved driveway of a yellow plantation-style cottage with a big banyan tree in the front yard.

"Nice digs!" I said, admiring his tropical yard as we climbed the four steps to his front lanai.

"*Mahalo*! Make yourself at home," Aaron said as he opened his front door for me and then turned on the lights.

His home was small but charming. I could see to the backyard from the front door. Dark hardwood floors contrasted with white ship lap walls. Built in bookcases were filled with books and local art hung on his walls. A large flat screen TV sat across from a big cream sofa.

Aaron busied himself looking for the *hula* recording as I collapsed onto his sofa. I let my body sink into the comfortable cushion and sighed, feeling relaxed and happy.

"Ah ha!" Aaron waved a DVD in triumph and then stuck it in his DVD player and turned the TV on. "Can I get you anything to drink?" Aaron asked. "Water? Coffee?"

"Water would be great."

A video of some young men walking onto a stage began to play as Aaron left for the kitchen. The young men were bare chested and wore green grass skirts and green leafy leis on their heads and around their wrists. Some of the men had tattoos and some did not. I spotted the younger version of Aaron right away. He stood in the center of all the young men. Someone in the background started playing a drum and chanting and the men started stomping their feet and swinging their hips around.

My heart sped up, and I felt my face flush. I was completely captivated by Aaron's performance. Aaron had been just as gorgeous back in high school as he was now. The muscles on his legs strained as he moved back and forth on the stage, stomping, jumping, and squatting. I felt my body heat up at the thought of him in that *hula* costume now.

"Water, my lady?" Aaron placed a glass full of water on the coffee table in front of me and then plopped down next to me on the sofa. "So what do you think?" he asked, chuckling.

The young men finished their *hula* with a Hawaiian chant. Catcalls and cheers erupted on the video as the young men walked off stage.

I guzzled down some water before answering to try to hide my blush. "Wow, that was impressive," I finally said, still watching the end of the DVD.

Aaron laughed.

I finally turned to looked at him and he turned toward me. "This may sound weird, Liz, but I feel like I've known you forever."

"Yeah." I nodded. "I feel the same about you."

He smiled. "But I don't really know that much about you yet! I want to know everything!"

"Yikes!" I laughed. "Everything?"

Aaron raised his eyebrows and nodded.

I thought this might be a good time to 'fess up about my hair. But how to do it? "Well, I was an only child, my parents died in a car crash about five years ago."

"Oh God, Liz! I'm so sorry!" Aaron frowned.

"And I have a rare disorder called Alopecia Universalis." I looked at him, waiting for his reaction.

"You have Alopecia?" he asked, looking confused. "That's not your hair?"

I was surprised he even knew what Alopecia was.

"It's a wig." I pulled back the side to reveal my head underneath. "You really couldn't tell?"

Aaron shook his head.

"You've heard of Alopecia before though?"

"Oh sure, my aunt has it." He reached up and ran his fingers through the hair on my wig. "Amazing!"

I got excited. "I can't believe you know someone with Alopecia. I've never met anyone else with it."

"Oh, well then, you are going to have to meet my aunt ASAP!" Aaron declared.

"I can't wait!" I told him. "Does your aunt wear wigs?"

"Not anymore, she got tired of them. Said they were cramping her style." Aaron grinned.

"She sounds like quite a lady."

"She is, she is," Aaron agreed. "She's gonna love you! She has a sailor's mouth, too!"

I laughed.

"When did you first get Alopecia?" he asked.

I told him all about getting that first bald spot and then everything else that happened afterward, including losing all the hair on my body in my senior year in high school. I told him about all the wigs I had tried over the years, blond wigs and red wigs, short and long, curly and straight, until finally settling on the shoulder-length, straight brunette wig that I currently wore. I told him about getting tattooed eyebrows, how much that had hurt.

He pushed my bangs out of the way and studied my eyebrows. "I never even noticed."

"So tell me more about you!" I said, suddenly feeling self-conscious.

"Well." He looked reflective. "I'm an only child as well; my parents are still alive but divorced and remarried. And I had to have my tonsils removed when I was ten years old." He paused and then added, "And I've had strep throat three times. Not fun! I do not recommend it. At all!"

"Oh no!" I laughed. "I'm sorry! I've never had strep. And I still have my tonsils."

"Oh yeah?" He grinned mischievously. "Let me double check that for you!" He leaned in. "Say ahhhh ..." he ordered.

"I will not!" I laughed and pushed him away.

"Come on!" He started tickling me.

I twisted away from him. "No!" I sputtered between laughs.

I started falling backward, and Aaron fell with me, cushioning my fall. I tried to catch my breath. Aaron had his arms wrapped around me, and I could smell his cologne.

"What cologne is that?" I asked, sniffing.

"Polo Blue. You like it, don't you?" he teased. "Inhale my manly scent!" He snuggled closer to me.

I laughed again and tried to push him away. His lips were on mine then. I stopped struggling and relaxed in his arms, melting with his kisses. His touch was both familiar and electrifying. I was on fire again. I wanted him.

I suddenly felt nervous. What was going to happen next here tonight? Right now I wanted to tear Aaron's clothes off and kiss every inch of his body. But I refused to allow my hormones to take over this time.

Aaron groaned and pulled back to study me. "Liz, Liz, Liz," he said in a sexy, gruff voice.

"Aaron, Aaron, Aaron," I mimicked him.

He laughed and then sighed. "I better get you home."

"Yeah." I pouted. Half of me wanted to stay and continue what we had started and half of me wanted to wait. I knew we would get there but just not yet.

Aaron kissed me again. "Are you climbing tomorrow?" he asked.

"Yeah, me and Lily are going."

"I wish I was," he said with a frown. "I've got some campaign business to attend to."

"Oh," I said, biting my lip. "What's going on?"

Aaron got up and helped me up too. "Well, with the elections less than a week away, we're getting out in the public eye as much as possible to get attention and more votes." He grinned at me. "It's a miracle I was able to cut out a few hours to spend with you tonight. But don't worry, things will calm down considerably after the elections."

"Even if you win?" I asked hesitantly.

"Well, I mean things will definitely change for me if I win. But not that much. I'll have plenty of time to spend with you, I promise!"

I nodded.

"I'll take you climbing and teach you all my mad skills. And have you ever surfed?"

"A few times."

"I can teach you that, too!"

Noe had been trying to get me into surfing and although I had tried it and I had been able to get up on a surfboard a few times, I preferred the thrill of scaling a mountain over the thrill of riding a wave.

Part of me hoped Aaron would win but another part of me hoped he lost. I felt terrible for half hoping he would lose, because I knew Aaron would make a great mayor. He could help facilitate some much-needed changes to the city, including helping the homeless.

"Do you need to use the bathroom before we go?" Aaron asked.

I shook my head.

"I do! I'll be right back and then I'll drive you home."

I sat back down on the comfy sofa and closed my eyes.

The next thing I knew, it was morning.

* * *

The sound of birds woke me early and I bolted up in confusion. I was not in my bed. I was in a man's room by the looks of it. A green blanket covered me. I inhaled and smelled Aaron. I must be in Aaron's room. I was still wearing my wig and the blue dress from last night. What happened?

I got up out of the bed and my head pounded from the effort. Oh no, a hangover. Had I really had that much wine last night? I wandered down the hall to the living room to find Aaron snoring on the couch.

Wow, he was adorable laying there asleep with his hair all messed up like that. I went to sit next to him and he muttered something in his sleep. I must have passed out on the couch last night and being the gentleman that he was, he moved me to the bed and took the couch for himself.

Aaron opened his eyes and a smile spread across his face. "Good morning!"

I smiled back. "Good morning! Sorry I fell asleep on you last night!"

"I have that effect on women," he joked and then tried to pull me down for a kiss.

"No!" I protested. "I have morning breath!"

"I don't care about that! Come on! Give me a kiss!" He puckered his lips out and closed his eyes.

I laughed and gave in.

He got up and drove me home and then Lily picked me up to go climbing soon afterward.

"So did you have a good time last night? On your date?" Lily asked as soon as we were on our way to the North Shore.

"Yes, I did. Thanks for asking." I smiled and sighed.

"Have you seen the local news this morning?" Lily asked next.

"No." I didn't normally pay attention to the news.

"Oh." Lily chewed on her lip.

"Why?" I asked, getting suspicious.

"Well, you *are* the news this morning." Lily glanced at me.

"What?" I didn't understand.

"Pictures of you and Aaron have been published. From the Halloween party and last night at Alan Wong's."

My eyes bulged.

"Everyone is speculating about you and Aaron."

"Oh shit." I covered my mouth with my hand. "Sorry!" I had never thought about the possibility of getting photographed with Aaron. I hadn't noticed anyone taking pictures around us. I grabbed my cell phone and did a search for local news. I found the pictures of Aaron and I. They were from far away and out of focus.

Lily tried to reassure me that the pictures were good and it was a positive thing, nothing to worry about. But I didn't like being the center of attention.

It was a hot day and by the time Lily and finished the hike to the top of the mountain, I had forgotten about the news. We were trying to catch our breath and cool down when a petite Asian girl with long hair pulled back in a tight ponytail breathlessly approached us. "That hike up the hill is killer!" she said as she took a frilly white handkerchief out of her pink backpack and started wiping the sweat from her face.

"Yeah, it weeds out the weak, that's for sure," Lily said.

"Hey! My name is Charlotte but you can call me Charlie," the girl said.

"I'm Lily, and this is Liz," Lily said, pointing to me.

Charlie nodded. "I just moved here, and I thought I'd check out the popular climbing site on the island." She smiled sweetly at us.

"Oh, you climb?" Lily asked.

Charlie said she had been climbing all over the world for about five years. She was able to travel a lot as an international lawyer.

"I've climbed in Australia, New Zealand, Greece, Spain, and lots of places on the mainland—California, Oregon, Utah."

"Cool, cool!" Lily said, impressed. "I've climbed in Australia and some places on the mainland, but I haven't had a chance to get to Greece yet. That's my dream destination! What was the climbing like there?"

"It was pretty epic!" Charlie beamed. "There is a lot of rock to climb there and the water is pristine!"

"Do you sport climb or trad climb?" Lily was trying to determine how experienced this girl was.

"I've done both but I prefer sport. I can lead as well." Charlie pulled out her harness, and Lily nodded at all the equipment Charlie had attached. There were some things I had never seen before. Everything was pink. I wasn't really into pink.

Lily nodded. She seemed satisfied. "Where are you from originally?"

"Thailand."

I cringed, thinking of Ken, my old boss from the yacht club.

"Well, you can climb with us if you want," Lily suggested, looking at me for approval. I nodded, agreeing. "What level do you climb at? We mostly stick to 5-8 and 5-9 runs because Liz is just learning."

"Oh, that's great! It's been a few months since I've climbed, I could use a nice, easy warm up on a 5-9!" Charlie put her white hanky back in her backpack.

I narrowed my eyes and studied this new girl. Was that a little diss at me and my beginner climbing skills or was I just being too sensitive?

"What's this route rated?" Charlie pointed at the nearest route.

"This is Smokestack, it's a 5-8," I said, finally speaking up. "It's got a tricky start but then it's a great climb after that. Lots of choices for hand and footholds."

"Oh, fun!" Charlie nodded.

"Lily." Jill suddenly appeared around the bed. "I'm so glad you're up here!" She walked over to us. "Hey, Liz! Could you possibly spare Lily to belay me on Rainy Wish really quick? I'm waiting for Pat to show up, but he just texted that he's gonna be late."

"Oh yeah!" Lily checked with me. "Would you mind? You can set up Smoke Stack while Jill and I do Rainy Wish...."

"Sure," I agreed. Rainy Wish was a hard run, a 5-10, and I didn't know how to lead belay yet. I didn't want to hold Lily back from a climb that was more her speed.

"Great!" Lily and Jill headed over to the Rainy Wish route, about twenty feet away.

"So where are you from, Liz?" Charlie asked as I started pulling my rope out of my bag.

I told her I was from California.

"Oh...." Charlie started putting her harness on. She looked like she knew what she was doing. "Have you climbed Maple Canyon?"

"No...." I admitted. "I just got into climbing this year, here in Hawaii." I tied one end of the string running through the bolt at the top to the end of my rope.

"Oh, what a shame. Good climbing in Cali."

"So I've heard." I started pulling the other end of the string through the bolt at the top.

"Well, when you go back home, you'll be able to get into climbing over there now," Charlie suggested.

"Maybe," I said. But I realized that I didn't see myself going back to California. California wasn't home.

"I'll belay you; you can go first," she volunteered. "That way you can show me how you do the tricky start that you were talking about!"

"Great, thanks...." I finished running the rope through the bolt, got my harness on and strapped the rope through the harness.

"Okay, let's check each other," I said. I went through all the checks and everything looked good.

"Okay." I smiled at Charlie and she gave me a thumbs up. "Climbing!" I announced and started my ascent. I pointed out the tricky parts to Charlie as I went up. It took me a minute to get past them and then I was climbing more easily up the rock. Charlie wasn't keeping me on a very tight belay at all; it was even looser than Lily. "Hey, Charlie, can you tighten me up, take up the slack a little more?" I yelled down, mid-way through the climb.

"Sure thing, Liz. Sorry!" Charlie yelled back. Immediately the rope tightened.

"Great! Thanks!" I yelled back.

I continued moving up. I looked back down at Charlie, who was looking up at me smiling.

"Nice job!" Charlie yelled.

"Thanks!" I replied.

I was nearly to the top of the route when my foot started to slide as I was trying a new foothold. I could feel myself starting to fall.

"I think I'm going to fall!" I cried out, warning Charlie below. The rope was too loose for a fall. I needed Charlie to take up the slack.

But there was no response from Charlie. I started panicking. My handhold wasn't very good, and I couldn't get my foot to hold to the rock here. If I fell, it wouldn't be pretty. The rope was so loose. I looked down to see what Charlie was doing and saw her talking to another climber.

"Charlie!" I screamed.

Just then, my hand slipped from its fragile hold on the rock and I was airborne.

* * *

Time stopped. My heart dropped to my toes. My heart pounded madly. I couldn't pull in a breath. My life flashed by. And then other lives flashed by. For one brief moment, I saw everything clearly. I am a soul, separate from this body and all the other bodies I have ever inhabited. I have lived many lives.

Just as the rope caught me, I saw myself as a young, ancient Hawaiian girl, felt myself tumbling off a rocky cliff into an angry ocean in the middle of a deadly storm. And then the rope was yanking me back from my fall and my vision. The impact pulled me into the side of the mountain, and I crashed into the rock, scraping up my elbows and knees in the process. I couldn't seem to get my arms or legs to work, and I bounced back into the rock again, scraping myself up a little more. Finally, I gained control of my limbs and the next time I swung toward the rock, I pushed myself away with my feet. Motionless at last, heart racing and mind swirling, I tried to get my breathing under control.

"Oh my God! Oh my God! Oh my God!" Charlie cried repeatedly from below. So she was finally paying attention now. "I'm so sorry! Are you all right?"

I looked down at this girl I didn't know, who I had just foolishly trusted with my life. Something about her was off.

"I'm okay," I told her weakly, "Just a few scrapes."

"Oh my god! Thank god! Oh my god! I don't know what I would have done if you had been hurt!" Charlie started going off about what had distracted her. She was being a bit melodramatic. I tuned her out. I wanted to hold on to the experience I'd just had. What I had seen. What I had felt. What I had realized. It was sort of like a dream. I felt like it would all slip away if I didn't work at remembering it right now.

Lily suddenly appeared next to Charlie below. "What happened? I heard screaming!" she asked, out of breath from running over.

"Liz slipped and fell but everything's okay!" Charlie smiled brightly at Lily.

"You okay, Liz?" Lily asked, looking up expectantly at me.

"Yeah, just a few scrapes," I told her, laughing it off. "Wouldn't be a good climbing day without a little blood!"

Everyone agreed.

"Do you want to finish the climb?" Charlie asked.

"No!" I shouted and then realized that I had been a little abrupt. "I was pretty much at the top when I fell anyway," I added more casually.

"Really?" Lily appraised the situation. "That was a long fall."

I rolled my eyes. Yes, it was. I was halfway down the route now.

"Could you just lower me the rest of the way down?" I asked Charlie, with obvious irritation in my voice. "Slowly!" I added with emphasis.

Charlie did as I asked. As I finally touched back down on solid ground, my tensed-up body started to relax. I let out a deep sigh and then immediately started taking off my climbing gear. I was a little shaky. Lily tried to examine my cuts but I pushed her away. "I'm okay."

"You're leaving?" Lily asked, surprised to see me packing everything up.

"Yeah, I need to go take care of something." I was going to go see Fred. Maybe he could help me understand what had just happened. "You can climb with Jill and Pat—they're more on your level anyway." I threw my backpack over my shoulders.

"Okay...." Lily sounded unsure. "Are you sure I can't persuade you to stay?"

I smiled and shook my head. Lily pouted.

"Oh! Liz!" Charlie cried out a bit dramatically. "Don't go! Please forgive me! I don't normally let things like that happen when I climb. Let me make it up to you. Let's do another route!"

I shook my head. There was no way I was ever going to let her belay me again.

Lily sneered at Charlie and then gave me a big bear hug. "I'll see you later, okay?" She studied me.

"Yeah, yeah, of course!" I said and smiled. "Have fun with Jill and Pat."

"It was nice to meet you, Liz," Charlie said as I turned to leave.

"Yeah, you, too," I lied. "Maybe we'll see you up here again sometime." I certainly hoped not!

"Oh, you definitely will!" she said, which almost sounded like a threat.

But that was crazy. Wasn't it? I was just being paranoid.

* * *

I sped all the way to Fred's house, my mind spinning. Had I really just remembered my past lives?

I felt so fragile, like death was just around the corner. Would it be in the form of a car accident? I tried to slow down.

I screeched to a stop in Fred's driveway and ran to his front door. I knocked on his door and waited. Then knocked again. No answer.

I went around back. Maybe he was meditating out on the beach again. I spotted him sitting with Kiana on their back *lanai*. They were sipping coffee and reading books.

"Hey!" I called out.

"*Aloha!*" Fred brightened when he saw me.

"Liz, what a nice surprise!" Kiana smiled.

They put their books down and got up. Hugs and kisses were exchanged.

"We thought you were climbing today," Fred said.

"I was."

Kiana noticed my frazzled state. "What's up? Did something happen?"

"You could say that." I looked back and forth at the two.

Fred and Kiana looked expectantly at me, waiting for me to explain.

"I fell on a route today," I started. "A long way."

"Oh my god!" Kiana noticed my injuries then. "Let me get some ointment and bandages."

I nodded, and Kiana went off in search of supplies.

"Sit, sit!" Fred pulled a chair out for me. I gingerly lowered myself into the chair. Fred looked me over with concern. "Are you okay?"

"I think so."

Kiana returned and got to work cleaning my wounds, applying ointment and then bandages.

"It was so scary, I thought I was going to die." I looked at Fred. "As I was falling, my life flashed before my eyes. And then other lives flashed by."

Kiana stopped what she was doing. She looked at Fred and then back at me.

"What did you see exactly?" Fred asked.

"A lot of things. But what really sticks out is I saw myself falling off a cliff. At night. In a terrible storm." I swallowed hard. "I felt myself falling into the raging ocean. I felt myself ... dying."

"Oh no." Kiana squeezed my hand. "I'm so sorry, honey."

"Could this be why I've always been afraid of the ocean?" I looked to Fred for confirmation.

Fred nodded. "Most likely."

"Wow." I took a deep breath in. Let it all out. "It was terrible. I can feel the fear, the pain." I started to cry; I couldn't hold back the tears anymore. "I feel like death is coming for me. What is wrong with me?"

Kiana pulled me into her arms, and I laid my head on her shoulder. Fred got up and joined us then, putting his big arms around us both.

"You are re-experiencing a death from a prior life," Fred explained. "It's fresh for you now, as if it just happened. But it will fade."

"It will be okay," Kiana soothed. Her embrace calmed me. She pulled back and studied me. "Come, you need to lie down and rest."

I didn't protest. She led me back to a guest bedroom and pulled the covers on the bed down for me. I sat on the bed, exhausted. She removed my shoes for me and helped me lay back. She pulled the covers up over me as I sank down into the fluffy mattress. I closed my eyes. "Release all the tension," Kiana said in a quiet comforting voice. "Relax your feet, your legs, your hands, your arms." I relaxed all my muscles one by one. "Just breathe." She kissed my forehead. "Sleep, my sweet heavenly *lei*. We'll be here for you when you wake up."

My sweet heavenly *lei*. That sounded familiar. As I drifted off to sleep, I wondered where I had heard that before.

I dreamt of simpler times from long ago. I saw Aaron, remembered the name Kanoa. I saw his sister, Noe, but her name had been Nani then. I saw Fred and Kiana. I even saw John; how funny that he had been my brother Keoki. And I saw Peter, whose name had once been Pika.

* * *

I woke up late Sunday morning feeling groggy and disoriented. Where was I? I sat up and looked around the room. The room had Kiana's style and touch. The comforter was a vibrant red, the sheets white. The floor was a dark wood. The sun streamed in through the sheer white curtains on the window, and I could hear the sound of waves crashing on the beach. Why was I here?

Then I remembered my fall from the day before. The images of myself in so many different lives came back to me as well. And I remembered my dreams during the night. But I knew deep down that they were not just dreams. They were memories.

Kiana opened the door and peeked her head in. She smiled. "Oh good, you're awake!" She came in and sat on the bed next to me. "How are you feeling?" She studied me.

"Confused," I admitted. "Is it morning? What time is it?"

"It's Sunday morning," she told me. "You slept for over eighteen hours."

"Oh my God!" I was shocked.

Kiana chuckled. "You were exhausted; you needed the sleep. But you're probably hungry now." She kissed my forehead and then rose and walked toward the door. "We made a big breakfast; come join us as soon as you freshen up." She pointed to a pretty red-and-white floral sundress on the chair next to the bed. "You can use the bathroom across the hall."

"Okay," I said, feeling numb.

"Take your time." Kiana smiled again and closed the door behind her.

I looked under the covers. I was still in my climbing clothes from the day before. I had bandages on my right knee and right forearm covering the scrapes I'd gotten from crashing into the rocks after falling. I lifted the heavy covers and tried moving. Every muscle ached, but I slowly got myself out of bed and then walked to the window. It was just another beautiful day in paradise. The sun shone brightly, light breezes rustled the leaves of the palm trees and the blue ocean sparkled.

I spotted the naupaka flower bushes along the edge of the backyard and my breath caught as I realized the legend had parallels with what I was learning about my past life. But, no! Impossible!

I shook my head and let the thought go. That was just silly. It was just a legend.

I took a long and very hot shower, and then brushed out my wig and put on the sundress Kiana had left for me. Then I went in search of Kiana and Fred. I found them on the back *lanai*, much as I had found them the day before. Sitting and reading books. But this time there was an assortment of breakfast foods to choose from and a big pot of fresh coffee.

"Liz!" Fred spotted me first. "You look much better today! How do you feel?

"I'm starving!" I said as I grabbed a big tropical-looking muffin with coconut and pineapple bits. I took a bite and plopped down in an empty chair.

Kiana and Fred glanced at each other.

"This is great!" I said with a mouthful of muffin. I poured some juice and took a long sip. "Are they homemade?"

"Yes," Fred told me. "Kiana is a genius in the kitchen." He winked at her. "Especially with the sweet treats!" He patted his stomach.

I grabbed a plate and started adding eggs and fruit to it. "Thank you for all the food!" I said, eager to dig in. The eggs were cold but delicious.

Fred chuckled as he watched me devour the food. When my plate was nearly empty, he cleared his throat. "So."

I looked up. Swallowed.

Fred raised an eyebrow. "Do you want to talk about what happened yesterday?"

I bit my lip. Nodded.

"Do you still remember what you saw? Your past lives?"

"I think so." It was hard to believe. Hard to admit to. "Yes."

I studied him. I could picture him wearing the *ali'i* cape and helmet that I'd seen at the Bishop Museum.

I looked at Kiana. I pictured her scolding me and then hugging me. As only mothers do.

Kiana smiled and a tear fell down her cheek.

"We knew each other," I said. "Before."

Fred smiled. "We did."

"This is crazy!" I said "You guys had already recalled your past lives? With me? Hadn't you?"

They both nodded.

Everything was starting to make sense.

"Let's meditate," Fred suggested.

Fred, Kiana and I all walked down to the beach together. We sat near the water in cross-legged positions. Fred and Kiana rested their hands lightly on their laps and closed their eyes. I closed my eyes and tried to clear my mind. Memories of me falling, bits and pieces of my past lives, and images of my new friends continued to creep into my mind. I pushed them away each time I caught myself.

Chapter 24

"Five Mai Tais, please," Noe shouted out to a passing waiter.

"You got it." The waiter, a hunky surfer, smiled at us and hurried on.

I looked around at all the happy people in Duke's, the perfect place to relax on a Sunday afternoon. The restaurant was on the beach in the middle of Waikiki. The bar was always busy on Sunday afternoons because of the live band playing local music on the outdoor patio. Noe, Lily, Kai, John and I were lucky to have snagged a booth with an umbrella on the deck facing the band. People of all ages danced together down on the patio. Hot girls in bikinis and old grandmas in muumuus. Cute guys in board shorts and dads dancing with their kids. Tourists and locals alike.

I wanted to relax and enjoy myself. But my thoughts were jumbled. I couldn't stop thinking about everything that had happened the day before. And I still felt like death was coming for me. I tried to clear my mind.

"Have you had the Mai Tais here?" Noe shouted to be heard above the music. "They're the best in the islands!"

"Yeah, I know! I've gotten a bit blitzed on them before," I shouted back.

Noe laughed at that, and the others nodded in agreement.

I couldn't help but see my friends differently now. I was seeing everything differently now. Did Noe remember anything from her past lives? Did John? Or Kai or Lily? I didn't want to die yet, not when I had just found these wonderful people! I needed more time. *Gods above, please give me more time!*

"Sorry I couldn't make it climbing with you yesterday!" Noe was saying.

I smiled at my good friend. "That's okay. I know you prefer surfing!"

"Which routes did you climb?" Noe asked.

"I wasn't up there long actually," I explained as our drinks arrived. "We met a new girl up there, and she belayed me on Smoke Stack." I took a big sip of my Mai Tai. "I fell." I showed Noe my scrapes.

"Oh no!" Noe examined my injuries and frowned.

"She fell halfway down Smokestack," Lily told Noe.

"What?" Noe's eyes bulged.

"No worries!" I brushed it off and smiled. "I survived."

Noe raised her glass. "To surviving a big fall."

We all clinked glasses and then took a long drink. I could feel the alcohol relaxing me. I sat sipping my drink and watching people dancing. And then I spotted Aaron. My heart skipped a beat. Butterflies fluttered in my stomach. And then my heart sank as Charlie appeared out of nowhere, leaning in to whisper something in Aaron's ear. In disbelief I watched as she kissed him! On the lips! Passionately!

What the hell? Charlie and Aaron? The room spun. I suddenly felt like I was in a bizarre dream. This could not be real.

"Liz? Hello! Earth to Liz!" Noe teased, laughing.

"What?" I asked, turning my attention back to Noe. "Sorry! What?"

"I said...."

I tried to listen to Noe, but it was useless. My mind was trying to sort out what I had just seen. Were Charlie and Aaron dating? Did Charlie know that I had started to date him? Had she stalked me up on the mountain yesterday? That bitch could have killed me!

I looked back out at the dance floor. Charlie was looking directly at me, smiling a self-satisfied little smile. As if she knew I had been watching. I looked away. What the hell?

"Liz!" Noe grabbed my hand. "Where are you right now? Are you sure you didn't hit your head yesterday when you fell? Seriously! What's up?"

"Sorry, I was distracted," I mumbled, feeling sick to my stomach. I looked back out to the dance floor but Aaron and Charlie were gone now. I guzzled the rest of my drink.

I felt anger slowly building up inside of me again. My old defense mechanism was back. I was hardening and closing down. Doubts filled my mind. Aaron didn't really feel anything special for me. He was just another player. I had just been played again. People were terrible. I should never open up to anybody again.

"I'll be right back," I said suddenly, jumping up from the booth.

Noe gave me a confused look and then nodded.

My adrenaline pumping, I hurried back to the ladies' restroom. It was empty. I stood in front of the mirror, studying my reflection. I was ugly. I was broken. I shouldn't be here.

Three girls in sundresses entered the restroom, smiling and laughing. I quickly ducked out, trying to avoid eye contact. Instead of heading back to the table, I started walking briskly toward the parking lot where I'd parked my car. A strange-looking man walking toward me with a package in his arms made me imagine that he was going to pull out a gun and shoot me. I ducked inside a gift shop, trying to hide until he passed by. Back on the street, I jumped as a loud motorcycle sped by. I was getting more and more agitated and I didn't want to be around people anymore.

I jumped in my car, slammed the door shut, started the engine and squealed out of the parking garage. I took off down the main road in Waikiki. I just wanted to escape, but I kept getting stuck at stoplights. I scowled at all the happy tourists walking around in their sundresses and swimsuits. In the back of my mind, I knew I shouldn't allow my anger to build and act out like this. But I didn't care. I felt strong and in control. I let myself go.

As soon as I got out of Waikiki, my phone started ringing, but I ignored it. I pumped up the Nine Inch Nails and reveled in my anger. Just like the good old days.

I pulled into my driveway, turned the car off and grabbed my phone to see who had called. It was Noe. I listened to her voicemail.

"Hey, Liz, where did you go? I've been looking everywhere for you. You've got me worried. Please call me back ASAP."

I grunted and walked toward my house. Maybe I would, maybe I wouldn't. My phone rang again. I expected to see Noe's number again, but it was Aaron this time. I ignored it.

"Uggghhh!" I unlocked my front door and then slammed it shut behind me. I screamed and threw the still ringing phone across the room. It hit my coffee table, knocking the Bible I had forgotten all about onto the floor.

I lost it then. I collapsed to the floor in a heap and started crying.

Koko ran in from the back of the house then and started licking my face, breaking the momentum of my pity party. I stroked his fur. "Good boy."

I could almost hear Fred's voice telling me to let go. So I sat up straighter, took a deep breath and emptied my mind. I immediately felt more space, more peace. I looked around. It was weird, but everything had been closing in on me before, suffocating me, and now everything seemed to open up.

I noticed the Bible lying open on the floor so I crawled over to it. It was open to Luke Chapter 6. My eyes fell to verse 27 and 28.

But to you who are listening I say: Love your enemies, do good to those who hate you, bless those who curse you, pray for those who mistreat you.

I snorted. What were the chances that the Bible would fall open to this page? With the very message I needed to hear at this moment.

Remembering Kiana's request to read the Bible with an open mind, I grabbed the Bible and my laptop and went outside to my *lanai*. I sat at the table and as I waited for my laptop to boot up, I randomly flipped the Bible to Matthew chapter 5 verse 38: *You have heard that it was said, 'Eye for eye, and tooth for tooth.'*

I continued reading on to chapter 42: *But I tell you, do not resist an evil person. If anyone slaps you on the right cheek, turn to them the other cheek also.*

"Really?" I asked incredulously. Two verses about how to react when you are mistreated?

I jumped onto the Internet and typed into the Google search engine *Luke 6:27-28 Buddhist similarities*. After clicking on several links, I found an introduction to the Dhammapada, a Buddhist scripture, on Wikisource. I started reading the chapters:

1:1

The mind is the basis for everything.

Everything is created by my mind, and is ruled by my mind.

When I speak or act with impure thoughts, suffering follows me

As the wheel of the cart follows the hoof of the ox.

1:2

The mind is the basis for everything

Everything is created by my mind, and is ruled by my mind.

When I speak or act with a clear awareness, happiness stays with me.

Like my own shadow, it is unshakeable.

1:3

"I was wronged! I was hurt! I was defeated! I was robbed!"

If I cultivate such thoughts, I will not be free from hatred.

1:4

"I was wronged! I was hurt! I was defeated! I was robbed!"

If I turn away from such thoughts, I may find peace.

"Whoa!" I breathed. The Bible and the Dhammapada were saying nearly the same thing! The Bible seemed to be saying that we should turn the other cheek in order to get into heaven someday when we die. Whereas the Dhammapada seemed to be stressing that it benefits us in the here and now if we are able to just let things go instead of acting out against those who harm us.

I read on:

1:5

In this world, hatred has never been defeated by hatred.

Only love can overcome hatred.

This is an ancient and eternal law.

I liked that. Anger had never helped me in any way. Sure, it felt good to go on the defensive when someone had wronged me. That good feeling never lasted long though, and I always ended up feeling even more miserable than before. It was time to end that cycle.

I was let down with myself for getting so angry back at Duke's but I had caught myself pretty quickly. I realized what a big deal that was. I was making progress! I vowed to keep working on it.

I continued reading the Bible and Googling similarities with Buddhist verses until I heard someone knocking on my door. I looked up in a daze and realized that it was getting dark. Where had the last few hours gone?

When I got to the door I found Noe standing there, fuming.

"Girl!" she huffed as she pushed her way in. "Why the hell did you run off from Duke's without saying a word?"

"I'm so sorry, Noe!" I bit my lip. "I freaked out and came home and forgot to call you back!"

"I've been freaking too! Damn it! I've called you a million times already! Why you no pick up?" Noe was sliding into speaking pidgin. That meant she was really pissed at me.

"I'm sorry!" I explained to Noe what had happened back at Duke's as I looked for my phone. It was still lying on the floor under the table where I had thrown it earlier. I went to retrieve it and saw that I had missed nine calls! I had missed Noe five times, Aaron twice, Kiana once and Fred once. I had four voicemails.

She apologized for getting so upset with me. But she chastised me for not turning to her for support. "We're going to work this all out, babe," she said. "Before you assume anything bad is going on here, talk to Aaron."

I tried to call Aaron but I got his voicemail.

We went outside to the back *lanai* and sat at my table and I opened up to Noe about remembering my past lives. About Kanoa and Nani. Pika. She took it pretty well.

"I have felt an unusual close bond with you ever since the first time we met." Noe suddenly jumped up, smacking her palm against her forehead. "Oh my God!" She pointed at me. "It's you! You and Aaron! You and Kanoa! You guys are what set off the naupaka flower myth way back then!"

I rolled my eyes. "Come on!" I shook my head. "No! That's just crazy!" But the idea wiggled around in my head.

"Damn!" Noe paced. "You realize you have to quit your job at Ali'i Properties?" She looked at me.

I groaned. I had been thinking the same thing.

* * *

I got to work early Monday morning full of apprehension. No one was in yet so I slid my resignation letter onto Peter's desk and then practically ran back to my office in a cold sweat. I did not want to see Peter.

I wanted to go about this as normally as possible, so instead of just not showing up to work anymore like Noe had suggested, I was giving my two weeks' notice. All day long, I kept expecting Peter to come raging into my office demanding to know why I was leaving him. But he never made an appearance and by the end of the day I started feeling relief. Maybe he was just going to accept my resignation and give me the silent treatment. I could handle the silent treatment.

"Working late, huh?" Elena commented as she popped her head in my office.

I nodded. "Gotta get these reports done for Peter's meeting Wednesday. I'm almost done."

"Okay, well, I'm taking off. It's just you left. You want me to lock the door?"

"Yes, please!"

I spent the next thirty minutes polishing up my reports. After the third review, I sighed happily. Perfection. I shut my computer down.

I gathered my stuff together and then shut the lights off in my office and the outer offices. As I was about to turn the handle of the big front office door, I realized I'd left my phone on my desk. I hustled back and felt around in the dark for my phone. And then I heard voices.

"So does she or does she not know anything about the bones?" a woman's voice asked.

"I do not believe that she knows anything," Peter replied in a clipped voice. "I think she was just inquiring because she was interested."

Lights flickered on in the hall. I grabbed my phone and dropped down to the floor behind my desk.

"You better be right," the woman warned. "Because we're finished if it ever gets out that we never moved those bones."

I nearly gasped. No wonder Peter had reacted so strangely when I'd asked about the bones before. I would be in serious trouble if they found me eavesdropping right now.

"You worry too much," Peter said as he walked by my office. I held my breath.

"One of us has to." The woman's voice sounded vaguely familiar, but I couldn't place it.

It sounded like they were headed back to Peter's office. I heard a door close, and it was quiet again for a while. Should I try to sneak out now?

I popped my head up from behind my desk and then slowly stood. I tiptoed to the door and peeked out in the hall. Peter's office door was shut, light streaming out along the bottom. They must be in there.

I took a deep breath and then started speed walking to the front office door.

"Liz," Peter demanded, stopping me in my tracks. "What are you doing here?"

My heart stopped. I whirled around. Peter was standing in his doorway. I decided to play innocent. "Oh, I forgot something." I held my phone up. "What are you doing here?"

Peter narrowed his eyes.

Charlie popped her head out then. I felt lightheaded suddenly. Charlie?

A smile grew on Charlie's face. "Oh, she so totally knows," Charlie said smugly.

I tried hard to look confused. "Knows what?" I asked, still going for the innocent play.

"Oh, Liz." Peter shook his head.

I gulped. And then I turned to run.

I got tackled to the ground a mere foot from the front door. Peter was on top of me, his face bright red and his eyes bulging. The scar on the side of his nose seemed to have turned red. He had turned into someone else, someone truly frightening. I could see him with a Mohawk in another life. "You ungrateful little bitch," he growled and then he punched me in the stomach. I gasped for breath and curled into a ball.

Charlie stood over me and laughed. Crazy thoughts filled my head. Noe had been right; I should have just stopped coming into work. Was Aaron mixed up in all of this? I was in serious trouble here. This was it, the end.

Peter got up and started whispering with Charlie, clearly debating how to get rid of me now. Decision made, Peter headed back to his office and Charlie made sure the front door was locked. She turned the lights off.

I started crawling toward the door. How cliché, I thought.

"Where do you think you're going?" Peter asked, walking back toward me with rope.

He got down on his knees and started to roll me over. I tried to fight him, but I was no match for Peter. He flipped me with ease. Once he'd gotten me on my back, I turned to begging instead. "Please!" I wheezed, still unable to fully catch my breath. "I won't tell anyone."

Charlie laughed. "Right! Bitch, your time is up!"

Peter tried to tie my hands together, and I saw my opportunity to do some damage. I kicked him in the balls as hard as I could. He doubled over in agony, moaning and cursing, and I scooted away from him. But I wasn't able to get far before Charlie grabbed my feet. I screamed and tried to kick my way out of her grasp.

"Stop fighting!" Peter yelled and then he kicked me in the stomach.

I doubled over in pain. I was stunned. I couldn't breathe, let alone move.

Peter picked me up and threw me over his shoulder like a sack of potatoes. He carried me back to his office. Charlie followed us, giggling. He threw me roughly on his sofa and then walked over to his wet bar and poured himself a drink. He looked at me lying helplessly there, still gasping for air. He shook his head and then downed his drink in one gulp.

"Liz, Liz, Liz." He sighed, put his glass down and poured himself another drink.

I started to panic, imagining all the horrible things Peter might do to me. And then I could practically hear Fred's voice telling me to stay present. I emptied my mind and a calmness came over me. I would get out of this. I would not be a victim anymore. I looked around the room, trying to work out a way to overcome Peter and Charlie.

"How do you guys even know each other?" I managed to wheeze, trying to buy time.

Peter finished his second drink and then slammed it down. "Charlie is my daughter." Peter kissed Charlie on the forehead and Charlie beamed. Peter turned and poured his third drink.

I gawked at them. What a family!

Charlie grinned at me. She went to Peter's desk and rooted around for something and then sauntered over to me with rope in one hand and scissors in the other.

My heart raced. I tried to scramble away from her but I was weak from getting punched and kicked and she was surprisingly strong. She straddled me, held me down and tied the rope around my wrists. And then she very lightly ran the tip of the scissors across my cheek, down my neck and to my breasts. Then she started cutting my dress away. I clenched my teeth and glared at her. I had just bought that dress, damn it! When she was done, she pulled the dress away, leaving me in just my bra and underwear.

"Not too bad, not too bad," Charlie said, admiring my half-naked body. "I can see why Aaron was attracted to you." She grabbed my left breast with her free hand and squeezed it hard. I winced. She smiled and then placed the sharp end of the scissors between my legs. She slowly applied more and more pressure until I winced again. "Not into the rough stuff, huh?" Charlie laughed and then she slapped my face hard. I couldn't help it; a tear ran down my cheek.

"Charlie!" Peter growled angrily. "Why must you torment her?" He sounded a bit tipsy.

"Because it's fun, Daddy!" Charlie said with a huff.

"Let's just get this over with already." Peter sounded unhappy. He motioned for her.

"Ah, you're no fun sometimes," Charlie pouted. She squeezed my breast again and then got off of me. She went to Peter. They mumbled back and forth for a minute and then Charlie started toward the office door. "I'll be right back!" she said cheerfully as she left.

A plan was forming in my mind. I tried to move my hands. The rope wasn't as tight as Charlie probably should have made it. I might be able to wiggle out of it.

Peter finished his third drink. He put it down with another thud. Looking at me and shaking his head, he said solemnly, "It didn't have to go this way. This is all on you." He started walking toward me.

A sudden chill in the air gave me goosebumps, and I felt a whoosh of air go by. The scent of flowers overpowered the room. Peter smelled it, too. His eyes widened as he became distracted by it, then something unseen caught Peter's foot midstride and he stumbled. It was now or never. I finished freeing my hands from the rope, jumped up, and grabbed the Koa club on the wall above the sofa. Turning and screaming, I swung with all my might, aiming at Peter's head.

Peter's eyes bulged as the club hit the side of his head with a satisfying crack. He fell with a thud to the floor.

"Daddy!" Charlie cried from the doorway. She held the scissors up and, with a murderous look in her eyes, charged me.

"Come on, you crazy bitch!" I said as I swung the Koa club back, ready to knock out Charlie next.

Someone yelled, "Freeze!" Charlie stopped in her tracks and turned to the door. Aaron stood there pointing a gun at Charlie.

"Aaron, baby!" Charlie's whole demeanor changed. "Liz just knocked my daddy out! She's crazy! She's trying to kill us! Please help us!"

"No!" I shrieked. "They were going to kill me! I overheard them talking about how they never moved those bones they found during digging last year. They just started building their luxury condos right on top of a massive burial site."

"What?" Aaron seemed surprised. He couldn't possibly be involved with these two nut cases.

"She's lying, baby!" Charlie whined again.

"Shut your mouth," Aaron growled through gritted teeth, "and drop the scissors."

Charlie pursed her lips and contemplated her options. Finally, with a huff, she dropped the scissors.

"Kick them over here," Aaron demanded.

She kicked the scissors out of her reach.

Aaron picked them up. "I called the police and they'll be here any minute."

Charlie started to cry. She knelt down by her father's side and shook his limp body. Peter groaned but didn't move.

"Are you okay?" Aaron asked, glancing at me.

"Yeah," I said. "What are you even doing here?"

"I've been trying to find you," Aaron explained. "I ran into Noe; she told me everything,"

"Oh." That seemed like a lifetime ago. "Everything?"

"Yeah, everything," Aaron stressed. "About your experience Saturday and remembering your past lives. About Peter. About seeing Charlie and me at Dukes. I wanted to tell you that Charlie is just an ex trying to stir up trouble." He looked pointedly at Charlie and then back at me. "But you've probably figured that out by now."

I nodded.

Aaron went on, "I went to your house but you weren't there. I thought to check here, and when I got off the elevator, I heard a scream so I called the police."

I nodded again and then shivered.

"Here, put my shirt on," Aaron said, unbuttoning his shirt.

I suddenly remembered that I was practically naked. Blushing, I folded my arms across my chest and nodded.

Two policemen showed up then and I explained everything to them. Aaron winced as I described what Charlie had done to me. One of the policemen handcuffed Peter, who was finally beginning to come to. The other policeman handcuffed Charlie, who was sobbing hysterically now.

As the policemen escorted Peter and Charlie away, Aaron wrapped his arms around me in a big hug. I rested my head on his shoulder and sank into his embrace. I felt safe again at last.

"I'm so glad you're okay!" he whispered.

"I'm so glad you showed up!" I said, breathing a sigh of relief.

"It looked like you were taking care of things all by yourself!" he teased.

I chuckled. "I was pissed and overdosing on adrenaline!" I shivered again, remembering how the room had gotten cold suddenly and smelled of flowers right as Peter tripped. I pulled back to look at Aaron. "I think I had some supernatural help."

Aaron raised his eyebrows. "Oh?"

"I felt this really cold burst of air and I swear I smelled flowers right before something seemed to trip Peter mid-stride."

"Really?"

"I know it sounds completely insane!" I said, my face warming with embarrassment.

"No! I believe you!" Aaron reassured me. "I believe our spirit ancestors can protect us when we need them most."

"Our *aumakua*?" I asked.

Aaron nodded solemnly. "Yes."

We both looked around the room as if we might be able to see some kind of spiritual presence. But it was just the two of us. I thought of my great-grandmother. I thought of the sea turtle I had come across in the ocean that fateful day so many months ago. I thought of the presence I had often felt in my house. My great-grandmother's house.

"Let's get out of here," Aaron said, taking my hand and leading me to the door.

I nodded but then turned back to grab all of my personal belongings. I had no intention of ever returning.

* * *

I went to see Fred and Kiana the next morning and told them all about what had happened. They were just hearing about it on the morning news and were glad to see that I was truly okay.

As we watched the news together, I learned that Peter and Charlie were being charged with multiple counts of fraud, bribery, kidnapping and attempted murder and bail was set at ten million dollars. Two people at Ali'i Properties had come forward to offer testimony against Peter. And the fact that the prior controller had been missing for several months came out. She was being presumed dead. I shivered at the thought that I had almost had a similar fate.

"Karma is a bitch after all," I said, feeling satisfied that Peter would finally get what he deserved. "It might take a while, like several lifetimes, but it will get you!"

Fred nodded. "Peter will have plenty of time and opportunity to learn from this and work on correcting his karma now. We just started a Buddhist meditation and mindfulness training program at the prison a few years ago."

"Oh?" I tried to imagine Peter meditating.

"And a yoga practice as well," Kiana added.

"I'd love to see Peter doing yoga in an orange jumpsuit!" I laughed.

The news channels were all over the story and wanted to interview me and Aaron. So we sat down with a reporter three days before the elections. Of course, Aaron became Honolulu's next mayor with seventy-three percent of the vote.

I got a new job with Homes for Hawaiians, a nonprofit helping to address the homeless crisis. They were working on innovative ideas such as turning old busses into portable homeless shelters and washrooms.

Aaron and I spent all of our free time together. We wanted to live life to the fullest, so every weekend we spent our time outside climbing, hiking, snorkeling and kayaking. And occasionally I would just hang out on the beach with a good book and watch Aaron surf.

A couple of weeks after the elections, after everything had calmed down a bit, Aaron took me out for dinner. We went to Buzz's Steakhouse across from Kailua beach. As we entered the restaurant, other diners approached us, congratulating us and shaking our hands. I blushed at the attention, but Aaron loved it and happily chatted with everyone.

Once we were seated and had placed our orders, I brought up the topic of dreams.

"Do you remember when you asked me about having odd dreams? That day we ran into each other at Mokuleia?"

"Yes," Aaron said. "Yes, I do!"

"Well, I've been dreaming about you since the first day I saw you surfing," I finally admitted.

"Ah hah!" Aaron grinned. "I thought so! You tried to brush it off and change the subject that day, if I remember correctly."

I bit my lip and nodded.

"So what am I like in your dreams?" Aaron asked with a playful look in his eyes.

"You're a hunky ancient Hawaiian ..." I paused for effect "... *hula* dancer!" I said with a big grin.

Aaron laughed. "Of course I am!" And then he suddenly got serious with me. "We belong together, Liz. We've always belonged together." He pulled a ring out of his pocket. A simple white gold band with a square blue diamond.

My eyes nearly popped out of my head. I had not expected this!

Aaron got down on one knee and the whole restaurant became silent. "I realize now that I never knew love until I found you. I want to be with you forever, and I don't want to waste one more minute. Will you marry me?"

I looked into the eyes of the man I adored. I loved him more than I ever knew I could. He was all mine. And I was all his. "Yes!" I said, as tears fell down my cheeks. "Of course!"

Aaron slid the ring on my finger and the other diners erupted into applause as we kissed.

The waitress brought our dinners out then along with a complimentary bottle of champagne to celebrate our engagement. Everyone in the restaurant cheered when Aaron popped the cork. "Champagne for everyone!" Aaron declared then and everyone cheered again.

After dinner, we crossed the street to the beach to watch the sun set. We took our shoes off in the sand and then walked hand in hand in silence. I kept looking down at the ring on my finger and back up at Aaron and smiling. The sky was turning brilliant shades of orange and red as the sun began to set. I felt at peace.

Aaron stopped to pick up a flower in the sand. He grinned and handed it to me. "Look at it."

I looked down and didn't realize at first why he wanted me to look at it. But then it hit me. This was a naupaka flower but it was different. This one had all its petals.

I looked back up into Aaron's eyes, surprised and breathless. A new naupaka flower was growing? One with all the petals? This could mean only one thing!

We stood there for a moment, studying each other. And then we fell into each other's arms.

About the Author

J.L. Eck was born in 1971. Her family moved around a few times when she was a child and as a result she has always been a bit of a nomad. Jaimie has lived in Utah, California, Washington, Arizona, Michigan, Hawaii and Oregon.

Ever since she was just a child, Jaimie has always loved reading and she always wanted to be a writer. But in college she took a different path earning an MBA and then working in management in the business world. When she moved to Hawaii in 2006 she was radically transformed by the islands and she decided it was time to follow her dream of writing.

Over the years, storytellers have told several versions of the myth of the naupaka flower. Some versions involve the goddess Pele and her sister Naupaka. Other versions involve a princess named Naupaka who falls in love with a commoner named Kaui. J.L. Eck took the idea of a princess falling in love with a commoner and let her imagination go wild. Naupaka Blooming is the end result.

Jaimie met her soul mate and husband in Hawaii and they now live in Portland Oregon with their three-year-old daughter and two dogs.

Jaimie is currently working on her next novel – a paranormal thriller/romance:

…a beautiful American Indian woman with a chip on her shoulder. …ado Springs, Colorado, she takes her frustrations with the world …criminals she chases down. But one fateful day, as she closes in on the biggest crime ring she's ever dealt with, she nearly loses her life in a scuffle with the bad guy. Luckily, Jack Campbell, a ruggedly handsome detective from a nearby precinct, arrives on the scene and saves her life.

As Summer lies in a state her doctor's call "locked in syndrome", unable to speak or move except for blinking or moving her eyes, but fully aware of everything going on around her, Jack attempts to pick up on the case where Summer left off. Summer is drawn to Jack but she has questions about him and doesn't fully trust him.

After a visit from her grandfather who she hasn't seen in twenty years, and in frustration with her predicament, Summer accidentally learns how to astral project her spirit. As she explores her newfound abilities from her hospital bed she plots revenge against those who put her there. Will she ever wake up from this nightmare? And is Jack the hero of the story or the villain?

You can read Jaimie's blog and sign up for extras as well as be the first to know when her new books will be released on her website at www.jleckthewriter.com

You can also follow Jaimie on Facebook, Twitter, Instagram and Pinterest.

Thank you so much for taking the time to read my story! If you enjoyed it, will you please consider leaving a short review? Reviews are incredibly important to authors. I read every review and I hope to see yours soon! Thank you!

Made in the USA
Monee, IL
02 September 2019